T0011255

Attending a theater p

Victoria had lost count of the number of times she had attended one, yet she'd never been more excited about going to one than she had been today. Since she'd woken up this morning, a thrill had lived inside her, knowing that she'd be attending with Lincoln. That same thrill had remained throughout the entire evening.

Truthfully, it was still there and the day was over. Furthermore, if she was being completely honest with herself, she knew that thrill was going to remain right up to the wedding. She liked acting as if she and Lincoln were a couple. Which was completely unlike her. She'd never wanted to be part of a couple.

This was different, though. She wasn't really part of a couple. Perhaps that's where the thrill came from, that she and Lincoln were only pretending.

However, when the pretending ended, nothing would have changed. Nothing about her life.

Author Note

The growing popularity of the entertainment industry during the Gilded Age is portrayed in the background of this story. Circuses, fairs, vaudeville shows, sports competitions and other activities, including bicycle riding, kept the young and old of this time busy. As did inventions. Every year brought new inventions, gadgets or ideas that affected lives for years to come, such as the telephone, light bulb and camera, to name only a select few.

All of that provided fun opportunities for Lincoln and Victoria to spend time together while they sought to overcome barriers that were destined to keep them from having their happily-ever-after. I hope you enjoy their journey!

A COURTSHIP TO FOOL MANHATTAN

LAURI ROBINSON

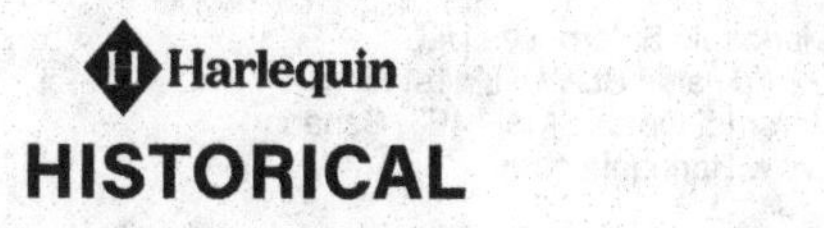

If you purchased this book without a cover you should be aware that this book is stolen property. It was reported as "unsold and destroyed" to the publisher, and neither the author nor the publisher has received any payment for this "stripped book."

Recycling programs for this product may not exist in your area.

ISBN-13: 978-1-335-59620-8

A Courtship to Fool Manhattan

Copyright © 2024 by Lauri Robinson

All rights reserved. No part of this book may be used or reproduced in any manner whatsoever without written permission.

Without limiting the author's and publisher's exclusive rights, any unauthorized use of this publication to train generative artificial intelligence (AI) technologies is expressly prohibited.

This is a work of fiction. Names, characters, places and incidents are either the product of the author's imagination or are used fictitiously. Any resemblance to actual persons, living or dead, businesses, companies, events or locales is entirely coincidental.

For questions and comments about the quality of this book, please contact us at CustomerService@Harlequin.com.

TM and ® are trademarks of Harlequin Enterprises ULC.

Harlequin Enterprises ULC
22 Adelaide St. West, 41st Floor
Toronto, Ontario M5H 4E3, Canada
www.Harlequin.com

Printed in U.S.A.

A lover of fairy tales and history, **Lauri Robinson** can't imagine a better profession than penning happily-ever-after stories about men and women in days gone past. Her favorite settings include World War II, the roaring twenties and the Old West. Lauri and her husband raised three sons in their rural Minnesota home and are now getting their just rewards by spoiling their grandchildren. Visit her at laurirobinson.blogspot.com, Facebook.com/lauri.robinson1 or Twitter.com/laurir.

Books by Lauri Robinson

Harlequin Historical

Southern Belles in London

The Return of His Promised Duchess
The Making of His Marchioness
Falling for His Pretend Countess

The Osterlund Saga

Marriage or Ruin for the Heiress
The Heiress and the Baby Boom

Twins of the Twenties

Scandal at the Speakeasy
A Proposal for the Unwed Mother

Sisters of the Roaring Twenties

The Flapper's Fake Fiancé
The Flapper's Baby Scandal
The Flapper's Scandalous Elopement

Diary of a War Bride
A Family for the Titanic Survivor
The Captain's Christmas Homecoming
An Unlikely Match for the Governess
A Dance with Her Forbidden Officer

Visit the Author Profile page
at Harlequin.com for more titles.

To my wonderful friend Robin for being
with me on this journey since day one!

Chapter One

The newly fallen snow that had coated the ground in glistening white when she'd boarded the train this morning had all disappeared. Although the distance between Tarrytown and the heart of New York City was only twenty-five miles, the small town and big city were worlds apart. They both had their assets and liabilities, their benefits and disadvantages, their beauties and ugliness.

Out of the windows on one side of the train, the Hudson River flowed, rippling in some areas, and catching the bright early-March sunshine. Along the other side of the train were towns and cities, showcasing ever-changing scenery of well-mannered homes and businesses, as well as factories puffing black smoke into the air and shantytowns where workers of those factories lived in a squalor that was inconceivable to those who had never noticed them. It wasn't so much a case of not noticing them as it was a choice to ignore them.

That was her opinion, and Victoria Biggs had plenty of opinions. On all sorts of topics and, try as they might, other people's justifications or arguments rarely made her change her mind. Stubborn was what her mother called her, and set in her ways. Two things that her mother claimed were the reason she was a bridesmaid and not a bride.

Victoria disagreed.

She was a bridesmaid because her dearest friend was getting married. Audrey Dryer had been her best friend all through finishing school, and the two of them hadn't let a mere thirty miles diminish that friendship since their school years had ended. Even though the ride between their homes often consumed over three hours due to the trains stopping numerous times at small depots along the way, they managed to see each other often.

As far as not being a bride, Victoria knew that hadn't happened because she hadn't met a man who'd made her want to enter the life-altering bonds of marriage, despite her mother's and grandfather's ardent efforts. That may have already happened if she wasn't so set in her ways, and if her life was different.

If her family lived within one of the neighborhoods of the city, most notably, Manhattan, where Audrey's family lived, her family would be accepted into the blue bloods' society, but Tarrytown was just far enough away for them to be considered outsiders, despite the size of their bank accounts and the charities her family supported.

That wasn't completely true. Living in the right neighborhood wouldn't have given them an entrance into the most upper class. There were too many variables, all of which mattered to society. Old money, generations of it, decided the hierarchy of society. Though her grandfather, Emmet Biggs, was a rich man, his funds weren't from old money. He'd acquired his wealth, which he generously shared with her, her mother, her younger sister, and several charities, during the gold rush in the Rocky Mountains.

As a young man, he'd headed west with little more than the clothes on his back, where he'd not only found gold, enough to amass a fortune, but also the love of his life.

Her grandmother had been a saloon gal, who had married her grandfather before he'd struck it rich. They'd raised a son in the wilds of Colorado, who also met the love of his life. Victoria knew the story well. Her mother had been a farmer's daughter. Her father hadn't cared. He'd loved her mother, and her mother had loved him with all her heart.

Both she and her younger sister, Eva, had been born in Colorado, lived their earliest years in a large white house where the booming of the stamp mill crushing rocks was so familiar that the only time they had noticed the sound was when it had stopped. After a brutal winter when tragedy had struck, taking the lives of both her father and grandmother due to pneumonia two months apart, and then her baby brother had died upon birth, her grandfather had packed up her mother, her, and her sister, and hauled them back East. To Tarrytown, close enough to New York City for them to have access to the assets and benefits of the city, but far enough away that they didn't have to witness the disadvantages and ugliness.

She understood that her family's history was different from the gentry's, who lived and breathed their own sets of rules and regulations, which in many ways limited her sources of finding a man she'd consider marrying. However, the main limiting factor was herself. The only man she would ever marry would be the love of her life, and she would have to be the love of his life, too.

That's what her grandparents had had, and what her parents had had, and she wanted no less.

None of the suitors who'd knocked on her door had come close to meeting her expectations, and despite what she was told, she would not lower those expectations. She'd rather be an old maid.

An old maid who loved mysteries. Loved solving crimes. She always knew the culprit in a book before it was revealed.

She glanced at the paper-wrapped picture frame sitting on the seat between her and the window. That picture held proof that her suitors had only been interested in courting her because of her grandfather's money. A fresh bout of anger rose up inside her, and she slowly breathed through it, telling herself to keep her reaction to what had happened under control. Elwood Kelley would be punished for his actions. This was a real-life mystery that she already knew the answer to, but needed a bit of help to prove it.

Elwood had no idea that the timing of his thievery had been completely inept. She'd already planned on traveling to Manhattan and staying the next month with Audrey, helping her friend prepare for her wedding next month. An April wedding was the wish of every society bride. By May, families were prepping to move to their country homes for the summer, and once they returned in the fall, winter holiday parties quickly got in the way of weddings. Leastwise, those were the justifications she'd heard about the goal of having a spring wedding. In her opinion, if two people loved each other what month they wed held very little importance.

The clanging of a bell announced the train was approaching the Grand Central Depot, and Victoria allowed her smile to hold a hint of conceit. Elwood had no idea that during her stay in Manhattan wedding preparations weren't the only thing she'd be doing. She would be acquiring the services of Audrey's father, a very well-known lawyer, to assist her in seeing that Elwood paid his dues for his thievery.

It wasn't just herself that she was concerned about when it came to men after nothing but money. She had her younger sister, Eva, to consider. By the time Eva was of age to marry, men would know that they couldn't pull one over on the Biggs sisters.

Her smile was still on her lips a few moments later, when she stepped off the train and onto the platform of the elaborate train shed that protected passengers from the weather upon their arrival at the station. The overhead trussed roof arched high above the platform that led to three separate waiting rooms and the depot itself. The decorative glass and metal windows and doors were just a glimpse of the overall grandeur of the depot. No costs had been spared by Cornelius Vanderbilt in building the station to show the world who was at the top of the ladder when it came to the railroad and steamboat industries.

The depot was lovely, but in her opinion, it was a glaring reminder of how, above all else, the elite valued a man's wealth, power, and status. In her opinion, character, honesty, and respectability were often overlooked in comparison to a man's wallet, and that didn't impress her in the least.

Holding on to the paper-wrapped picture, she attempted to see beyond the crowd, looking for Audrey, or perhaps Mr. Carson, their driver. He'd picked her up at the station on some of her previous visits.

"Would you like me to carry that for you, Miss Biggs?"

She twisted at the sound of her name and nearly dropped the picture. How had she missed seeing Lincoln Dryer amongst the crowd? Tall, and quite handsome, for years he'd made something go soft inside her. She'd always credited that to him being Audrey's older brother. Tightening her hold on the somewhat awkward and not overly small—large, in fact—parcel, she found her voice. "Mr. Dryer. I expected Audrey or perhaps Mr. Carson."

"I'm sure you did," Lincoln said. "My sister had an appointment with the dressmaker this morning, and William—Mr. Carson, is overseeing your luggage being loaded into the carriage. Would you like me to carry that for you?"

His repeated question didn't faze her as much as he did. She hadn't seen Lincoln in several months. During her last visit, he'd been out of town, and it appeared as if she'd forgotten his extraordinary handsomeness. It wasn't just his face, with shimmering brown eyes and thick brows, straight nose, and firmly curved chin. His sandy-colored hair added to his good looks, as did his wide neck and broad shoulders, and… Well, simply all of him. Blinking, just to change the focus of her vision, she replied, "No, thank you. I'll carry it."

Someone rushing by jostled her and Lincoln caught her elbow. "Are you sure?"

"Yes, I'm sure." Clutching the paper-wrapped picture tighter, she hoisted it up a bit, flinching slightly as the top of it hit her beneath the chin.

He gave her an incredulous look, somewhere between a frown of confusion and a grimace of disgust. Along with a smile. It was a plastered-on smile. She knew. Hers was, too. A picture of this size was a bit odd for someone to be carrying around.

"I don't want the glass to get smudged," she said. That was the ultimate truth. She'd even placed a thin board over the glass, so the paper wouldn't touch it.

His nod could have been confirmation in his own mind

that she was as mad as a March hare, which is what her grandfather was known to call people at times.

"I brought it along to have it cleaned," she said, using the same excuse that she'd used at home when leaving with the picture. "It's a framed picture that my grandfather adores."

There was barely a change in his expression. "Very well." He gestured towards the doorway. "Shall we?"

"Yes, and thank you for meeting me. It wasn't necessary."

"Mother believed you'd have several pieces of luggage due to the length of your stay," he said.

"Oh, yes, well, that is true." Usually, she only had one or two pieces, but that had always been for much shorter stays.

Other passengers hurried around them, as if they were in a rush to get a list of things accomplished today and didn't have time to dally. The city was like that. Everyone was always in a hurry and she believed they must all fall into bed completely exhausted by the efforts it had taken them to keep up with the pace around them all day.

"I hope the train ride was satisfactory," Lincoln said when they exited the depot and the hustle and bustle surrounding them eased as people dispersed in all directions.

Accepting his attempt at small talk, she replied with her own, "Oh, yes. It was fine, thank you. We had a fresh inch or more of snow this morning."

"We had about an inch, too," he said. "This time of year it doesn't last long."

The herringbone pattern of the bricks that made up the street didn't show a hint of snow, nor of water from melting snow. Whatever may have been there had disappeared beneath the feet of moving people.

"The carriage is right over here," Lincoln said, once

again touching her elbow. "William will be along shortly with your luggage."

At the black carriage, he looked at her paper-wrapped parcel again. "Would you like me to hold that while you climb in?"

Keeping the glass from being smudged was still her greatest concern. A single smudge would spoil her chances of proving it was Elwood who'd stolen from her grandfather. "I'll just set it on the seat," she said, leaning into the carriage and doing just that. Then she stepped up on the single footstep and climbed in the carriage as he held her elbow. The carriage had a fringed canopied top with two seats both facing forward, one for passengers and one for the driver. Behind the back seat was a square boxed area for cargo. She picked up the picture and sat down, holding it on her lap.

Noticing her dress, she used one hand to tuck the powder blue material behind her knee, giving Lincoln space to sit.

The smile on Lincoln Dryer's face grew even more painful as he held it in place while climbing into the carriage. He'd tried his best to get out of this errand, to no avail. His mother's insistence had won out. She'd been correct, it wouldn't have been proper to have Victoria waiting alone in the carriage while William collected her luggage, and sending a second servant wouldn't have been the proper way to welcome a guest, either.

Normally, such a small request wouldn't have bothered him. He simply knew what his mother was up to, and wasn't going to stand for it. Now that Audrey's wedding was only a month away, his mother's attention had already moved onto the next family wedding.

His.

That was not going to happen. Perhaps someday, but right now he had his own goals and ambitions to see to. Things no one else knew about, yet.

However, besides that, it wasn't just himself he was considering. His mother's attentions were also focused on Victoria. Though he knew her, as she had been Audrey's friend for years, he didn't appreciate his mother trying to force that into becoming more than it could ever develop into being.

Twisting his shoulders, he tried not to crowd Victoria as he settled onto the seat.

There wasn't much room in the carriage to begin with, and her holding that huge paper-wrapped picture made the quarters tighter. Who hauled a picture on a three-hour train ride so it can be cleaned? Wasn't that something a servant could do? They did at his house. Maybe that was why. Audrey could have said that Mrs. Owens, their housekeeper, could clean it. Mrs. Owens was a marvel at many things. Their house ran with every cog oiled because of her.

He'd known Victoria for several years, because of Audrey. Besides visiting each other at their homes a few times a year, the two women wrote letters back and forth weekly, long ones covering all sorts of topics including birthdays, illnesses, and gossip of the latest scandals. His sister loved sharing Victoria's thoughts on all the subjects they wrote about with the rest of the family, and had been counting down the days until Victoria's arrival. Audrey had been shocked that their mother had scheduled an appointment with the dressmaker for this morning.

Lincoln hadn't been shocked.

His mother had claimed that Victoria was practically family, and had previously hinted that it would be wonderful if she truly became a part of their family. He'd never taken the bait and wouldn't now. Although, Victoria was pretty, and he couldn't remember another time when she'd acted odd—as in carrying around a three-foot-by-two-foot paper-wrapped picture—but he had things to do before marriage was something he'd contemplate.

Considering she would be at his house for the next month, and he knew his mother would be plying her match-making upon Victoria as much as she was him, Lincoln figured this was the opportune time for him to set things straight. "How is your family?" He'd never met her family, but via Audrey's enthusiasm in sharing Victoria's letters, it felt as if he knew them.

"They are all fine," she answered. "They'll be at the wedding."

"I'm sure they'll miss you this next month," he said, trying to find a way to enter into the topic. He didn't want to hurt her feelings, and that was making him somewhat tongue-tied, which was as odd as the picture on her lap.

"My sister will be home on break for two weeks starting next week," she said, "so they'll be busy catching up on everything with her. She hasn't been home since the holidays."

He nodded, and glanced over his shoulder, towards the station, looking for William, who had yet to appear.

"How are things at your law firm?" she asked. "Audrey says you'll be made partner soon."

Because his family had his life all planned out for him, his father had been ready to make him a partner as soon as he'd passed the bar exam. He had other plans, his own plan, and had suggested they wait a few years. For as long as he could remember, he'd been going to work with his father and studying law. He enjoyed practicing it, but really wanted to enforce laws on a larger scale. Laws already in place that would benefit people, all people, not just those with enough money to pay lawmakers to do biddings on their behalf. There was too much of that happening, and it was getting worse, not better. It may take a few years, but he would run for office. State attorney general was his goal, and he wouldn't let anything get in the way of that.

He twisted his neck enough to study her profile, wondering if he should tell her that. She truly was a lovely woman. The mass of her auburn hair was pinned up and the crown of her head was covered by a nonobtrusive blue hat, the same shade of blue as her dress, with just enough white lace to make it look nice. The same could be said of her dress. It was a simple, almost delicate gown, with only small amounts of lace here and there, not some sort of dressmaker's masterpiece that was so full of lace, ribbons, feathers, ruffles, and other whatnots that it was nearly impossible to know if there was a person inside the material or not.

He'd heard his mother tell Audrey a time or two how a dress made her look pretty, and he always thought that peculiar. In his mind, it should be the other way around, that the woman should make the dress look pretty. That a dress should fit her in a way that *her* beauty shone through, not the dress's.

However, he was of the opposite sex, so clearly didn't understand women's fashion. He merely noticed Victoria's style. It had been impossible to miss her stepping off the train. Not even the huge package she'd carried distracted from her natural beauty. Besides an overall gracefulness, her eyes were so blue they stood out from her dark brows, lashes, and hair. Her mouth stood out too, because her lips curled up slightly, appearing to be in a perpetual, natural smile.

She twisted her neck, looked at him.

He sucked in a breath at being caught staring at her, but didn't look away. He had to get this over with. "I believe we should get something straight right from the start."

Her dark brows drew together in a frown.

"I'm not interested in marriage and there is no reason for you to think, or hope, otherwise." That sounded harsher than he'd intended, and had caused something inside him to flinch.

Her eyes grew round and her mouth formed an O shape, then closed and formed another O shape, before she shook her head and asked, "What?"

He hadn't meant to shock her, just wanted her to know and accept the truth. "My mother has been attempting to *arrange* a marriage for years without success. It's not going to succeed this time, either."

Shaking her head, she opened her mouth, but before words came out, she glanced over his shoulder and closed her mouth.

"Forgive the delay," William said, climbing up into the carriage's driver's seat. He turned about and tipped the brim of his black wool hat at her. "Miss Biggs, it's a pleasure to see you again."

The carriage jostled as two trunks were loaded into the box behind the seat by two men, as she replied, "It's wonderful to see you, too, Mr. Carson. I apologize for having so much luggage this trip."

"No inconvenience at all, miss," William said. "I do believe we found all of it."

Lincoln witnessed two more trunks and then two tapestry bags being loaded before asking, "Is that everything?"

She twisted and, after scanning the luggage, nodded.

He tuned and gestured to William to proceed into navigating their way through the traffic surrounding the station.

As the carriage rolled out of the station, onto Fourth Avenue, under her breath, she asked, "What's not going to succeed?"

"My mother's matchmaking," he said just as quietly.

She gasped. "Audrey and Jake—"

"Not them. Me," he whispered. "I'm not marrying you."

"Me? You!"

"My mother has tried her best to…" He paused, because she had covered her mouth with one hand a moment ago, but now he realized that had been to cover laughter, which had become too strong to contain behind her hand.

"Me and you?" She laughed harder.

He wouldn't call it a rejection, yet couldn't deny the smart that stung him in the chest vicinity. "You may think it's funny, but I don't."

"You don't?"

"No, I don't," he whispered, not wanting William to hear. "We are going to be thrown together for the next month and I don't want any disillusions to be formed during that time."

"Disillusions?" She shook her head and her eyes narrowed as she glared at him while whispering, "The only disillusions are in your head. I am not here to find a husband. In fact, I'm here to get away from the array of men knocking on my door, thinking I will fall at their feet. A desperate maiden, well on her way to becoming an old maid who needs a husband so badly that she'll forget the good sense she was born with. I haven't forgotten my good sense, nor will I."

"I never said—"

"You didn't have to," she interrupted. "The implication was utterly clear."

This was turning out to be more awkward than he'd imagined. He hadn't meant to insult her, or imply she was desperate for a husband. He just knew his mother. "I simply wanted you to be prepared for my mother's efforts."

"Prepared?" She shook her head. "I am fully *prepared* to help my friend with her wedding and nothing more, including disillusions about you or anyone or anything else!"

He could try to dissolve the misunderstanding that had clearly occurred. The lawyer in him could argue the strongest and weakest points. Why hadn't he started out that way? It was like his brain hadn't engaged and the words had just started flowing. The wrong words. Or words in the wrong order.

He drew in a deep breath and tried to find them now, the right words and order, but all he was able to conclude was that the tension filling the air could make the two-and-a-half-mile trek to his house the longest one on record.

Chapter Two

Normally not one to lose her temper so easily, Victoria wasn't sure if it had been mortification or anger that had caused her to respond so vehemently. Most likely it had been a combination of the two, because when she'd espied him staring at her, she'd feared he'd been reading her mind. How she'd been thinking that if any one of her suitors had been more like him, she might've been more lenient in getting to know them. He met all of the characteristic criteria on her mental list for a husband, as in personality, integrity, being an overall good person. His handsomeness was certainly undeniable, but that was more of an added benefit in her opinion.

Handsome men could be just as unsavory as homely men.

Obviously.

The fear that he'd read her mind had turned into mortification when he'd begun speaking of marriage, and had grown into anger at his assumption that was the reason she was here. Looking for a husband, and that it could never be him.

She'd already known it could never be him, but having it spoken so directly had sent her ire to unimaginable heights. She fully understood her standing in society and that a man of his stature, of old money, would never be interested in her, but hadn't needed it tossed in her face.

The picture on her lap added to her anger, because it was proof that men were, and would only ever be, interested in her only because of her grandfather's money. Men who didn't have their own money and wanted it to move up in society. Everyone knew that old money ruled New York, but new money could open doors, and that's what the men seeking her attention wanted. Doors opened for them into society.

"I apologize, Victoria," he said quietly. "It was not my intent to upset or insult you."

Due to past visits, she knew him well enough to believe that hadn't been his intention, and she couldn't blame him for believing she was like so many other women in the city who were hoping to get him to the altar. Audrey had mentioned that in many of her letters, as well as how many of them were silly, lovestruck society girls who drove him crazy. However, she also knew Roseanne, his mother, and knew he was mistaken in his thoughts about her matchmaking the two of them. "You did not upset, nor insult me. I am fully aware that I am not a member of the blue bloods."

"Not a— What's that supposed to mean? You are as much a member of society as I am."

That was hardly the case, but she wasn't going to argue with him any longer. Drawing in a deep breath, she said, "Let's just leave this conversation as is, knowing we both understand what was said."

He nodded and was silent for a moment, but then whispered, "Just for the record, I don't agree that you are not a member of society."

Her own stubbornness wouldn't let her remain silent, either. "For goodness' sake, Lincoln, this is not a trial, nothing needs to be on *record*."

"I am fully aware of that."

"Then you should be fully aware that there is no reason to argue your case."

"It's not my case, it's yours. You're the one who said it."

"Because it's true."

"Tell me why you believe that."

She sucked in a breath and held it at the frustration that was growing inside her, at him and the thought that the driver might hear their whispering. "This is ridiculous."

"Yes, it is."

She knew he wasn't agreeing to what she'd been referring to. "I meant this conversation."

"That's what I'm referring to."

"No, it's not. You're referring to one specific point, I'm referring to the entire conversation, which has been ridiculous since it started. Once again, I suggest we end this discussion."

"Why? So you can claim the last word?"

"No." Thankfully she had a very viable answer and smiled as the clip-clop of the horses' hooves slowed. "Because we are turning into your driveway."

He glanced at the house, then back at her.

She smiled and focused on their arrival. It truly had been a meaningless conversation that had nothing to do with her reason for being here.

The house her grandfather had built for them in Tarrytown was large and very lovely, with all the modern conveniences, and she loved living there, but there was something about the Dryer home, about being in the heart of the city, that instilled a sense of exhilaration inside her whenever she was here. Life in the city was different than in Tarrytown, and that thrilled her deeply embedded sense of curiosity in many ways.

Fifth Avenue hosted some of the most extravagant mansions and brownstone homes in all of New York City, and the Dryer house was one of them. Their ancestors had been in shipping since the Revolutionary War. One of Audrey's great-uncles still oversaw the shipping company and lived a block up the road, in a house just as large as the one where they'd just arrived. Made of stone and brick, with marble pillars and floors, the Dryer home encompassed a large corner lot, was four stories tall, and one side overlooked a section of Central Park.

Audrey, with her blond hair fashioned in a Newport coiffure and wearing a beautiful light green dress with a stand-up collar, was on the steps near the side door, waving ecstatically, and shouting, "You're here! You're here!"

Despite the frustration of the ride, Victoria was elated to see her friend. "I am! I've missed you!"

"I've missed you, too!" Audrey exclaimed.

Lincoln stepped out as soon as the carriage stopped. "Give me your picture while you step out. I'll be careful with it."

Victoria hated to take the chance of the glass getting smudged, but couldn't hold on to it while climbing out and there was no place to put it, except for on the seat like before, but this time she'd have to turn around, which would be awkward and seemed senseless with the way Lincoln was holding out his hands. "Please hold it by the edges," she said.

"I will." He took the picture as she handed it over, and he still had a free hand to assist her out of the carriage.

Before she could ask for her picture, Audrey engulfed her in a huge hug.

"I'm so happy you are here!"

Victoria returned the hug. "Me, too!"

"Come," Audrey said, releasing the hug and taking a hold of Victoria's hand. "The dressmaker is here, waiting to take your measurements for your bridesmaid dress. It's such a lovely design and will look so wonderful on you."

"I need to see to my luggage," Victoria said, glancing at Lincoln.

Audrey didn't release her hand. "Curtis will see to that."

Curtis was their butler, and though Victoria trusted him, she still wanted to take the picture inside herself. She dug her heels into the stone steps, but Audrey pulled harder.

"I can't wait for you to see the material samples," Audrey said. "It's a lovely shade of rose red, muted of course, because no one would want bright red for a wedding this time of year."

Victoria sought an appropriate response, but wasn't having much luck.

"I will carry your picture up to your room," Lincoln said. "By the edges."

"Thanks, Linc," Audrey answered as if he'd been talking to her and won the tug of war, pulling Victoria into the house through the side door.

Victoria had no choice but to hope that Lincoln wouldn't smudge the glass as Audrey pulled her down a long, marble tiled floor, while talking nonstop about dress patterns, materials, and so many other things, Victoria gave up trying to comment. Until Audrey mentioned her father.

Stopping so hard and fast, Audrey had to stop too, Victoria asked, "Your father isn't home?"

"No, he's down in Florida, something to do with the shipping company, but don't worry, he'll be home in plenty of time for the wedding."

Victoria's stomach sank. "When will that be?"

"He promised to be back a week before the wedding." Audrey frowned. "Why? It's nothing to worry about."

It was to Victoria. She wanted an investigation into Elwood started immediately. Otherwise, he'd think he'd gotten away with it completely.

"Victoria?"

She shook her head, and told a white lie, something she rarely did, until lately when it came to the picture Lincoln was carrying upstairs to her bedroom. "I was just thinking about you, all the events before the wedding."

"Oh, you are such a wonderful friend." Audrey hugged her again. "Don't worry. Linc promised to fill in for Daddy at all the necessary events."

She couldn't ask him to fill in for her, yet found a smile. "That's nice of him."

"He's the best brother ever, just like you're the best friend ever."

Lincoln delivered the picture to the room assigned to Victoria, and immediately left the house again, this time to go to the office where he should have been all morning. The firm employed a large number of top-notch lawyers, and with his father out of town, it was his job to oversee the cases they accepted, and won. They had a loss now and again, but for the most part, they didn't take on a case without fully believing they'd win—by following the law. Other firms could be bought off. Not theirs, and he was proud of that.

Corruption had no boundaries or limits, and the current political environment was making it worse. There wasn't a business or resident in the city that wasn't affected by it, and what bothered him the most was that politicians weren't willing to do anything about it, because they were being enriched by it. As long as they continued to buy votes, it wouldn't end.

What he wouldn't give to get a case where he could go after one of them. Prove how corrupt they'd become and get them expelled from their seats. It was the only way to stop it, and if someone didn't do it soon, the city would be in ruin. No longer be known as the Empire City, the home of America's national and international business.

As the carriage traversed through the traffic, Lincoln glanced to his left, to the seat where Victoria had sat holding on to her picture, and couldn't stop a grin from forming. He hoped she got her picture cleaned. The grin slipped as he wondered about her statement concerning her not being a member of the blue bloods. High society had their rules, but the only rule concerning entrance was money, and her grandfather had plenty.

His father had handled some investments for Emmet Biggs, and the money was there. More money than many families who felt they wore the crowns of society had in their coffers. Yes, it was new money, but old money—as it was referred to—was changing. Times were changing.

Maybe she felt that way because she didn't act like so many flighty society girls. She didn't giggle nonstop, or talk constantly, or drop things, waiting for a man to pick them up, or twist an ankle and insist upon being carried, or a number of other ridiculous actions that he'd been the target of too many times to count.

However, she could argue. He'd never experienced that with her before, and despite the subject, sparring back and forth with her, while keeping their voices low, had been entertaining.

He could recall it as entertaining now. At the time, he hadn't found much amusement in it. He'd never had such difficulties attempting to get a point across. She would find out what he was referring to soon enough. His mother was relentless.

Yet his mother could also be sly, and probably wouldn't be as forward with Victoria as she was with him. He would just sit back and watch, and when the time came, he could say *I told you so.*

Until then, he'd just ignore it all. Her, and his mother's ploy.

Work would allow him to put that plan in place, so that's what he did. Worked. He went into the office early and stayed late, and planned on continuing to until after the wedding.

His plan worked the rest of Monday and Tuesday, but by Wednesday, his mother was on to him and caught him before he left for the office in the morning.

"Audrey and Jake will be taking a ride in the park this evening," she said. "You and Victoria will accompany them."

"They're engaged," he responded, while spreading orange marmalade on his toast.

She merely stared at him from the other side of the table, giving him the *I'm your mother and you will listen* look.

"They no longer need a chaperone," he added.

Pouring coffee form the silver pot into a floral china cup with matching saucer, she shook her head. "You will not be accompanying them as a chaperone. You will accompany them so Victoria will not be left home alone."

He sliced his toast in half and picked up one piece. “Does Victoria want to go?”

“Of course, she wants to go.”

“How do you know? Did you ask her?”

Her lips puckered and she pointed the spoon she’d used to add sugar to her cup at him. “Do not talk with food in your mouth.”

“I didn’t. I’d already swallowed.” He held the toast up near to his mouth for a second bite, but spoke first. “Did you ask her if she wants to go?”

“No, but she does. The two of them haven’t gone anywhere except shopping since she arrived.”

He swallowed his toast and took a drink of coffee before saying, “She’s only been here a day and a half.”

“It will be three days this evening. She arrived on Monday and this is Wednesday. I’ll expect you home for dinner. Jake will be joining us, then the four of you will go riding.” She lifted her cup and took a sip before adding, “You promised you’d fulfill all your father’s duties while he’s absent.”

Lincoln considered pointing out that hours-wise, Victoria had been here less than forty-eight, but chose not to. He set his napkin on the table and stood. “I will, but father wouldn’t go riding with them in the park.” On his way around the table, he paused and kissed her cheek. “Have a good day, Mother.”

Keeping his smile hidden until he was out of the room, he then added a chuckle to it. He would be home in time for supper, and would go riding, so Victoria could see exactly what he’d been attempting to explain to her.

That thought and a smile hung with him all day. Although, he did experience an odd tightening in his chest once in a while when thinking about Victoria. She was innocent in all this, even though he had warned her. That could be the true sense of why she didn't consider herself a part of high society, for the mere fact her family wasn't as cutthroat as some.

He wouldn't define his mother as such, either. She was a kind and caring person, except for when it came to the subject of him getting married. Not even she would consider him marriageable if she knew the real him. The man who was far more interested in fighting corruption than going about town with a wife on his arm and having the main goal of procreating the next generation of Dryers.

That would come someday. His family would need the next generation to continue the name and the successes of previous generations, but he was only twenty-six and had years before he'd need to procure a son. By then, he would be an elected official, enforcing laws that would make this world safer and more secure than the current conditions provided for.

Until then, a wife would only be in the way.

Young women wanted a man's undying attention, a fantasy life of love and adoration. When the time came for him to choose a wife, it would be a woman mature enough to understand that respectability and security would make them happier in the long run, because it didn't fade over time. He'd already seen men, friends of his, who had been so love smitten they couldn't think straight, then married only to be miserable within months of the wedding. Two were already seeking divorces and there were others who'd come to him seeking legal advice on ways to get out of the situations they now found themselves in with women they'd once claimed to love and now couldn't stand to be in the same house as.

He felt sympathy for his friends, but at the same time, he couldn't help but think how those men should have thought things through rather than rushing to the altar. A fraction of impulse control would have benefitted them greatly.

Then again, perhaps they didn't know all that he knew. How marriage had ruined lives before, including his uncle's.

If his mother knew his inner thoughts, she wouldn't be so intent to marry him off, especially to Victoria, because the entire family liked her and wanted the best for her. Maybe he should point that out to his mother.

He quickly forwent that thought. She'd simply try to convince him how wrong he was, and that could make matters worse.

Thumping his pencil on the stack of papers on his desk, he glanced at the clock hanging on the wall. Most days he was surprised when he looked up and realized it was past time to go home. Today, barely a few minutes ticked by between glances.

Victoria had to know that the two of them would be accompanying Audrey and Jake for a ride in the park this evening, and he wondered what she thought about that. If she was beginning to see through his mother's request or not. He also wondered what she thought about him being right.

Giving his head a shake, he shoved all thoughts to the back of his mind and put his focus on the papers before him. John Webster was selling his downtown department store to Blackwells, who had several other stores throughout the city. It was a simple sale, and he'd written dozens of such contracts practically with his eyes closed. This one should be just as easy. He just couldn't seem to keep his mind on it.

Needing a way for that to happen, he picked up the telephone and called John Webster. Once the line was connected, he said, "Hello, Mr. Webster, it's Lincoln Dryer."

"Hello, Mr. Dryer, thank you for considering my case."

Case? Lincoln quickly scanned through the paperwork, looking for who had taken the original request to write up a sales contract. Seeing no name, just a letter from Mr. Webster requesting a contract for the sale, he said, "It's my understanding you are selling your department store."

"That's what they're calling it," Mr. Webster said.

A shiver tickled Lincoln's spine, and he gave himself a second to determine if he wanted to go down a road that was sure to be dirty, but already knew the answer. "Would you be interested in having a consultation on this sale?"

The silence on the other end of the line was his answer. Webster was being coerced into selling. Something that was becoming too common.

"If you aren't interested in selling," Lincoln said. "I might be able to help. We could set up a time to meet."

"They know where I am at all times."

Lincoln's assumptions were stacking up like bricks. "I have some shopping to do, at your store, around three tomorrow afternoon."

"I could be in the men's department."

Because he'd never bought anything at Webster's store, that might appear too obvious to onlookers. "Make it the women's department," Lincoln said. "I have to purchase a gift for my sister's upcoming wedding."

"Excellent. Thank you, Mr. Dryer. Good day."

"Good day," Lincoln said, hanging up the handpiece. Was he getting his hopes up, or could this be the case he'd been hoping for?

* * *

Victoria stared at the list Roseanne Dryer had created with disbelief. Audrey's mother was a lovely woman whom Victoria had always adored. She still did, and her disbelief wasn't so much at Roseanne as it was to herself, because she was wondering if Lincoln been right.

Every event between now and the wedding, and there was a long list of them, had her attending them with Lincoln. Even a ride in the park this evening. She understood that the wedding greatly increased the number of parties, balls, and outings that Audrey would want to attend, but that didn't mean Victoria had to attend. It didn't mean that Lincoln had to, either. Especially things like riding in the park, or attending the theater, and other things that had no relation to the wedding.

Nothing close to this had ever happened on her prior visits.

"Is there something wrong, dear?" Roseanne asked, taking a sip of her tea.

"I'm just thinking about Audrey," Victoria said. "She and Jake might like to attend some of these events alone, together."

"They'll have the rest of their lives to be alone together." Roseanne looked towards the doorway through which Audrey had disappeared a few moments ago.

Although neither Victoria nor Audrey had seen a grease spot on Audrey's dress, Roseanne had and Audrey had left to change into another dress. Glancing back down at the list, Victoria said, "Lincoln may have to work late again."

"He'll be home tonight, and will be at each of those events." Rosanne lowered her voice to near a whisper. "The truth is, dear, I'm worried about Lincoln."

A tiny shiver rippled over Victoria. "Why?"

"He's the eldest, everyone expected him to marry first. Though he acts like that doesn't matter, I know it's on his mind." Roseanne lowered her voice even more. "He's not courting anyone, so without you, he'd have to attend all these events by himself, which would just add to his embarrassment."

Victoria highly doubted Lincoln was embarrassed to not be courting someone. He'd been adamant about not being interested in marriage during their carriage ride from the train station on Monday. "Perhaps it would be more of an embarrassment for him to be seen with me."

"Oh, heavens no! Why would you say such a thing? You're practically family. That's why it's perfect for you and him to attend functions together." Roseanne picked up her cup again. "It the perfect solution for everyone."

No, it wasn't, but Victoria couldn't voice that. Lincoln was going to be quite smug if his theory proved true. Which would also prove her wrong. "Perhaps Lincoln doesn't want to attend all of these functions."

"Of course, he does. He fully understands the importance of the entire family supporting Audrey and Jake in their decision to marry." Roseanne smiled. "Just as I know you understand how important your support is. It means so much to Audrey to have you here and to share this very special time with her."

Victoria hadn't questioned Audrey's request to come and stay with her for an entire month, but now wondered if it had even been Audrey's idea. Traveling from Tarrytown for dress fittings and a few mandatory events wouldn't have been an issue. That is what she and Audrey had discussed in their letters, until the one Audrey had written last week, asking for her to come and stay for the next month. Victoria had readily agreed, but it hadn't just been for Audrey. Getting away from the onslaught of suitors had excited her to no end. It seemed as if Audrey's wedding had put some kind of urgency in her mother when it came to finding her a husband. The number of men invited for dinner the past few weeks had been ridiculous.

"Well, now that we have that settled," Roseanne said. "I have a few things to see to."

Victoria stood as Roseanne rose and accepted a kiss on the cheek before Roseanne left the room. With the list in her hand, Victoria left the sitting room, too, and made her way through the massive house to the second floor, where she found Audrey now dressed in a lovely pink-and-white gown and instructing a maid to have Mrs. Clark examine the dress that she'd just removed for a grease spot on the front of the skirt.

"I never did see the spot that Mother could," Audrey said as the maid exited the room.

"I couldn't see it, either." Victoria sat down on the sofa in the sitting area of Audrey's bedroom, having formed a conclusion that there wasn't a spot. Roseanne had simply wanted a private opportunity to give her the list and attempt to convince her to go along with it.

"What's that?"

Victoria handed the list to Audrey. "A list of outings between now and your wedding date." The two of them had shared many secrets over the years, and never having withheld a single one, she added, "That Lincoln and I need to attend with you and Jake."

"Oh, that will be fun."

"Fun? Don't the two of you want to be alone?"

Audrey sat down on the bed and looked at the note. "This will give us more time alone. You and Linc can cover for us while we slip away for a few moments." Her grin was filled with delight, and the shimmer in her eyes said there would be a lot of kissing between her and Jake when they *slipped away.* Audrey insisted that there was nothing like kissing the man you loved.

Although she'd never held back from saying anything to Audrey, Victoria simply couldn't accuse Roseanne of matchmaking as Lincoln had. She decided to try another route. "Your mother said she's worried about Lincoln."

Audrey sighed and handed her back the list. "She is. My wedding has increased the pressure on him to get married. I've written to you about how the socialites are coming out of the woodwork after Lincoln. Mother is afraid that one of them might try to trick him into marriage. You know, create a scandal. It would be first one in our family and could be detrimental to all of us. That would be terrible, and even worse if it happened right before my wedding. It could ruin it."

A scandal had been known to ruin a wedding or two, and Victoria pressed a hand to her chest, where her heart had started to pound harder. She hadn't thought of it along those lines, and had to admit how much sense it made. "It's that bad? There are that many women after him?"

"Yes," Audrey said while nodding vigorously. "You'll see on Friday when we attend the ball at the Christie mansion. I wrote to you about when Eloise Watson pretended to twist her ankle and insisted that Lincoln carry her off the dance floor last month. She'd wanted him to carry her into the library so she could rest her ankle. He was onto her ploy and instead carried her over to her brother, handed her to him and suggested they find some ice for her ankle. Eloise was furious, and that's just one of the things that has happened lately. Sheila Butler pretended to faint and Kathrine Foster dumped punch down the front of her dress and handed Lincoln her handkerchief to wipe it off."

Appalled that a woman would act so forward, Victoria asked, "She didn't?"

"Yes, she did."

Victoria let out a long sigh. Lincoln was wrong. His mother wasn't matchmaking, she was simply trying to save him from a scandal, and that meant one thing. There was no choice but to go to all of the functions on the list with him.

Chapter Three

Lincoln hadn't been home for the evening meal the last two nights, but Victoria wasn't surprised to see him in the front parlor when she and Audrey entered the room prior to dinner.

Jake, with his coal-black hair and his down-turned mustache that always made him look like he was frowning, was also there and Audrey left her side to greet him.

As the couple met and took a hold of each other's hands, Victoria chose to give them their privacy and made her way over to Lincoln, who had crossed the room as soon as she'd entered it and now stood near the credenza hosting before-dinner drinks. "You didn't have to work late tonight, I see."

He grinned and shrugged while taking the top off a decanter. "No, I didn't."

"Didn't have a choice, did you?" Victoria asked. She didn't know why she felt the need to tease him, but knew that Roseanne had said he'd be home, and he was, per his mother's instructions. That didn't make her happy. In fact, it increased her empathy for him. He was being targeted, but it wasn't by his mother, as he thought.

"No more of a choice than you have to go riding after dinner," he replied, while handing her one of the glasses of sherry that he'd poured.

They had their backs to Audrey and Jake, and were both

talking softly, to keep from being overheard. She took a sip of the sweet wine before saying, "Your mother is not matchmaking, she's merely worried about you."

"Is she?"

"Yes." Lowering her voice even more, she said, "She wants to avoid a scandal."

He stared at her over the rim of his glass as he took a drink of the amber liquid with somewhat of a dullness in his eyes. "That's her excuse?"

"It's not an excuse, and I would think you would want to avoid one, too," she replied, trying hard to not become frustrated that he didn't believe her.

"In that case, I suppose I should be grateful that you are going to save me from one, too."

He'd never caught her attention, nor struck her nerves, like he was during her stay this time. "I very well could."

Twinkles formed in his brown eyes. "Victoria to the rescue." He leaned closer. "I don't need to be rescued. I'm perfectly capable of saving myself."

"What about everyone else? Your family?"

"I can save them from a scandal all my own, too." He lifted a brow. "I have been for years."

His attitude was exasperating, but so were her inner reactions to him. Not wanting to admit, or for him to know, he was making her heart beat too fast, she lifted the glass to her lips, but before taking a sip, whispered, "You should have a tail to go with your braying."

He lifted a brow. "Are you calling me an ass?"

There was no conceivable reason for her to be enjoying having done exactly that, in a roundabout way, but she was. Shrugging, she took a sip of her wine.

"What are you two whispering about?" Audrey asked

quietly, coming up behind them and sticking her face between their shoulders.

Looking at Lincoln, Victoria answered, "Animals."

However, at the very same moment, he said, "Asses."

She nearly choked on her own saliva, and stared at him. "Which are animals. Ones that bray."

"They do," he said. "They also kick."

"And are stubborn," she replied. "To a fault."

"Like some people I know."

Eyes still locked with his, she said, "I know some, too."

"I'll just take this glass of sherry," Audrey said, reaching between them to pick up the glass off the credenza. She backed away with the glass in her hand. "And leave you two alone."

Victoria knew she should walk away, too, but instead shook her head at Lincoln. "Asses?" she hissed.

"You started it," he said.

"I did not."

"Yes, you did. I was simply standing here, minding my own business when you walked over and—"

"Oh, hush up!"

"Why?"

In spite of the fact that they were whispering, she still bit back a retort that would be too long if she said all that was on her mind about his own beliefs and abilities and shot him a glare that said it instead.

He frowned. "How did you master that look? You aren't a mother."

Once again telling herself not to answer, she shook her head.

Grinning, he asked, "No last word?"

She was about to just call him an ass again, using the word this time, but was interrupted by someone else speaking.

"Oh, I wish your father was home," Roseanne said.

Both Victoria and Lincoln turned about, and watched as his mother walked across the room from the doorway she'd just entered.

"Look at the four of you," Roseanne continued. "You all look so adorable. Victoria, dear, that dress makes you look so nice. Yellow is your color, and Lincoln, your gold vest matches her dress perfectly."

As Roseanne turned her attention and compliments on Audrey and Jake, Victoria glanced at Lincoln. He did look nice in his black suit, white shirt, and gold vest, which was close to the color of her dress.

He was looking at her, too, the length of her, which made an odd warmth form in her stomach and spread. All the way to her face when their gazes met.

"She's wrong," he whispered, then took a drink from his glass. "That dress doesn't make you look nice. You make that dress look nice."

The warmth inside her heated up, and she could feel her pulse throbbing, even though she was sure he was still simply trying to get her goat. She had to draw in a deep breath before finding the ability to say, "You look nice, too."

He chuckled. "For a moment, I thought a cat got your tongue."

His ability to fluster her had hit a new level. "Just accept the compliment."

"Thank you." Giving her another slow glance, he added, "She was right about the color. You look good in yellow."

"Thank you," she said, only because he had thanked her for her compliment.

"It gives your face a glow."

She drew in another deep breath at yet another increase in her pulse.

"Or is that just a blush?" he asked. "Are you blushing?"

This time, she listened to herself and walked away, and kept walking even as his soft chuckle followed her. Taking a seat in the armchair adjacent to the sofa where Audrey and Jake sat, holding hands, she told herself to concentrate on the conversation already happening between them and Roseanne. It may have been about the wedding, or a number of other topics. She truly had no idea because the hand that settled on the back of her chair near her shoulder made concentrating impossible.

Lincoln was doing his best to unnerve her. She had no doubt about that. She also had no doubt that he was doing a very good job at doing exactly that. The question was why? He'd never been anything but friendly and kind during all of her other visits. They'd spoken, even joked, but in a different way. A more distant way. Nothing like this.

Who was she trying to fool? She knew why. He was trying to prove that his mother was matchmaking. It took her less than a split second to determine that she would prove to him that Roseanne wasn't. Everyone was worried about him being tricked into a scandal, and he should be, too. He had to know that could ruin Audrey's wedding.

A pit formed in her stomach. Good heavens! If a scandal did happen, it would be her fault. Preventing one was why she was here. She was sure that was why she'd been asked to come for a month.

Lincoln had no idea what had gotten into him—as his mother would say—other than he'd never realized just how fun it was to bicker with Victoria. A teasing bicker. She was so quick to respond and that made it enjoyable. Then again, maybe he did know what had gotten into him. She wasn't trying to force him to the altar. Women, and before them, girls, had been trying to do that for years, and that had made him stay away from even innocent fun that could be had with the opposite sex. He didn't have to worry about that with her. He was free to just be himself, with no worries that his actions or behavior would give her the wrong idea. That had never been an option for him before, and he wasn't opposed to it, even though he probably should be.

She did look nice in that yellow dress. Like the one she'd worn the other day, it wasn't overly busy with lace and ribbon and things that would have taken away from the fitted waist and flowing skirt that highlighted her a sculpted, well-defined shape. Her face was admirable, too. It had a glow to it, even when she wasn't blushing.

He bit back a smile at that memory. She had been blushing while he'd been complimenting her. They truly had been compliments. He'd noticed how lovely she looked as soon as she'd walked into the room, which had been why he'd instantly crossed the room and poured himself a second drink. If he hadn't, he wouldn't have been able to tear his gaze away from her, and might still be standing in the parlor, simply staring, and wondering why he'd never noticed her in the past. Then again, his mother had never implanted herself into her matchmaking role as she was this time.

Just as his mother had planned and insisted, they were now on horseback, riding through Central Park as the stars grew brighter and the air colder.

Jake and Audrey rode ahead of them, most likely whispering sweet nothings to one another. They were quite smitten with each other, and oddly enough, considering his attitude towards marriage, he was happy for them. He didn't have concerns of their marriage turning into something neither of them wanted. Namely because Jake was not like him. Jake already had the career he wanted and was ready for the next step in procuring a future for his family. Like many men in the city, Jake was following in his father's footsteps. Theirs was the newspaper business, and Jake had taken over as editor-in-chief last year, after being a reporter for several years.

Lincoln couldn't think of a better man than Jake to marry Audrey. They'd known each other for years, and had been smitten with each other for nearly just as long, yet had chosen to wait for marriage until Jake had been promoted into a position that would indeed secure their future. Not only financially, for his family was very well-off. Jake had the time for marriage, for a wife His job no longer drew him out into the streets in the middle of the night to report on some dastardly deed, or a fire that could spread along blocks of businesses, or inclement weather that could bring the city to a standstill. All things that would have sent Audrey into a worried panic.

Furthermore, Audrey was not like so many socialites. She'd patiently waited for marriage, knowing that would give them time to make sure they were making the right decision.

"How much longer do you think they'll want to ride?" Victoria asked.

He and Victoria had silently been riding side by side behind the happy couple, and he glanced her way. "Getting tired?" They had ridden thorough a large portion of the park, at a slow, dull walk.

The expression on her face was enough to make him grin, even before she spoke. "Bored," she replied. "Aren't you? The horses are."

He agreed fully and gestured towards the couple ahead of them. "Maybe we wouldn't be bored if we were whispering sweet nothings to each other."

She let out a huff of disgust. "The horses would still be bored."

He laughed. It shouldn't be this fun to frustrate someone, but she made it enjoyable. Just like she made the green cape she was wearing over her yellow dress look lovely.

"We could have a race," she suggested. "To the footbridge. It's not far."

He knew how far it was to the footbridge and that the path to it was straight. However, more importantly, he knew she was comfortable and confident in the saddle. She and Audrey often rode during her stays here, and he'd accompanied them a time or two. His third consideration was for others. The pathway was wide, and so far had been relatively clear of park patrons. He brought his horse to a stop and confirmed her suggestion. "Just to the footbridge?"

Stopping her horse next to him, she looked at him expectantly, but also with a shine of excitement in her eyes. "Yes."

He glanced at her horse. The bay mare had a good temperament and was sure-footed, which was why that was the animal he'd chosen for her to ride this evening. Determining there was no real danger in providing her request, he asked, "On three?"

Her smile lit up her face. "On three," she agreed while readjusting the reins in her hands and leaning forward in line with the mare's neck.

"One," they said together.

"Two."

"Three!"

The horses lurched forward at the same time, and reached a gallop in unison. He steered his animal left, while she went right and they raced past Jake and Audrey. It had been some time since he'd raced for the fun of it. Samson, his horse, was faster than her mare, but he wasn't focused on winning. The laughter echoing in her wake was like a win in itself.

Though the ride was swift, it was smooth and he felt as if he was at his leisure watching her ride. It was a sight to see, her green cape flying behind her, lit by the stars and the moon, and a gas lamp now and again. There were very few, if any, society girls who would dare be seen galloping through the park. Perhaps he should have qualms about that, but at the moment, her pleasure was more important. She was clearly enjoying the race, and truth was, he was, too.

They raced along the gravel path, side by side, past trees, flickering flames inside the glass globes of the light poles, and trimmed hedges. The footbridge was in sight and they both surged forward, when suddenly, out of nowhere, a dog ran onto the pathway and froze as if in shock at the horses racing forward.

Lincoln steered his horse far to the left to make room for Victoria, and pulled up on the reins, but she didn't slow or steer in either direction. He shouted, "Dog!" but at that very same moment, her horse soared into the air.

Lincoln's heart leaped into his throat, and remained there as Victoria's horse sailed over the dog, made a smooth landing, and continued onward in a gallop.

The entire event had only taken a matter of seconds, but in his mind, and his pounding heart, it had been much longer.

Samson danced with impatience, and Lincoln eased off the reins, urged the horse to race after Victoria while the dog ran off in the opposite direction.

He arrived at the footbridge as she was slowing her horse into a walk, to let it cool down. "What were you thinking?" he asked, fear of what might have happened burning inside him. "You could have broken your neck!"

"My neck? You mean thc dog's neck, had I run into it."

He grasped a hold of the rein running along her horse's neck, bringing it to a stop. "I mean your neck if you'd fallen off!"

"Fallen off?" She laughed. "I've been riding longer than I've been walking."

"I don't care! That was dangerous!"

"Jumping over a dog? I'd say it would have been more dangerous to run into it. There wasn't time for me to do anything else."

"Yes, there was. I swerved!"

"The dog wasn't in front of you!"

"You are the most—"

"You're just mad," she interrupted.

"Yes, I am!"

"Because I won!"

Lincoln took the time to draw in a deep breath, but it didn't help. "I don't care who won. You could have gotten seriously hurt with a stunt like that."

"It wasn't a stunt," she said. "It was to save a dog's life. Now, will you kindly release my horse so I can cool her down?"

He let go of the rein and followed as she walked her horse over the short wooden bridge. A million and one things were still floating in his mind. Front and center was her and the injuries she could have acquired. "How would your family have felt if you'd gotten hurt?"

She didn't respond.

He rode up beside her. "Or mine? Think about Audrey and Mother."

"Think of the scandal that would have created," she said with feigned exaggeration.

"I'm not worried about a scandal." He let out a pent-up sigh. "I was worried about you. Nothing more."

The clip-clop of horse steps echoed behind them. They both turned, then reined in their horses to wait for Jake and Audrey to catch up.

"We heard yelling," Audrey said. "Did something happen?"

"A dog ran into the road," Victoria said, glancing at him.

"Oh, no!" Audrey pressed a hand to her chest as she glanced at both of them. "But you're all right? Both of you? We didn't see a dog."

"We're fine," Victoria replied.

"It ran off," Lincoln said, forgoing the need to explain anything more.

Audrey gave them both a long, somewhat perplexed look, before she smiled at Jake. "We are getting cold and are going home for some hot chocolate."

"We'll join you," Lincoln said, but his gaze was on Victoria.

"Yes, we will," she said, and nudged her horse into a walk.

The ride home was quiet. At least it was between him and Victoria. Jake and Audrey could still be whispering sweet nothings. They were behind him, so he didn't know. They could very well be whispering about other things.

Him things. He wasn't one to lose his temper easily, and his sister knew that. She also knew he'd been mad.

He still was, but had lost a lot of his steam. Victoria hadn't known a dog would run into their path, and jumping over it had been a better solution than running into it. She hadn't had time to swerve, not at the speed they'd been going, and he could blame that on him. He could have slowed the race simply by letting her take the lead. If he had done that, she would have had time and room to swerve around the dog.

Therefore, the truth was that he was culpable in what had happened.

As soon as they'd handed the reins of their horses over to the groom, he cupped her elbow to escort her to the back door of the house. "I apologize for shouting at you," he said quietly. "That was very rude of me, and I agree that jumping over the dog was the smartest choice."

She stopped and turned to stare up at him. "Oh, dear, that had to hurt."

"Excuse me?"

"Apologizing, agreeing with me, and calling me smart, all at the same time?" She huffed out a tiny breath. "That either had to hurt, or you like eating crow."

He pinched his lips together, mainly because he couldn't think of a comeback. Normally, he would have, but her smile was blocking his ability to do much other than admire the shine on her face at besting him.

"Are you two whispering again?" Audrey asked. "Should I be wondering about something?"

He and Victoria turned around to face Audrey, then glanced at each other, before he said, "That's for us to know and you to find out."

Audrey giggled as she and Jake walked past.

Victoria was looking at him with eyes wide. "Why did you say that?"

"What?" he asked, not understanding her concern. "It was an answer to her question."

She shook her head. "Don't you realize what you just did?"

He had to think for a moment as to what she was referring to, and glanced at his sister and Jake walking in the house. Nothing came to mind. "I was joking. It was a joke."

"She doesn't think it was a joke." Victoria pointed at the door. "Everything right now is about their wedding. I bet you a dime to a dollar that she thinks you—we—are whispering about something to do with that. The wedding."

Lincoln was still dumbfounded, yet a hint of reality struck. She could be right. "Like what?"

She stared at the house door for a moment. "I don't know. A gift, maybe. Something unique and different."

He felt deflated, because that was probably exactly what Audrey was thinking. "What would be a unique and different gift?"

"I don't know, but I bet that's what she's thinking, and expecting. Something out of the ordinary."

He agreed. That would be exactly what Audrey was expecting. Luckily, another thought formed. Having Victoria with him would make his visit to Webster's tomorrow appear more natural. He'd planned on picking up a little something, just to make the visit legit, but she would have more of an idea of something unique and out of the ordinary. "What are you doing tomorrow afternoon?"

"Nothing that I know of, why?"

"I have to go to Webster's Department Store in the afternoon. Can you meet me there at three? Help me pick out something?"

"I guess so."

"Good. I'll tell William, he'll be prepared to take you in the carriage."

"What are you going to buy them?"

"I don't know, hopefully you'll see something." He put pressure on her elbow to escort her to the house.

"Me?"

"Yes, you."

"You're the one who said—"

"Not so fast," he interrupted. "If you'd have just accepted my apology, we'd have kept right on walking into the house and no one would have caught us whispering again."

She huffed out a breath before hissing, "Oh, hush up."

"Gladly." He grinned at getting the best of her, and he opened the house door.

Chapter Four

William was indeed ready to give her a ride the following afternoon, and they arrived outside of the department store a few minutes before three in the afternoon. The stone building was massive, six stories tall and taking up half a block. Huge bronze and glass doors along with tall sparkling display windows took up the entire lower floor. Victoria knew what was on every floor, for this was one of her favorite stores. Webster's had items that couldn't be found anywhere else, and she never missed a shopping trip to it whenever she was in the city.

The carriage had barely rolled to a stop when Lincoln appeared next to it on the sidewalk. Victoria told herself the hitch behind her breastbone was merely excitement at visiting the store, not at seeing him. Yet she did admit that he looked as handsome as ever in his gray suit, burgundy vest and neatly tied ascot.

"Are you ready to go shopping?" he asked, while holding out a hand.

She hooked the handle of her small leather purse over her wrist and made sure her green cape was still tied beneath her chin before taking a hold of his hand. "I am. Have you decided what you're going to purchase?"

"No, that is completely up to you."

There was still no reason that she could comprehend why it was so amusing to bicker with him at every turn, yet couldn't stop from doing just that. "She is your sister."

"She is your best friend, and I'm sure you know her likes and dislikes more than I do." He stopped near the massive front doors. "This is a large store."

"Have you never been here before?"

He shook his head. "I never go shopping."

"You don't?"

"No."

"What about Christmas or birthdays?"

He shrugged. "Mother tells me what she'll buy for Audrey and Father from me, and Audrey tells me what she'll buy for Mother from me."

She should be shocked, but as he'd been talking, she'd remembered shopping with Audrey for a birthday gift for their mother from him during a visit last fall. "There's never anything you need to purchase?"

"Clothes from my tailor, shoes from the shoemaker. Anything else, I just tell someone what I need and they get it for me."

Just because it was the truth, she shook her head at him. "I feel sorry for you."

"Why?"

She grasped a hold of his hand and tugged him towards the door. "Because you have no idea what you're missing."

A doorman opened the door and held it for them, and in every direction, there were employees ready to help. Shop girls wearing freshly pressed green-and-white-striped dresses, and male clerks wearing starched green-and-white-striped shirts, white bow ties and gray pants.

"The first floor is seasonal merchandise," Victoria explained. "At Christmas time last year, they had huge trees in the windows, all decorated, with little trains beneath them on miniature tracks, and this entire floor was full of toys. The second floor is household goods and materials, the third floor is children's, the fourth is women's, and the fifth is men's."

"The sixth?" he asked.

"Offices, I assume."

He chuckled. "I certainly brought the right person with me. Shall we take the elevator or the stairs?"

"The stairs," she said, tugging him along the central aisle that led to the wide marble staircase. "That way you can see everything below as you walk up and down."

"Very well, the stairs it is."

She hadn't been here since Christmas, and scanned the display tables, shelves, and floor displays as they walked up the stairway. Umbrellas, lawn chairs, badminton and croquet sets, as well as many other spring items were nicely displayed, including a variety of bicycles. She had yet to try riding a bicycle, but was very curious about them.

At the top of the steps, they turned to continue on the next set of steps, and she asked, "What floor did you want to start on?"

"Women's."

"Women's?"

"Yes. Audrey is a woman."

She had put some thought into what he could possibly buy, and felt the need to point out, "I know she is a woman, but you are buying a wedding gift, so it should be something for both her and Jake. I assumed we'd looked for something on the household floor."

"Oh, well, maybe, but let's still start on the women's floor."

She readily agreed, in part because he might have something in mind, and because she wanted to see the newest displays. This was where she'd purchased the leather purse with its stiff handles and clasp that she was carrying. She'd never seen them anywhere else and everyone who'd seen hers had wanted their own. Every woman, that was. She also had the most wonderful pair of lined gloves for winter wear that she'd purchased here last fall.

"This is a big store," he said. "A nice store."

"Did you expect elsewise?"

"I don't really know."

Shocked, she asked, "Surely you've noticed it while driving by?"

"On occasion, but I never wondered what was inside."

Still in utter surprise, she asked, "Why not?"

"I suspect because I have other things on my mind," he replied.

"Such as?"

He shrugged. "Work, cases, clients."

That didn't surprise her. She knew from past visits and Audrey's letters that he was very committed to his work. "Well, I imagine this is the most popular store in all of the city," she said. "You can find things here that you can't find anywhere else."

"Interesting. Did you have a difficult time getting away from the house?" he asked as they traipsed to the third set of stairs taking them to the fourth floor.

"No. I simply said I had some shopping to do. Audrey was busy with correspondences and your mother was having a luncheon with her library charity group."

Her eyes had already gone to a display of what appeared to be shorter than usual skirts when they arrived at the top of the steps for the women's floor. A man was standing there. Not a clerk, because he was wearing a black suit.

"Mr. Dryer," the man said.

Lincoln shook hands with the man. "Mr. Webster, allow me to introduce Miss Biggs. She's come along to assist me in purchasing a gift for my sister."

"Miss Biggs, it's a pleasure to meet you."

"Likewise, Mr. Webster," she said, wondering why Lincoln had said he'd never been here. He clearly knew the owner. In all the times she'd been here, she'd never seen Mr. Webster before. Not that she should have. It's just seemed odd for him to have met them at the top of the stairs.

"Victoria, if you don't mind, I'd like to speak with Mr. Webster for a few moments," Lincoln said. "Perhaps you could have a look around, see if anything catches your eye?"

She knew a dismissal when she heard one, and didn't mind because his conversation was none of her business. That's what she told herself in an effort to quell her curiosity. "Certainly. Excuse me."

There was much to see, things she wanted to examine closer, yet none of it was stealing her attention. She moved to the clothing racks, yet kept an eye on where the two men had moved closer to the wall, almost hidden behind a dress form wearing a lovely yellow brocade cape.

Mr. Webster was perhaps a few years older than Lincoln, and had a narrow black mustache and long sideburns. The two of them appeared to be in a deep discussion about something.

"May I help you?" a young sales girl asked.

"I'm just browsing," Victoria replied, turning her attention to the rack of shorter than normal skirts.

"These are part of our new rational clothing line," the

sales girl explained. "They are clip skirts." Lifting the bottom of a skirt the girl demonstrated how the skirt had several buttons and buttonholes near the hem. "These are perfect for bicycling. You can unbutton the side and button them around your knees so the material is out of the way while pedaling. We also have new corsets that have elastic, making them far more comfortable."

"Interesting," Victoria said, very fascinated.

"We also have bloomers right over here." The sales clerk turned to another rack. "Many women find them even more practical while riding."

The bloomers reminded Victoria of men's pants, just prettier because they came in an array of colors with lacy hems.

"Do you ride?" the sales girl asked.

"No, I have not tried it yet."

"Oh, you must. I ride my bicycle to work every day."

"You do?"

"Yes, it's much faster than finding a cab. Mr. Webster allowed me to purchase one on payments. Several other employees, too. We love them." The girl gestured towards the staircase. "We have a wide variety of bicycles for sale on the first floor. The new safety bicycles, with two wheels the same size, are much easier to control than the ones with the large front wheel, and the chain guard protects…"

As the girl continued, several things went through Victoria's mind. Much of it was about how she did want to try and ride a bicycle, especially the new ones that were becoming the rave, but she also was amazed by how well informed the sales girl was about the subject. However, foremost on her mind continued to be Lincoln. He and Mr. Webster were still talking behind the mannequin.

She couldn't help but wonder if Mr. Webster was a client of Lincoln's. The idea of asking him about her case had crossed her mind more than once. She truly didn't want to wait until his father returned.

Lincoln listened with deep interest as John Webster continued his reasons for needing to sell the store. According to John, his father, Alfred Webster, who had started the store twenty years ago, had been murdered in the alley behind the store late one night last November. The police had determined it had been a random robbery. That "thugs" had assumed he must have had money on him, perhaps a deposit for the bank, but John said nothing had been removed from his father's pockets, and that his father never transported deposits to the bank himself. Nor had any thugs ever been arrested.

Then in January, John had received an offer from a brokering agency to sell the store. When he'd refused, he'd begun receiving messages that if he didn't sell, what had happened to his father would happen to him. Webster didn't want to sell, but had a family to think about, especially now that the threatening messages had begun to include his wife and children.

Lincoln may have heard of Alfred Webster's death, but couldn't say for sure. Obituaries filled the newspapers weekly and the retail market had not been one that his law firm had been overly involved in. "You believe Blackwells is coercing you into selling your store?" Lincoln asked, for confirmation of what he'd just heard.

"It's not Blackwells," John said. "It's Alderman Kelley. He's got his thumb on the mayor and is ruling businesses in the city with his taxes and tariffs. He's also now the owner of Blackwells. He bought them out, all four stores, last year. Though he's using an investment company, making it look like he's not involved. I'd asked my lawyer to write up a contract, but he refused, afraid to get involved. I'll understand if you feel the same."

"I have no qualms about getting involved," Lincoln said. In fact, this was exactly what he'd been looking for. It sounds like Kelley was trying to get rid of all competition for his other department stores.

"Let me further my explanation," John said. "It might change your mind about agreeing. The brokering agency suggested a contract wasn't needed. I insisted it was due to my father's will, which isn't completely true, but I was hoping to buy enough time to find a lawyer who was not afraid of taking on Kelley. He's buying up retail businesses—actually, his investment companies are—and could soon own all the major retailers in all the boroughs, from furniture companies to department stores. He's attempting to build himself a monopoly."

Lincoln knew Phillip Kelley had been taking kickbacks from deals he'd made during his political career for years, but he hadn't known the extent of it. How Kelley was using front companies, like the investment ones that John was talking about. That could explain why even though there was plenty of suspicion, the ties directly to Kelley hadn't been apparent.

"He has the mob protecting him, too," John said. "They are under his thumb as much as the mayor."

"That's how he keeps getting elected," Lincoln supplied. "The mob is out there, coercing the poor neighborhoods that Kelley's the only one they can vote for, or they'll lose their meager jobs, apartments, or their lives. He's using every avenue to coerce votes."

"I love this store," John said. "My father loved it. Worked hard to make it one of the most popular in the city, and I have money to fight this, but I do have to think about my family. Their safety."

"Of course, you do," Lincoln said. "Do you know of other owners facing buyouts?"

John shook his head. "No, I don't. There are more, I guarantee it, but they are afraid of talking. They know what happened to my father. It wasn't a random robbery like the police say, but there's no proof. Nothing I can do."

Lincoln nodded. He knew that Victoria was watching them, and that others could be, too. "I'll need a copy of your father's will because there very well could be a legal way to tie it to any sale, and I'll need any and all information you have on Kelley and his investment companies."

"I'll tell you all I know, but I don't know how much help it will be."

"It'll help, and I'll also put my own investigators on it, but I think we should keep this under wraps for as long as possible. We don't want anyone knowing I'm working on it. You can write up all you know, courier it to my office. I don't think we should be seen together, nor should we trust telephone lines." Though he didn't say it, he wondered if he'd already said too much on the telephone yesterday.

"I will include a few social engagements that I will be at in the coming weeks with the papers I send to your office," John said. "Perhaps we could briefly speak at them."

"Perfect," Lincoln said. Figuring they'd spent enough time alone together, he then said, "Now, I need to buy a gift for my sister's wedding. Something unique and different. Out of the ordinary, for her and her soon-to-be husband."

"May I offer a suggestion?" John asked after a thoughtful moment.

"Please."

"We are the only store that sells the new diamond-framed safety bicycles, for now anyway. They are becoming very popular with the younger crowd."

Lincoln nodded, slowly at first, but then the idea really resonated. He didn't know much about bicycles, other than that they were growing in popularity. That alone was something that Audrey would enjoy. "I think that's an excellent idea. Bicycles."

"Allow me to show you them to you," John said. "They are on the ground floor."

They walked around the display tables and racks full of women's clothing to where Victoria was examining a display of hats. Lincoln had noticed how she'd kept an eye on him and John during their conversation, and wasn't surprised when she stepped around the table to meet him.

"Have you found anything?" he asked.

She smiled at both him and John. "I've found a floor full of wonderful things, but I'm afraid not anything suitable as a wedding gift."

"Mr. Webster has provided me with a suggestion."

Her perfectly shaped brows arched in question. "Oh? What is that?"

"Bicycles," he replied, watching her expression.

Her face took on a glow as her smile grew. "I never thought of that. Audrey would be so surprised, I'm sure she would. I believe Jake would, too."

"That's what I thought," Lincoln agreed.

"Well, then, shall we go down to the first floor?" John asked. "We have several models to choose from."

Once on the first floor, it didn't take long to pick out two bicycles and arrange to have them delivered to the house next week. Lincoln figured he'd give them early, just to satisfy his sister's curiosity. "Is there anything else you'd like to look at while we are here?" Lincoln asked Victoria after John Webster had left them and he'd paid for the bicycles.

"No, I can come back another day," she replied. "I do believe you picked out very unique gifts. Audrey is going to be shocked, and excited."

He agreed, and wondered if he shouldn't have purchased a third bicycle, considering how Victoria had examined the bicycles with what he'd considered a longing gaze. "Shall we be on our way, then?"

"Yes."

Lincoln had never thought much about being seen with someone, and perhaps was only now because of the issues that John Webster was facing. The entire store was most likely being watched. Today, he noticed people looking his way. Men and women, and had to note that it wasn't him they were admiring, it was Victoria. Though most of her peach gown was covered by her green cape, the colors went well together, which wasn't by chance. The green silk scarf that matched her cape was looped over the top of her hat and tied beneath her chin in a way that enchantingly framed her face. "Is there anywhere else you wish to stop this afternoon?" he asked as a doorman opened the large glass door for them.

"No, I'll just have William take me home."

"William isn't here." He gestured up the road, where his

carriage and driver waited. "I assumed you'd ride home with me. I'm done for the day."

"Very well."

His carriage was enclosed, which he was glad about because the day had turned blustery and gray, suggesting it could rain before they arrived home. "Thank you for your help today," he said, once they were settled on the single seat.

"You're welcome." Looking at him, she asked, "Is Mr. Webster a client of yours?"

With client privacy in mind, he replied, "I'd never met him before today. Who better to ask for a unique gift than the store owner?"

She nodded. "True." After a brief, thoughtful moment, she asked, "Do you have a lot of clients right now?"

"Enough, but I had completed my work for the day before leaving the office, if that's what you're worried about."

She glanced out the window on her side of the carriage. "No, just curious."

Noting the sky turning darker outside his window, he asked, "What is on your agenda tonight?"

"Nothing. Audrey is having dinner with Jake and his family tonight. You?"

"Nothing," he replied, with a shake of his head, whereas in all actuality, he'd be making a few telephone calls to find out more information on the death of Alfred Webster as well as the company that had purchased Blackwells. A thought formed, and considering she was much more educated on department stores and shopping than him, he asked, "Have you ever been to a Blackwells department store?"

"Yes. Many times."

"Did you like it?" he asked, fishing for more information.

"I used to, but the last few times I've been to the one close to Tarrytown, I've been disappointed. The store had been purchased by someone else, and they don't have the same quality of merchandise that they used to, nor the variety. I was looking for a new lamp to replace one that had been accidently broken, and found one, but I really don't care for it."

"How long ago was that?"

"January."

"How do you know they are under new ownership?"

"I asked." A moment later, she continued, "I didn't recognize anyone working there and always had in the past. I'd also noticed that their hours had changed. They are now open on Sundays. I didn't share that with my family because I knew it would upset my grandfather. He's set in his ways and believes no one should work on Sunday." She let out a sigh. "Their prices have also changed, increased substantially, and that hurts the residents of Tarrytown. They can't afford to pay extravagant prices for everyday needs. Yet with other stores closing, Blackwells is the only option for things."

He probably shouldn't take advantage of her knowledge of shopping and stores, but he trusted her opinion. "Why are other stores closing?"

She shrugged. "From what I hear, they can't compete with Blackwells, which doesn't make a lot of sense, because Blackwells had been there for years and it wasn't a problem in the past."

He asked several other questions about Tarrytown and the businesses as they traversed the city streets, wondering why Kelley would have purchased that store when it wasn't in his district. It all simply added to his list of things to have investigated.

Luckily, they arrived home before the rain hit. Once there, he went to his second-floor study and made notes from his conversation with her and with John Webster, before he telephoned a few trusted men to research more information.

He'd just returned the receiver to its holder when a knock sounded on the door. "Come in."

As the door opened and Victoria appeared in the doorway, Lincoln rose to his feet, then quickly crossed the room to hold the door as she carried her paper-wrapped picture into the room.

"May I show you something?" she asked.

"Certainly." Once she was in the room, he closed the door. "May I help you with that?"

"No, I have it. I'll set it on the table, if that's all right?"

"Sure."

The room was large, hosting shelves filled with law books, framed maps, and awards on the walls from his school days, a fireplace hosting a fire just large enough to chase off the chill from the rain pelting on the windows, and a couch, table and chairs, besides his desk. The table was on the far side of the room from his desk, and he crossed the room to click on the light above the table.

She'd already set down the picture and was carefully removing the paper, then she lifted a thin piece of wood off the frame and set it aside with the paper.

"That's a nice picture," he said, simply being kind because in truth, he didn't see anything about the painting of flowers worthy of hauling it so far or keeping it so protected.

"I lied," she said, kneeling down. "It's not one of my grandfather's favorites, it's simply one of three that hang in our drawing room." Eye level with the picture lying on the table, she gazed over the glass. "You might have to kneel down to see it."

He walked around to her side of the table and knelt down next to her. The picture didn't catch his attention nearly as much as the faint, floral scent filling his nostrils. He'd noticed her perfume earlier in the day, and liked how it wasn't overpowering. It matched her personality, which wasn't overpowering, either.

Her gaze was still on the picture, and he tried to focus, to see what she was looking at. The light from the bulb overhead was reflecting off the glass, and in order to see better, he raised a hand to block the shine from the bulb.

She grabbed his wrist. "Don't touch it."

"I wasn't going to touch the picture," he said, amazed that someone could be so protective over a painting.

"Can you see that?" she asked, releasing his hand to point at the side of the picture. "Right there. Along the side, do you see those four fingerprints?"

He saw smudges on the otherwise clean glass that might be fingerprints, but didn't move to get a better look. "I'm sure Mrs. Owens can clean that for you."

"I don't want it cleaned." She grimaced while shrugging. "That was another lie. They were both just white lies for good reason."

"Oh? What's the reason?" he asked.

"Those are fingerprints, and I'm going to use them to prove who stole ten thousand dollars out of my grandfather's safe."

Concern and shock rippled through him. "Ten thousand dollars?"

She nodded. "Yes. Right there, along the side of the picture, you can see where someone grasped a hold of the frame to move the picture. The prints prove it."

"They could be fingerprints, but they don't prove anything."

"Yes, they do. This picture hangs in front of my grandfather's wall safe. There are hinges on the back for it to swing open. The hinges are on the opposite side from the prints. Proving that's where someone grasped a hold of it to swing it open and reveal the safe door. I hung a different picture in its place when I took this one down."

Lincoln scratched the back of his neck. She was convinced of her beliefs. He, though, had more questions, several questions, and started with the most relevant. "How did they get inside the safe?"

"They had asked my grandfather to put something in there, and must have watched him open it, figured out the combination."

He was concerned for her. Having money stolen was no little issue, especially ten thousand dollars, but she was grasping at straws. "Victoria—"

"I'm not imagining things, Lincoln."

"I wasn't close to suggesting that." He chose another route. "Is whatever the fingerprint person had asked your grandfather to put in the safe still there?"

"No, because he asked my grandfather to retrieve it for him, again, while he was in the room. It was a watch, that he said he didn't want to lose, but then asked for it back when I refused to go for a walk with him. However, then he stayed for dinner, but before dinner, he used the water closet. I think that's when he stole the money. The rest of us were in the front parlor, waiting for dinner to be served." She stood up and set the wood back over the glass. "This past winter, I read an article about how a suspect in a murder case was proven by her fingerprints."

Rising to his feet, he didn't know if he should be humored or concerned over her choice of reading material, but he had another more pressing question. "Why did you refuse to go for a walk with him?"

"For one, it was cold outside, and for two, I didn't want to go for a walk with him." Changing the subject, she said, "The article I read explained how everyone's fingerprints are unique, that no two are the same. Not even for twins."

Attempting to be as tactful as possible, he said, "Fictional stories about solving crimes can seem—"

"It wasn't fiction," she said. "And I know some people might think my grandfather foolish for keeping so much money in his safe, but he doesn't have a lot of trust in banks and insists that we need to have enough cash on hand so that if anything were to happen to the banks, we'd still be able to live comfortably."

The seriousness of her expression said that she fully believed in what she was saying, and he had to admit that her story was increasing his concern. Someone could have stolen money from her family. However, he was still looking for a solid line of reasoning. "Perhaps those are your grandfather's prints on the glass."

"No. He's the one who taught me to open it only by the frame, because smudges on the glass might alert someone that something is behind the picture. Furthermore, I'm the only one who goes in the safe. My grandfather rarely does. That day was unusual, only because of the request. Otherwise, he would have asked me to open it. That's what he always does. I opened it two days later, to take out some money for my trip here. I keep a tally and know exactly how much is in there at all times. The bottom shelf had five stacks of bills, ten thousand in each stack, and the top had eight-hundred and seventy-five, before I took some. I rearranged the stacked bills, so if my grandfather looks, he won't notice the missing money, because I don't want him to know until I've proven what happened."

"Why?"

"Multiple reasons," she said.

Questions were piling up in his mind and answers such as that were only creating more. He knew her family history, somewhat, mainly through Audrey.

"I'm wondering if you could help me prove my case?" she asked.

She didn't have a case, yet Lincoln couldn't say that. She was too convinced that she did. "How do you plan on proving whose fingerprints those are?"

"In a court of law. You will question him about being in the house that day, and then make him put his fingerprints on another piece of glass. The jury will see how they match perfectly, and case solved."

He withheld the want to shake his head. "I'm assuming that's what happened in the book you read."

"Article. It was in an English law journal, and yes, that's how it happened. The jury saw the evidence and the woman had no choice but to confess."

If only things were that easy. She was looking at him with such expectancy, he hated to disappoint her, but couldn't indulge her, either. "In order to take a case to trial, we'd have to have enough evidence to charge this fingerprint person."

"I do have enough evidence. His fingerprints. He was at the house and ten thousand dollars was missing after he left."

"Did you contact the police? File a report?"

"No, I didn't want anyone to know. Can't you do that?"

Why did some people think lawyers were miracle makers? He'd encountered that before. "I'm sorry, Victoria, but there's not enough here to make a case." He gestured towards the picture. "Some smudges on glass—"

"They aren't smudges." She picked up the paper and laid it over the wood, folding it around the edges of the frame. "They are fingerprints. Four fingerprints belonging to Elwood Kelley."

Lincoln's spine stiffened. "Elwood Kelley? Alderman Kelley's son?"

She picked up the picture. "Yes."

More than concern was causing his nerves to spike. "How do you know him? Why was he at your house?"

"Because he's one of the suitors my mother has encouraged to call upon me." She walked towards the door. "I'm sorry I bothered you."

He opened his mouth to stop her, but closed it. Elwood Kelley was as corrupt as his father, and accusing him of stealing could bring down the wrath of his father on her entire family.

Lincoln quickly crossed the room and grasped a hold of the doorknob. "You didn't bother me. I'm very sorry for your loss of money, but I think you need to just let this one go."

Staring at the door, waiting for him to open it, she said, "Thank you for your opinion."

It was more than an opinion. It was a warning. One he

would have to make sure that she heeded. She could get hurt, seriously hurt, and he wouldn't allow that to happen on his watch. If anyone needed to be saved, it was her, not him.

Chapter Five

Victoria had done her best to act normal throughout the evening, but it had been very difficult with the amount of disappointment floating inside her. Lincoln hadn't believed a word she'd said. He'd been nice about it, but his expression had displayed his disbelief. The article she'd read hadn't been fiction. Nor had it been the only one she'd read about fingerprints. It had been proven that everyone had unique, one-of-a-kind fingerprints.

He hadn't even believed that. She'd seen his face when she'd told him those were Elwood Kelley's fingerprints. Just because Elwood was an alderman's son, it didn't give him the right to get away with theft.

Nor did it make him an excellent *prospect*, as her mother had said, even when Victoria had pointed out how much her grandfather loathed politicians. He didn't trust them any more than he did banks. Which was another reason why Victoria hadn't wanted her grandfather to know about the theft.

Perhaps she should have at least told her mother, but she wouldn't have believed it any more than Lincoln had.

If anyone's mother was attempting to matchmake, it was her mother. Elwood had just been one among many who had been invited to call upon her, despite having informed her mother that she wasn't looking for a possible husband.

Maybe all mothers thought marriage was the ultimate goal, and maybe it was, to the right man. That's what it was going to take for her, and she wouldn't settle for less. It irked her to think that others expected her to settle on nothing more than a suitable match. Both her mother and grandfather had found the loves of their lives, and it was only fair that they allow her that opportunity, too.

Trying to shut down her mind, because she didn't want to start thinking about if there was a right man out there for her, Victoria pulled the covers tighter beneath her chin as she rolled over in the soft bed and buried the side of her face in the pillow.

She shouldn't have shown the picture to Lincoln.

However, that wasn't going to stop her. It might take longer than she'd wanted, but she would prove that Elwood had stolen that money. She had to. For herself and Eva. The idea of either of them ending up married to a man who would squander away all that her grandfather and father had worked for goaded her to no end. Her mother simply didn't understand that.

One other thing did worry her. If Lincoln had said that there wasn't enough evidence for a trial, his father might, too. She hadn't contacted the police because she didn't want her grandfather to know that money was missing. Upon noticing the missing amount, she'd asked if he'd been in the safe. He'd then told her about Elwood asking to put his watch in the safe. Elwood had claimed the chain had broken and he didn't want to lose the watch. That had made no sense to her, he'd had a pocket he could put it in, but her grandfather had fallen for it.

If she had told him the truth, there was no telling what he might do. He was not only set in his ways, at times, his temper got the best of him and he could very well track Elwood down and confront him, especially if he'd learned Elwood's father was an alderman. She wanted to avoid upsetting her grandfather like that.

Avoid a scandal.

Huffing out a breath, she rolled onto her other side. She didn't want to cause a scandal for her family as much as Roseanne didn't want one for her family.

She'd find out if that truly was what Roseanne was worried about tomorrow night, at the ball held at the Christie mansion. According to Audrey, half of New York had been on pins and needles, awaiting their invitation to the ball that was being hosted in honor of Audrey's upcoming wedding.

Also according to Audrey, it would be where Victoria could witness the socialites vying for Lincoln's attention.

With everything else on her mind, that was a foolish thing to be looking forward to, but she did want to see how women were trying to catch his attention. More than that, she wanted to see if he was interested in giving his attention to any one of them, and who that woman might be. It wasn't a novel idea, that of a socialite looking to marry well, nor was it out of the ordinary for a handsome, well-educated, and rich man to be first on their list.

Lincoln was certainly all of those things, and would be a remarkable catch for some lucky woman. However, she knew him well enough to know that he wouldn't be interested in someone just for their looks, or for their family's money, which made her wonder exactly what he would be looking for in a woman. In a wife.

Or maybe she wanted to know why he wasn't interested in marriage.

Either way, she was looking forward to tomorrow night more than she normally would, despite her own issues at hand.

All of that was still on her mind the following evening, when she arrived at the Christie mansion. The magnificent home was aptly referred to as a mansion. Manhattan was filled with stately homes. Those building new ones were doing their best to master astonishment by building larger, taller, more elaborate homes, but some of the older homes, such as this mansion, out-brillianced all others. Set back from the road, the lush lawn, well-manicured even though it was early spring, offered a unique seclusion, a privacy that was rare in the city.

The home itself was massive, with marble pillars welcoming guests to the front door, flanked by large urns filled with blooming flowers. Obviously purchased for the party because there were no flowers outdoors blooming yet.

Inside, the home was breathtaking. Overhead chandeliers cast twinkling light on the marble floors and polished wooden walls, making them sparkle and shine as guests entered by the dozens, dressed in all the finery expected at such an event.

The ballroom was on the second floor, and visitors were invited to use either the sweeping, gold-carpeted staircase, or the caged elevator, manned by a uniformed attendant.

"Isn't this place grand?" Roseanne asked quietly as they followed Audrey and Jake up the stairway.

"Yes, it is," Victoria replied. "It's truly lovely." She and Roseanne had ridden with Audrey and Jake because Lincoln had telephoned at the last minute and said he'd been detained at work and would meet them at the ball. Roseanne hadn't been happy with his delay, whereas Victoria found empathy for Lincoln. The ball may be an important event for some, but to Lincoln, it was merely one amongst many that he was required to attend. She believed he would arrive in plenty of time to fulfill his duty, and felt he deserved a bit of compassion, for she didn't believe he'd been delayed on purpose.

She might have a different attitude towards his delay due to her grandfather, who often spoke of how her grandmother had worked side by side with him to build their fortune. How they'd supported each other in all aspects. As had her mother supported her father prior to his death and supported the idea of them moving to New York. There were times when she really missed how different things had been in Colorado than here. She'd been ten when they'd moved, so could remember plenty about her old life and could hold things in comparison. Which she often did, and those memories played an integral part of when, if, and to whom she would marry.

She fully understood that was expected of her—to marry and have a life that was focused on raising a family, but there, too, she wanted more. She wanted a life where she could support her husband in his business, work at his side, to build it into something they both could be proud of.

Roseanne tapped her arm, and pointed out people as they arrived in the lavish ballroom, whispering their names under her breath. Victoria had been to several balls since graduating, and recognized names and faces. Up until this moment, she hadn't thought of a consequence of Audrey's marriage. All of the parties and balls she'd attended, had been with Audrey. Usually just the two of them, because Jake had often been working as a reporter. Once Jake and Audrey were married, there wouldn't be anyone to attend such events with her. Granted, Roseanne and Audrey's father, Walter, as well as Lincoln had often been at the balls, too, but once Audrey was married, it would be unsightly for her, a single woman, to attend such events with Audrey's family.

All of the guests entering the ballroom were greeted by two young maids, carrying trays of nosegays for the women and boutonnieres for the men, for them to choose from. Roseanne took one with a yellow rose to match her gold dress, and Victoria chose one that had a large purple iris and small white lily of the valley bells.

"That dress looks so lovely on you," Roseanne said, straightening the nosegay that had just been pinned on Victoria's dress. "Lavender is your color, and that black lace on the collar and wrists is so delicate. It really makes you look pretty."

"Thank you," Victoria replied. The lavender dress was one that a seamstress in Tarrytown had sewn for her in preparation for unknown events concerning Audrey's wedding and this was the first time she'd worn it. Although Victoria had questioned the suggestion of black lace by the seamstress, she did like how the gown had turned out. The delicate black lace also ran the length of the open over skirt and added just enough to the dress without being too showy. Unlike many, she preferred her gowns to be simple and comfortable rather than worrying about what the latest fashions dictated.

It appeared that others in the room where the exact opposite. Some dresses were so full of layers, ruffles, lace, bows, and bustles that she imagined it would be impossible for those wearing them to sit down.

She thanked a servant for a crystal glass of champagne and sipped on it sparingly as she and Roseanne slowly made their way around the room, making the obligatory stops to say hello and engage in brief conversations. The main topic was the upcoming wedding, but Lincoln's absence was a close second.

Roseanne was quick to laugh and say *like father like son* as she explained that Lincoln had been held up at work but would make an appearance soon.

They eventually arrived at the far side of the room, where there was plenty of seating and a door that led to another large room housing an elaborate buffet. People were gathered in that room, too, especially around a massive swan ice sculpture where there were hundreds of crystal glasses filled with the sparkling champagne.

On the far side of the ballroom, a band, which in Victoria's opinion was only a few members shy of being a full-blown orchestra, played the music that was filling the room and encouraging guests to enjoy the highly polished dance floor.

Audrey and Jake were already dancing, with eyes for no one but each other, and Victoria felt a softening in her chest as she watched them. They truly were in love with each other, and she was so very happy for Audrey. Few knew, but Audrey had a passion for writing newspaper articles and had secretly been writing articles that Jake published in his newspaper for years.

"Miss Biggs, may I hope that you'd be so inclined to join me on the dance floor?"

Victoria turned slightly to face the speaker and a genuine smile formed. The tall, slender man with sparkling green eyes and red-brown hair was Ronald Woodroof, a friend of Lincoln's. Therefore, she'd met him on a few occasions during her previous visits and always enjoyed his good humor. "Hello, Mr. Woodroof. It's a pleasure to see you again, and I would be so inclined. Thank you."

He held out a hand to her. "The pleasure is all mine."

She laid her hand on his and walked onto the dance floor.

"Tell me, Miss Biggs, are you impressed?" he asked as they took up a position to dance, with his hand on her hip, hers on his shoulder, and their other hands clasped in the air between them.

"With the Christie mansion?" she asked, for clarification. "Who wouldn't be?"

"Those who are jealous," he replied as the music began. "Those who aspire to be at the top of the social ladder."

His usual cheerful face didn't quite match his words. "Do I perceive a hint of disdain in your tone?"

He chuckled. "You do. I have an aversion to show-and-tell sessions."

"Yet you are here," she replied.

"Duty calls." He lifted a brow. "Are you unaware that Nancy Christie is my aunt?"

If someone had made mention of that in the past, she hadn't retained the information. "My apologies. I was not aware of that."

"She is my mother's sister, and I love her dearly, hence my reason for being here." He gave a slight bow of his head. "Seeing you made my efforts to look presentable all the more worthwhile."

She laughed at his compliment. "I have never seen you not look presentable."

"Because I'm always on my best behavior in your presence."

Fully understanding his teasing held no deep basis, nor harm, she replied, "I'm happy to inspire good behavior. I only regret that doesn't extend to fabrications on your behalf."

He let out a theatrical moan. "Your disbelief in my sincerity is an injury upon my person."

She laughed. "I highly doubt that."

They sashayed around several dancers, before he said, "I can tell you something that no one will doubt."

"What's that?"

"There is about to be a spectacle."

"How do you know that?"

He was staring over her shoulder. "By the count of three, every woman aspiring to become a bride will be rushing across the room."

"Why?"

"Because Lincoln just arrived at the doorway."

Victoria did her very best to not turn around by keeping her gaze locked on his face. "Why do they not rush to your side? You are as eligible as him."

He chuckled. "Because I'm not out of reach." Meeting her gaze, he added, "If I've learned one thing, it's that when a woman is told it's something she can't have, she wants it even more."

Before she could ask what made Lincoln out of reach, Ronald danced in a half circle.

"See for yourself," he said.

Victoria could now see the doorway over his shoulder, where Lincoln had indeed entered the room. Just as Ronald had said, a spectacle was in the making. There was a complete rush of bustles, bows, and ruffles as women, more than she cared to count, made their way towards the door. Some so unabashed they were elbowing their way past others. A few had left partners on the dance floor in their hurry to arrive near the door, where Lincoln was obligated to wait for a red carnation boutonniere to be pinned on his suit.

She wouldn't have believed it if she hadn't seen it. "It was never like that before," she said, half to herself. Over the years she'd attended balls and parties with Audrey and Lincoln's arrival had never created such a fuss as this.

"That's because his mother had never announced his need to marry before," Ronald replied.

There was no reason for him to lie to her, but she couldn't believe it. "Roseanne wouldn't have done that."

"She didn't exactly," he said. "What she did do was tell Mrs. Collins that Lincoln's wedding would be next, meaning for her family of course, but by the time the gossips were done adding to it, despite his years of showing no interest in marriage, every young woman in town believed Lincoln was on the search for a wife and time was of the essence."

That she could believe. Gossip had its own wings that flew faster than anything else, and a simple statement could easily grow. "How do you know what Roseanne told Mrs. Collins?"

"My mother was at the luncheon when Roseanne said it, and though my mother understood that Roseanne had simply made a statement about her children, within days, a deluge of balls were announced. Marriage marts. Of course, many of those hosting the balls are claiming to be doing so in honor of Audrey and Jake, because that ensures Lincoln will be in attendance."

Victoria was once again facing the door, where Lincoln had received his boutonniere and was attempting to make his way through the crowd of young women. She had heard of marriage marts, where only the best families were invited to attend so parents could be assured that their offspring wouldn't be subjected to falling in love with someone from a lower class. Suddenly, the reason her mother was so excited for her to spend the entire month in the city made sense. All sorts of things were making so much sense. A wave of sympathy for Lincoln washed over her, but it only lasted until a thought formed. He'd said he didn't need to be saved, not by her. Well, she'd let this play out for a while and prove that he did. Because saving him from a scandal could work very well for her, too. In more than one way.

The song ended and she gave a slight curtsey. "Thank you, Mr. Woodroof, for the dance and the enlightening conversation."

Ronald lifted a brow. "I have more where that came from if you'd care to join me in a second dance."

"Oh? Such as?"

His smile grew as he once again held out a hand to her. "I happen to know who are most keen to convince Lincoln that he is interested in marriage, and could share names, even point out a few, if you would be inclined to know."

That information could come in useful, only because she was here to do a job, one that was growing more appealing by the moment. She once again laid her hand in Ronald's. "I would enjoy a second dance very much."

Trying his best to be polite and amicable, Lincoln edged his way through the crowd of women, all the while looking for a familiar face. He recognized many men and women in the ballroom, but was specifically looking for Victoria. Upon arrival, he'd instantly scanned the room, looking for her, but his vision had quickly become blocked by curls, feathers, and other doodads poking out of the hair atop the heads of the women who had formed a circle around him.

It would have been better if he'd arrived with the rest of his family, but his informant had arrived just as he'd been about to leave the office. The information he'd learned had been worth being delayed. Mainly because it had given him more reason to make sure that Elwood Kelley was no longer one of Victoria's callers. He couldn't prove her theft case, but he could put a stop to Elwood being one of her callers.

One of the women surrounding him stepped forward, completely blocking his path, and not so nonchalantly dropped her fan at his feet.

"Oh, dear me, look what I've done," she said, with a giggle, looking at him expectantly.

He held in a frustrated sigh, and though he'd rather not, he bent down to pick up the fan. The dropper, along with those standing next to her, lifted the hems of their skirts, high enough to expose ankles and shins. None of which drew his interest. What it did do was confirm that although he'd just arrived, he'd had enough.

Upon handing the fan to the dropper, he shouldered his way through the group, and didn't slow his speed until he reached the far side of the room. Where, unfortunately, he found no relief. Besides those who had followed him, he ended up face-to-face with Melody Harding. Mitch Harding, her father, was one of their law firm's largest clients and for years had suggested that a connection could benefit both families.

Although he'd adamantly voiced that a connection wasn't

needed, it hadn't deterred Melody. She'd been like a dog after a bone for months, and his mother's suggestion that his wedding would be next had added to Melody's pursuit.

"Lincoln," Melody said, blocking him from moving by adjusting his boutonniere with both hands.

She wasn't a homely woman. Some may call her nice looking. Her blond hair was a nice enough shade, and her face wasn't so bad, she just had never appealed to him. Perhaps because she was the perfect example of an idealistic young woman with fantasy dreams of a man being at her beck and call. "Melody," he said in response.

"Shall we find an attendant and some champagne?" she asked. "Or dance?"

"Sorry," he replied, scanning the dance floor as the music ended. "I'm looking for someone."

"Who?"

Lincoln wasn't about to admit who he was looking for, and was happy that he didn't need to, because Victoria was walking towards him, along with one of his good friends. "There he is right now," he said, though he hadn't been searching for Ronald.

"He?"

"Yes, Ronald Woodroof. Excuse me."

Melody latched onto to his arm. "I'll say hello, with you."

The hold she had on his arm would make dislodging it difficult, but he wasn't thinking about that. Victoria's gaze had locked with his and there was humor sparkling in her blue eyes. Eyes that were made even bluer by the light purple color of her dress. An elegant gown that enhanced her shapely curves to perfection. He didn't need her to save him from a scandal, but showing an interest in her might dissuade Melody.

"I see you made it," Ronald said as they walked closer.

"And I see you were keeping Victoria company in my absence," Lincoln replied.

Melody gasped, but Victoria merely smiled.

"I couldn't let her become a wallflower," Ronald said.

"I doubt that would ever happen," Lincoln said, looking at Victoria. Despite their bantering in the past, this time, he couldn't tell what she was thinking. Her expression hadn't changed. Not even when her gaze shifted to Melody.

"Hello," Victoria said. "I'm Victoria Biggs, and you are?"

Melody looked up at him, as if he should make the introduction, which would be proper, but he had no obligation to Melody. That might be considered a callous way to look at things, but she was the one who had latched onto him. Furthermore, he was impressed by Victoria's forwardness.

"I'm Melody Harding," she replied to Victoria. "Our families are very well acquainted. Have been for years."

"Is that so?" Victoria replied. "Harding? I can't say I've heard that name mentioned."

"My father is Lincoln's most prominent client," Melody proclaimed with indignation in her tone.

Victoria's smile never waned. "That explains it," she said quietly. "Lincoln takes client confidentiality very seriously."

Impressed with her response, he gave Victoria a slight nod.

Melody let out a small huff. "You're that friend of Audrey's."

"Yes, I am." Victoria looked at him. "Our families have been well acquainted for years."

Lincoln was chuckling inside, but had also had enough of Melody. "Shall we find Mother?" he asked Victoria.

"Oh, yes, that would be a very good thing for you to do," Victoria said. She turned to Ronald. "Thank you for the dances." She then looked at Melody and the hold she still had on Lincoln's arm. "If you will excuse us, Miss Harding?"

Melody bristled. "We—we, Lincoln and I, were going to dance."

Melody was doing her best to make more out of their friendship, and he was fully prepared to put it to a stop, but Victoria was already moving.

Stepping in front of Melody, Victoria said, "I think not." Then, as if she held a magic wand, Melody's hold was gone and Victoria's hand was around his arm. "Excuse us."

This time, Lincoln knew exactly what she was thinking as they walked away. "I didn't need to be saved," he whispered, because Ronald was walking on the other side of her. "There was no scandal in the making."

"I didn't suggest there was," she whispered just as quietly.

"Then what do you call what you just did?"

"I'm simply joining you to say hello to your mother, at your suggestion." She released his arm. "But if that's not what you wanted..."

He took a hold of her elbow, but didn't say more. Ronald had already glanced their way too many times.

She remained silent, too, as they walked to the very back of the room, where they found his mother seated at a table with Ronald's mother and aunt.

"Lincoln, darling." His mother rose and offered him her cheek.

He kissed her cheek. "Hello, Mother, my apologies again." He then greeted the hostess and Ronald's mother, and they spent several moments making small talk before he made an excuse of needing refreshment.

As the three of them walked away, Ronald said, "Looks like my uncle is now vying for my attention. If you'll excuse me?"

"Of course," Victoria said.

Lincoln gave a nod, seeing Ronald's uncle waving at him from across the room. He also noticed the cluster of women gawking his way and couldn't stop the sigh that escaped. He sincerely didn't want a repeat of the scene from when he'd arrived.

Victoria lifted a brow when his gaze landed on her again.

A waiter appeared at his side. Lincoln took two glasses off the tray and handed one to her. He had a decision to make. It should be an easy one, because it came down to one woman, poised and elegantly dressed, or a flock of lace-encrusted young girls full of giggles and batting eyelashes. The weight of his decision came down to consequences. If he chose Victoria, his mother would believe her matchmaking was working, and that was not only a consequence for him, it was also one for Victoria.

On the other hand, he truly didn't believe he had the patience needed to expose himself to the flock, which would not only tell his mother that her plan wasn't working, but tell Victoria that he didn't need to be saved.

In the end, the choice was easy, because there was one other underlying issue. Victoria's safety. He didn't need to know her entire list of past suitors. Elwood Kelly was unsavory, and that was enough for him to want to keep her away from other such suitors.

He emptied his glass in a single swallow and set it on a nearby table before asking, "Shall we dance?"

She took a sip from her glass. "I believe Melody is waiting for a dance with you."

"Don't play coy with me," he replied. "You know as well as I do that I had no intention of dancing with Melody."

"Your families are very well acquainted."

"So are our families." He took the glass from her hand and set it on the table.

She lifted a single brow and stepped forward, closer to him, then reached down and picked her glass up off the table. Without a word, she took a sip, as well as a second one, all the while keeping a stony gaze locked with his.

Impressed by how subtly she pointed out his shortcomings, he held in a grin. "My apologies. Would you be interested in dancing with me after you've finished your refreshment?"

"Why? Because I'm the lesser of two evils?"

His initial response was to say no, but he stopped himself and said nothing.

She laughed. "I believe I am, because if you dance with any one of those so eagerly awaiting such an opportunity, it will open the floodgate. However, if you dance with me, you're afraid that your mother will believe that her matchmaking is working."

"I could choose to not dance at all," he said, half pretending that she hadn't hit the nail on the head.

"You could." She took another sip of champagne. "And subject yourself to a constant deluge of picking up dropped handkerchiefs and fans throughout the evening."

All she said was true, and he truly wished he was someplace else. That they were someplace else and that this conversation wasn't relevant in any way.

Chapter Six

The expression that formed on Lincoln's face said that he'd rather be anywhere but here right now. Victoria could relate fully, but they were here, and her hope was to convince Lincoln to see things her way, that a union between the two of them—a completely platonic union—could benefit both of them.

She didn't want to spend the next month attending marriage marts and knew he didn't, either.

That was a conclusion she'd come to quite quickly and easily, and she had to admit, that helping him was very appealing.

She took a final sip of her drink and set it on the table next to his glass. "A month isn't all that long in the scheme of things," she said quietly. "Merely four weeks. Actually, it's closer to three now."

"Until the wedding?" he asked.

Glad he was following her line of thought, she nodded. "Yes. After which I will return home."

His nod was slight as he glanced around the room.

"There is already a long list of events, parties, and activities that we are expected to attend together," she said.

"Thanks to my mother."

"Yes, thanks to your mother." She glanced towards the

group of young women who hadn't taken theirs eyes off him and were gradually inching closer. "Have you ever considered that she created that list, paired us up so to speak, because she knows what she said in innocence, gossip inflated?"

"I think you're giving more credit, than credit is due."

She shook her head. "I don't. I believe your mother understands what happened and concluded that seeing us together in public so often could cause people to think..." Victoria paused to find the right words. "That you are not interested in pursuing others and that would prevent the chance of a scandal." She shrugged. "With a small amount of acting on our part, we could encourage others to fully believe that."

He stared at her for a long, stilled moment. "They could, but why would you want that?"

Being careful to not reveal too much, she smiled. "Because, like you, I am not interested in marriage. Not interested in being inundated with suitors who want nothing more than access to my grandfather's money."

"Like Elwood Kelley?"

That was the very subject she was hoping to avoid. She wanted to bring that up again later, after he'd agreed with her. He might then be willing to help her with her case. That line of thinking wasn't very ethical, now that she thought about it. "Yes." She quickly added more of an explanation, "Neither you nor I want to spend the next month attending marriage marts or dealing with the consequences of doing so alone. A partnership between us for the next month could be beneficial to both of us."

"A partnership?" he asked, with one brow raised.

"Yes, to, shall we say, fool a few people."

He held out a hand. "I think we should continue this conversation on the dance floor."

The crowd of young women had edged closer, and she couldn't deny the spark inside her at being the one to dance with him. The one to receive his undivided attention. She laid her hand in his. "All right."

He led her onto the dance floor, and soon they were gliding across the floor in a slow minuet. Dancing with him was easy. Comfortable, even though it increased her heartbeat. She could also feel the heat of his hand penetrating through the material of her dress at her waist, and how that heat spread throughout her body. Having never been so aware of a man while dancing before, she knew it was because of the room full of eyes watching them.

That was something she'd have to get used to, accept, if he were to agree to her suggestion. A month of pretending to be in a relationship with him wouldn't be difficult, and though some might be disappointed, it certainly wouldn't harm anyone. Especially not the two of them.

"Why are you not interested in marriage?" he asked.

She wasn't ashamed of her reasonings. "Because I will not settle for anything less than I what I truly want."

"What is that?"

"Love," she replied. "That is the only reason I will marry. He will be the love of my life, and I will be the love of his."

"Love?" he asked, as if skeptical.

"Yes. My grandparents married for love. My parents married for love, and I will, too. Currently, my mother and grandfather have forgotten that, even though I've reminded them frequently." She did understand one thing. "My grandfather is getting up in years, and his heart has weakened. He's fearful that there will not be a man around to take care of my mother, me, and my sister, were something to happen to him."

"That's why you didn't tell him about the stolen money?" he asked.

"Yes. The doctor has warned him about getting overly flustered or worked up, so I didn't dare tell him, or my mother. She can overreact at times, which can upset him, and so the circle goes."

"How will she and your grandfather react if we agree to work together, to make things appear to be something when it's not?"

Her family could be disappointed in the end, but they were already disappointed in her lack of interest in marriage. A month of pretending wouldn't change that. "Ours wouldn't be the first courtship that dissolved prior to marriage."

"The end of a courtship has created a scandal or two."

"We won't let it," she replied. "We can part as friends."

The music ended, but he didn't remove his hand from her waist or release her hand, therefore, she kept her other hand on his shoulder and her eyes locked with his. The tingling of a thrill shot though her, confirming how much she enjoyed challenging him, even in the tiniest way. She couldn't help but wonder if that's what it would be like to be a real relationship with him—but quickly shut down that thought. There was no possibility of that ever happening.

Neither of them moved, other than a blink or two, until the music began again. As they began to dance, Lincoln asked, "What if you happen upon the love of your life over the next month?"

"That won't happen."

"How do you know?"

She shrugged. "I just do."

"How?"

"Because I won't let it."

"You believe love is something you can control?"

"Of course it is." She'd had to learn to control her emotions years ago. As a child actually, when her father and grandmother died. The pain had been severe, but she'd had to learn to control it, because her mother had been devastated, barely able to function. Her mother still wasn't the same person she used to be. For a long time, Victoria had wondered if it had been because they'd moved away, left everything her mother had loved behind. As she grew older, she learned that wasn't true. Her mother loved her and Eva, and their grandfather, and even loved things about their lives now. Her mother had explained that a love between husband and wife was a different kind of love, one that couldn't be explained. It was felt. Victoria believed that, and had determined that the only way she would enter into such a life-changing event, which is what marriage would be, was when she felt that kind of love.

No one could fault her if she never found a man that she would love like that, for she was the only one who would feel it. Especially not her mother or grandfather. It had been eleven years since her father and grandmother had died, and neither her mother nor grandfather had ever considered getting married again. They claimed that when a person knew true love, they didn't ever want anything else.

Her throat was growing thick from memories. Or perhaps from knowledge. Her grandfather was aging, and ailing, and she knew his death, at some point, would break her heart. She feared that time, the pain it would bring. She hated losing things. Anything. That was another reason she had no desire to marry. A husband would expect her to turn the job of overseeing the family finances to him.

"What if you never find the love of your life?" Lincoln asked.

That was one thing that didn't worry her. "Then I will do what I'm doing now. Oversee my family's finances." Not waiting to see his reaction, she continued, "I understand some don't believe a woman is capable of that, but my grandfather has taught me well. I've been overseeing his investments for several years. Your father has assisted us with some of them."

"I am aware of that," he replied.

"Are you like others? Who don't believe a woman should be responsible for the family finances?" Her mother believed the household needed a man to guard the family fortune, which was the main reason for the line of suitors knocking on her door.

"Not at all."

Her thoughts were shifting to him. "Why don't you want to get married?"

"Several reasons."

"What are they?"

"You want their names?" he asked.

Her feet stumbled slightly.

Tightening his hold on her waist and hand, he quickly got her back in step.

"Whose names?" she asked. "The socialites who want to get you to the altar?"

"No. All of the friends I know who thought they were in love, got married, and regretted it almost immediately."

He was looking over her shoulder, but she knew it wasn't at people. He was thinking. Maybe coming up with a list of names to rattle off. That's how it had sounded, as if he knew a whole list of people who were unhappily married.

"My life has been planned out for me since I was born," he said. "How I'd go to school, college, become a lawyer, join my father's law firm, and get married. But no one ever asked me if that's what I wanted."

"You didn't want any of that?"

"Yes. I like being a lawyer, but I don't plan on working for the family firm forever."

Surprised, she asked, "You don't? Does your family know that?"

"No, no one but you knows that, because I haven't told anyone except you."

An odd sensation spread across her chest at his confidence in her. "I won't tell anyone," she assured. "What do you want to do when you stop being a lawyer?"

"I'll still be an attorney. The attorney general for the state of New York."

"You mean a politician?"

"Yes, you don't like politicians?" he asked.

"I don't believe that I know any," she replied, keeping her grandfather's opinions to herself.

"I want to run for office and enforce laws that will help people, all people, not just some, and until that happens, I don't have time for what others call love, or for a wife. Don't have time to worry if they are sitting at home lonely or not. May not have time for it afterwards, either."

There was something in his tone that made a tiny shiver tickle the back of her neck. It could be due to her grandfather, or it could be because she, too, would like to see laws made that truly would help people. "Well then, it sounds like our plan will work for both of us. After the wedding, we can part as friends, and neither of us will have any reason to attend any more parties or balls."

"For at least a few months," he said.

"Or more," she said, once again thinking about how she wouldn't have anyone to attend them with her. That was not going to please her mother, but in all honesty, it wouldn't bother her and that was a bridge she'd cross then. Now, she just had to act the part, and along the way, convince him to help her solve her case against Elwood.

Several things were floating about in Lincoln's mind, including his uncle Troy, who was where his loathing towards marriage had first come from. He hadn't seen his uncle, his favorite uncle, for over twelve years, because that's how long Troy had been in an English prison—a scandal that the family had kept hidden.

For a moment, he considered telling Victoria about Troy, how he'd married an Englishwoman during one of his ocean voyages for the shipping company, and how he was now serving time, accused of his wife's death and that of the man whom she'd been consorting with because she'd been lonely during Troy's absence, but his entire family had prohibited any mention of Troy years ago. The way his family had written Uncle Troy off, as if he'd never existed, goaded him deeply.

He trusted her, believed she wouldn't reveal his secrets, and he agreed with her that love was something that could be controlled. Why anyone would willingly subject themselves to something that was sure to fail was beyond him. Everyone had impulse control, they just needed to use it. Especially when it came to love and marriage.

Pretending to be interested in her for the short term wouldn't be difficult, and it would give him breathing room during all of the events he was expected to attend over the next few weeks. As well as for a time afterwards. Her, too.

Convincing the Manhattan elites that the two of them were courting would be simple. Actually, the two dances they'd already danced together were enough to fuel a good amount of gossip.

"So," he said, letting his thoughts settle. "Do we need to establish any procedures for this plan of ours?"

"Procedures?" She laughed. "You truly are a lawyer."

He liked having parameters, rules to follow. "Rules and guidelines are useful, they let everyone know what is expected," he explained.

"True," she said. "But I don't think we need to worry about that. All we have to do is pretend to have fun attending the events together. Pretend to like each other."

He already did like her, especially bickering with her. "So no more whispered arguments?"

She shook her head. "I can't agree to a promise that I can't keep. You are wrong about too many things for that."

"Me? What have I been wrong about?"

"Where do you want me to start? The train station where you didn't want me to have any disillusions? Even though I already didn't have any disillusions?"

The music stopped, and he lowered his voice to a whisper. "I explained all that. My mother—"

"Is doing all of this for your own good," she whispered in return. "When are you going to accept that?"

"When will you realize that she has ulterior motives?" He knew his mother better than she did, and didn't believe she'd accidently said anything that had been misconstrued.

"No, she doesn't."

They'd moved closer during their hushed conversation,

so close he was breathing in the scent of her floral perfume. Flustered, he asked a question that was really goading him. "Why would rather believe her than me?"

"Do you two ever talk?" his sister asked, suddenly appearing beside them, along with Jake. "Or just whisper at each other?"

"We talk," Lincoln replied. "When you aren't near to overhear what we are saying."

Audrey's face lit up. "You two are conjuring up something."

Lincoln met Victoria's gaze and silently laughed at what only the two of them knew. She was doing the same, and that was a unique sensation to share with her.

"We are going to get something to eat from the buffet," Jake said. "Would you two care to join us?"

Recalling the champagne glass incident, Lincoln gave Victoria a questioning look, allowing her to make the decision. She had a mind of her own, and he liked that she used it. That was simply one more thing that made her unique.

She gave a slight nod, before saying, "We would, thank you."

Lincoln laid a hand in the small of her back as they made their way off the dance floor and around the room, to the adjacent room. A full meal would be served in the wee hours of the morning, but a massive buffet was set out now for people to enjoy at their leisure. He liked how easy it was to be with her. How he didn't have to worry that any small action, like keeping his hand on the small of her back, would be taken as something with deeper meaning. She didn't have any ulterior motives, and neither did he. That wasn't true. They both had ulterior motives, but they each knew what those motives were.

After filling their plates with various cuts of meat, vegetable dishes, and fruits, they found a small table a distance away from the busy buffet and drink tables. As they ate and visited, he realized that this was a nice perk of having Victoria at his side. Normally, his only reprieve from an onslaught of young women was finding a cluster of men to hide amongst.

Actually, he normally only attended balls when required, but during those events, he had found clusters of men to act as a shield to the socialites.

Tonight, he was able to sit and enjoy the food and the company, including Ronald and a few others who joined their table. The conversations were fun, but he found himself more intrigued with watching Victoria as she laughed and joked with the others at the table.

She was very personable, and likeable. To most people. From the number of stares their table received, it was clear that word of the way she'd dislodged Melody from his arm had spread. That brought up the fact that their plan could have a negative effect on her or her character. He couldn't let that happen. There was no dire need for this deal or partnership that they'd come up with. He was perfectly capable of keeping the zealous young women at bay, just as he'd done most of his life. The main thing about their deal that did appeal to him was it gave him the ability to monitor her suitors. In his opinion, her mother and grandfather were not being diligent enough on that issue.

Feeling her gaze on the side of his face, he glanced her way. Something about her gaze told him to listen to the conversation happening around him, which he'd been ignoring while processing his own thoughts.

Tuning in, he instantly grinned, understanding that Ronald had mentioned bicycles, and was furthering his comment by explaining how he was working on a combustion engine to attach to a bicycle. Ronald was obsessed with combustion engines, insisted they were the future of the nation.

"I love bicycles," Audrey said, while looking at Jake. "But have only told Jake that because my mother is appalled by them and their increasing popularity."

Lincoln bit back a grin at the way Victoria grimaced. He turned his face away from the others as if looking over her shoulder as he asked, "Did you know how my mother feels about bicycles?"

"No," she whispered. "Did you?"

"No." Because their whispering was sure to draw his sister's attention, he turned back to the table. "If you will all excuse us." Switching his gaze to Victoria, he added, "I believe we are here to dance?"

She nodded and excused herself as he stood and held her chair as she rose to her feet. Moments later, as they walked away from the table, she asked, "What are you going to do?"

Although he knew that she was referring to the bicycles he'd purchased, he couldn't stop himself when it came to bantering with her. It was simply too much fun. "We are going to dance."

"I mean about the bicycles."

Once again, his hand found the small of her back, where it fit perfectly, and guided her to step in front of him as they walked through an overly crowded area. "They'll be delivered next week as scheduled."

She shook her head. "That might upset your mother."

Stepping back up beside her, he said, "I've been known to do that a time or two."

"On purpose? Because that's what buying those bicycles could look like."

They were keeping their voices low, and once again he recognized a hitch of enjoyment inside his chest. The sensation was as unique as her, and he wondered why he'd never felt anything like it before now. Until he remembered that they'd never interacted in the close proximity that his mother had forced them into this time. "Neither of us knew my mother had an aversion to bicycles when we purchased them."

"But we do now."

Keeping his hand on her back as they entered the ballroom, he said, "There have been other things that she was averse to at one time or another, but is no longer."

"That doesn't mean she'll change her mind this time."

"It doesn't mean she won't, either." Nodding towards the dance floor, he asked, "Would you like to dance, or would you rather watch the magician?"

"Magician? Here?" She twisted left and right, scanning the room, before looking back up at him. "Where? I haven't heard anything about a magician."

One of the things he'd never cared for when it came to the socialites pursuing him had been the stars in their eyes. On her, it was a completely different story. He liked seeing her eyes sparkle. "Hans the Magnificent is here. I met him downstairs upon my arrival. He's performing in the upper hall. Shall we go and see him?"

"Oh, yes, let's! I saw a magician on the street corner once, he knew exactly what card I'd chosen from the deck, every time."

Keeping his chuckles to himself, he asked, "Did he?"

"Yes, it was quite remarkable. Every card was different, but he knew which one I'd picked."

A set of marked cards wasn't that hard to manipulate, but he chose not to tell her that as they walked out of the ballroom, nor did he attempt to disillusion her when she told him about how the street magician had found a coin hidden behind her ear. There was no need for him to say anything about that trick, because as they walked along the wide hallway, she explained that her grandfather could perform that trick.

He knew plenty of people who performed that trick, too, and from what he'd seen of the magician downstairs, knew the man's stovepipe hat was large enough to hide more than a single rabbit, which was also a common trick. That was another bit of information he chose not to share with her, because he was looking forward to watching her reactions during the magic show.

The upper hall was smaller than the ballroom, yet still large enough to hold a considerable amount of people, and though a stage had been assembled near the front of the room, the show itself had not yet started because Hans the Magnificent was in the crowd, amusing groups of people.

Lincoln pointed out the man wearing the black stovepipe hat, tuxedo, and flowing black cape with his name embroidered in red across the back.

"Oh, my, he truly looks like a magician, doesn't he?" Victoria asked.

He couldn't say one way or the other what a magician should look like, so he merely nodded as they made their way across the room.

"Look," she whispered. "He's having them pick a card from the deck. Think he'll guess correctly?"

"I'm sure he'll guess correctly," Lincoln replied.

They arrived at the outskirts of the crowd in time to see

that happen, and Victoria joined in with the rest in clapping ecstatically.

"Aw, Mr. Dryer," Hans said, picking him out in the crowd. "We meet again." Walking closer, his black, waxed imperial mustache wiggled as he continued, "And look at your companion. There is none more beautiful." Hans then performed an exaggerated and sweeping bow before Victoria, removing his top hat halfway into his bow.

"Allow me to present Miss Biggs," Lincoln said.

"I'm sure you meant to say the lovely Miss Biggs," Hans said.

"Forgive me," Lincoln said, "I did indeed."

Pulling himself upright, the magician asked her, "Did you hear that?"

With cheeks turning pinker, Victoria replied, "Yes, I did."

"Oh, I don't mean Mr. Dryer," Hans said, wiggling his thick brows. "Although I'm happy to have set him straight. I meant the other sound."

"What other sound?" she asked.

Assuming a performance in the making, Lincoln remained silent, but smiled at the excitement on her face.

Hans leaned over the stovepipe hat he was holding with both hands and let out an extended sigh. "It's Harvey."

Lincoln shrugged as Victoria glanced at him.

She leaned forward and glanced into the empty hat. "Harvey? Your hat?"

"Oh, no, Harvey is not my hat," Hans replied, shaking his head while still staring at the hat. "Harvey is, well, a surprise for later, but beautiful women are his downfall."

"Who is he?" she asked, looking deeper into the hat.

"Oh, well, he's not going to stop begging until I give him

a peek." Hans held the hat closer to her. "Go ahead and lift him out."

"There's nothing in there," she said.

"He must be hiding," Hans said. "He can be shy. Don't worry, he won't bite, just reach in and grab him."

Once again, she glanced his way and Lincoln shrugged, then looked into the hat. After confirming it was indeed empty, he gestured for her to reach inside the hat.

A crowd was forming all around them, and with a shrug at him and a gleam in her eyes, she stuck her hand in the hat. "There's nothing in there," she said, moving her hand around. "Nothing at all."

"He's very good at hiding," Hans said, as a carrot suddenly appeared in his hand. "I'll try to coax him out." He dropped the carrot, complete with the greens still attached, into the hat, then stuck his hand inside and, a moment later, pulled out a small white rabbit.

"Oh, look at him!" Victoria exclaimed, clapping with the crowd.

Lincoln clapped, too, but was enjoying watching Victoria's reaction to the show more than the show itself. She was captivated, and seeing that captivation was downright enchanting.

"Harvey, this is the lovely Miss Biggs," Hans said to the rabbit then held him towards Victoria. "Miss Biggs, this is Harvey."

"Hello, Harvey," she replied.

"Would you mind holding him for a moment?" Hans asked her.

"Not at all." Victoria gently took the rabbit from Hans and nuzzled its furry head with her chin as she asked, "Where's the carrot?"

Hans tipped the hat over and gave it a shake, but nothing fell out. "He must have eaten it."

"That quickly?" she asked.

"Harvey!" Hans exclaimed, as if upset. "You have to stop doing your own tricks. I do apologize, Miss Biggs."

Lincoln noticed at the same time as Victoria, because Hans pointed it out, that her nosegay was gone and a carrot, with greens intact, was pinned to her dress instead. Lincoln was trying to figure out how that had happened, when Hans practically shoved the top hat into his chest.

"Hold this please, Mr. Dryer," Hans said, pressing the tall hat against his chest.

The hat juggled until Lincoln got a firm hold on it.

By then, Hans already had the carrot in his hand. "There, that's better," the magician said with a head nod.

Still holding the rabbit, Victoria gasped. "That's not my nosegay, that's Lincoln's boutonniere."

Lincoln glanced down at his lapel, where her nosegay was now pinned instead of his boutonniere. Hans had to have pinned it there while handing him the hat.

"How on earth did you do that?" she asked the magician.

Dangling the carrot in one hand, Hans gave her an elaborate hand-across-stomach bow. "It's called magic, my fair lady." Once upright, he collected his rabbit and hat, and turned to the applauding crowd. "Now, ladies and gentlemen, if you care to take a seat, the real show will begin."

Chapter Seven

Heart pounding with excitement, Victoria wrapped both hands around Lincoln's forearm. "That was amazing. How did he do that?"

"I don't know. I wouldn't have believed it if I hadn't seen it. Actually, I did see it, and am not sure if I believe it."

"Well, that's my nosegay pinned on you, and your boutonniere is pinned on my dress." She glanced down where the red carnation was pinned just above her heart that was fluttering like there would be no tomorrow. "I suppose we should switch them back."

"Do you want to?" he asked.

Any other man and she would have already removed it, simply out of propriety, or because it almost felt like a claim on her, or a claim on him, but because it was Lincoln, she didn't mind that. Probably because of the deal they'd struck. Whether that was it or not, she felt comfortable telling him the truth. "Not really. I want proof to tell others what happened. Audrey isn't going to believe it."

"Then we'll leave them," he said. "Come, let's find some seats for the show."

"You won't mind walking around wearing a nosegay?" she asked as they made their way towards the rows of chairs.

"Not if you don't mind walking around wearing a boutonniere."

He was looking down at her in such a way that her heart started pitter-pattering all over again. There was truly no reason. Other than perhaps the excitement of the magic trick was still living inside her. "No," she said. "I happen to like carnations."

"There you go," he said with a nod, and then gestured to two chairs in the third row. The closer ones were already taken. "You take the aisle seat," he said, stepping into the row. "That way you won't have to look over anyone's head. I'm taller. That won't bother me."

"Thank you." He was a very considerate person. It wasn't like she hadn't realized that before, she'd just never thought about it that much. He'd just always been Audrey's older brother.

"Can you see the stage?" he asked after they'd sat on the chairs.

Due to the man sitting in front of her, she did need to lean sideways and look up the aisle to see the entire stage. "Yes." Noticing the woman sitting in front of him, who had two huge peacock feathers in her hair, she said, "You can't."

The aisle between the rows of chairs was wide, and refusing to feel bad about her actions, because he needed to be able to see, she scootered her chair partway into the aisle. "Scoot your chair over."

"Good idea." He scooted his chair up next to hers. "Thank you."

Hans walked onto the center of the stage and excitement rippled through her. That had to be why. The way Lincoln laid an arm over the back of her chair and leaned closer so he could see between the man and woman in front of them had nothing to do with it. Nothing at all.

"Welcome, ladies and gentlemen," Hans said. "Allow me

to begin by introducing you to my lovely assistant, Matilda. She'll be assisting me to make the impossible, possible!"

Victoria clapped along with the others as Hans pointed to a dark-haired woman wearing a flowing dress of bright red, orange, and yellow silk.

"And some of you have already met Harvey," Hans continued. "He's a tricky one, so I'm going to put him right here in this wooden cage, so you can all help me keep an eye on him." Hans placed the little white rabbit in a wooden cage atop a table, and then, out of nowhere, the carrot appeared again, and he dropped it inside the cage, too, which Harvey instantly started munching on, making everyone laugh.

"I still wonder how he did that with our flowers," she whispered to Lincoln.

"Sleight of hand, I guess," Lincoln replied. "But he certainly was good at it."

"And quick. I didn't feel a thing, did you?"

"No, I didn't."

Hans began speaking again, and she forced her attention on the stage, yet found it somewhat difficult with Lincoln's arm still stretched along the back of her chair. That was, until Hans started pulling scarfs out of his sleeve. A red one, green one, yellow, orange, blue, purple, all tied together and the line of them just kept coming, piling up at his feet. Then he picked up the pile, rolled them into a ball and threw the ball into the air, where the scarfs all turned white and separated, floating down around him as simple white squares of cloth.

"How in the world?" she asked aloud.

Lincoln chuckled and patted her shoulder. "Look, the rabbit is gone. The cage is empty."

The cage was still on the table, but empty. Shocked, she laid a hand on Lincoln's leg. "Where did he go?"

"I don't know."

She didn't either, and didn't know how Hans completed many other magic tricks that took place on the stage, from juggling bottles to making things disappear, including his assistant Matilda after she'd climbed into a box on the stage. Matilda showed up in the back of the room, carrying Harvey. The room erupted in applause, and Victoria was disappointed to learn that was the end of the show.

"We can come back for the next show," Lincoln said as they rose from their seats. "He's repeating it every hour."

She stepped into the aisle while he slid both of their chairs back in line with the others in the row. "Do you want to see it again?"

"If you do."

The softening inside her chest caused her to place a hand over her heart. Audrey had always said that he was the best brother ever, but not having a brother herself, Victoria had never had anyone to compare him to. She would have had a brother, if Garth had survived, but he hadn't lived more than a few minutes. However, she had encountered enough men to know Lincoln was different. He was likeable. Even while bickering, she liked him. She liked being around him, too. He was fun, but also, she didn't grow tired of him. Some of the suitors who'd shown up at her house she'd been tired of before they'd removed their jackets.

"We don't have to," he said. "It was just a suggestion."

"Oh, no." She shook her head and stepped further into the aisle so he could step out from between the rows of chairs. "I'm afraid I was woolgathering. The show was fun, and I would like to see it again, but first I must find Audrey. She hadn't mentioned a magician, and I wonder if she knows about him."

"All right then, we'll go find her."

He cupped her elbow as they began to walk, and she contemplated how she didn't mind that. Him touching her. All it did was make her heart beat a little faster. Normally, just dancing with some men man could make her skin crawl. He didn't have that effect on her at all and she smiled up at him. "Thank you."

"You're welcome. I'm glad to see the frown is gone."

"What frown?"

"You were frowning while woolgathering a moment ago."

"Was I? I didn't mean to be. I was thinking about how Audrey was right."

"About what?" he asked.

"You. She said you are the best brother ever."

He chuckled as they entered the hallway. "You caught her on a good day."

"No, I didn't. She always speaks highly of you, and it's very nice of you to step in for her father at all these functions."

This time he laughed. "I'd be here whether my father was in Florida or not."

She believed that, and truly didn't want him to think that she had been frowning about him earlier. "I was thinking about brothers," she admitted. "I had a baby brother, but he only lived for a few minutes. He was born right after my father died, and was just too tiny to live. Too tiny to breathe."

"I'm sorry to hear to hear that," he replied softly.

"We never talk about him. My family. No one does. He was named Garth, after my father, but to this day, my mother never mentions him."

"Every family has someone they don't talk about," he said.

"Even yours?"

"Yes, even mine. For us, it's my uncle Troy."

She shook her head. "Audrey has never mentioned a Troy. Did he pass away?"

"No, she won't mention him, no one will, because he's in prison in England." He nodded towards the doorway leading into the ballroom. "There's Audrey and Jake."

"I just heard there is a magician performing in the upper hall," Audrey said, rushing towards them.

"There is!" Victoria replied, although her mind was on Lincoln, and how sad he'd sounded when he'd mentioned his uncle.

"Why are you wearing Lincoln's boutonniere?" Audrey asked, frowning as she glanced at Lincoln. "And he's wearing your nosegay?"

"The magician," Victoria said, and proceeded to explain how it had happened, as well as many of the other tricks the magician had performed.

The four of them attended the next performance of Hans the Magnificent, which was just as breathtaking as the first one. No one else had their flowers switched like she and Lincoln had, and hours later, upon arriving home, Victoria removed the red carnation from her dress and carefully laid it between the pages of a book, to preserve it.

The magician's performances had been remarkable, but Lincoln was who had made the evening memorable. She had never enjoyed a ball so much. Because of their agreement, she hadn't needed to worry about men asking her to dance. That had not only been a relief, it made her look forward to the list of other events that they would attend. It seemed strange, but having people think they were a couple, felt freeing to her.

Their agreement had worked out for Lincoln, too, because she'd remained at his side the entire time, and had easily dissuaded any eager socialites with little more than a smile. She hadn't felt bad about that, nor had it been difficult, because they were all silly girls who only had one thing in mind—getting him to the altar.

That would not happen on her watch.

Nor would there be a scandal.

Not even when they ended their partnership. They would part as friends. Remain friends. Just like she would remain friends with Audrey.

She'd never thought of him as a friend in the past, but this trip had changed all that and she was happy about that. They had so much in common. Especially when it came to marriage. It was so nice knowing that she didn't need to worry about saying or doing anything that might encourage him to believe that was her goal. He knew it wasn't, and she knew he had no ulterior motives.

She had no ulterior motives, either. Though, for a fleeting moment or two this evening, she had caught herself wondering why she didn't feel as if she was pretending. What she felt for him had felt real, natural, but then she'd remembered that they were friends. Nothing more.

The list she'd made long ago about finding the love of her life wasn't overly long, but it was specific. He—if there ever was a he—would be very much like her father had been. Kind, and caring, and funny. Very funny. Someone who would make her happy, make her laugh. Her father had made them all laugh, all the time, and she missed that, so very much. He'd made others laugh, too. Everyone had liked her father. And she had loved him. Loved him so much that sometimes her heart still hurt when she thought about him dying. Being gone forever.

Her father had been handsome, too, but that wasn't on her list. She would never fall in love with someone just because of their looks. She wouldn't fall in love with anyone that she didn't want to fall in love with. It was as simple as that. Just like she'd told Lincoln.

With happiness filling her, because there were times when everything felt right, and this was one of them, she patted the book holding the boutonniere between its pages. The book was one she'd brought with her from home, a mystery novel. She'd known how it would end—at least had been very sure of that—and had brought it with her because she knew she couldn't have waited a month to finish it. Having finished the book a few days ago, she'd been happy to know she'd been right about who the culprit had been and what he'd done.

She was right about Lincoln, too. About the two of them being friends.

Smiling to herself, she left the book on the dresser and proceeded to get ready for bed, already excited for the next event on the list Roseanne had created.

Lincoln normally didn't go into the office on Saturdays, but had this morning, because he wanted to go over the notes that he'd quickly written up last night while talking with his informant in order to have things fresh in his mind.

He and Victoria would be attending the theater tonight with Jake and Audrey. John Webster would be there, too, and Lincoln wanted a few questions front and foremost to ask when they encountered each other.

Yet the paper before him was empty because he kept thinking about Victoria, and how enthralled she'd been about the magician last night. He wondered if the play would have her as mesmerized as Hans the Magnificent had last night. Her nosegay was still on his dresser. In the small dish where he usually put the change out of his pockets. He hadn't known what to do with it. It was just a flower, but he hadn't wanted to throw it away.

Eventually, he'd have to.

Giving his head a clearing shake, he mumbled, "It's a flower. You have a case to focus on. One that could put you where you want to be."

It took more reminders like that to keep his mind on the task at hand. By the afternoon, when he left his office, he'd memorized a list of questions for John. He also had two nosegays in his possession.

Unable to get that flower on his dresser off his mind, and because he'd never bought one before, nor knew where to buy one, he'd sent his driver out to buy one for Victoria for tonight. However, then he'd determined that giving her one might raise eyebrows, so he'd sent his driver out to buy a second one for Audrey. Giving each his sister and Victoria one to wear to the theater tonight wouldn't raise eyebrows. Not even his mother would be able to read more into that.

Furthermore, there wasn't anything that needed to be read into. He merely felt bad that Victoria's flower from last night was drying up to nothing on his dresser.

Upon arriving home, he asked Curtis to have the nosegays sent up to Audrey's and Victoria's rooms. While the butler saw to the task, Lincoln made his way into the parlor, where he heard voices.

Audrey, Victoria, and his mother were in there, all three sitting on the sofa and discussing something on the large sheet of paper laid on the table before them.

"Hello, Lincoln, dear," his mother greeted. "We are putting together the reserved seating."

He gave a nod, but his eyes kept going to Victoria, as if he had no control over them. She was wearing a pink-and-white-striped dress, and looked as pretty as ever, so why was he noticing small things? Like how a few corkscrews of hair dangled near her temples, and how her ears were perfectly shaped. He'd never noticed a misshaped ear in the past, and noticing that hers weren't made no sense.

He had to clear a lump out of his throat while pulling his gaze off her. "Reserved seating for what?"

"Oh, darling." His mother sounded exasperated as she shook her head. "The wedding, of course."

He nodded, recognizing that he should have known that.

"Oh, and dear, dinner will be served half an hour early this evening. We'll need the extra time to arrive at the theater on time. It's opening night."

Hiding the thought that hit him, he gave his mother another head nod. "Very well. I'll leave you to your reserved seating work." Why hadn't he considered his mother would be attending with them tonight? She loved the theater and never missed an opening night of a new play.

Leaving the room, he sought out Curtis again. "I need you to send someone to buy a nosegay for my mother and have it put in her room," he told the butler.

"Right away, sir," Curtis replied. "Is there anything else?"

"No, that's all."

Curtis left and Lincoln made his way to the second floor, wondering how replacing a simple flower from last night had snowballed into three trips to buy nosegays. Yet, he was glad that he'd thought about the repercussions of only giving Victoria one. Neither of them expected anything from their arrangement. It was simply to fool others for the time being, but he didn't need his mother or sister to read more into it.

His actions confirmed themselves later, when all three women appeared in the drawing room wearing their theater finery, including the nosegays. All three were appreciative of his thoughtfulness.

A short time later, upon arriving at the theater, and noticing other women wearing nosegays—something he'd never noticed in the past—he was glad to have bought them.

The other thing he noticed, was the number of stares directed at him, as well as the whispering behind hand fans.

Although, in all honesty, he hadn't set out to notice the nosegays or the stares, he'd been searching the crowd for John Webster. He'd told himself to look for John in an attempt to not be caught staring at Victoria. However, not even that was working. Ever since he'd walked into the drawing room and seen her wearing an olive green gown that was again a simple dress with little embellishment other than the pink rose nosegay, he'd been having a hard time taking his eyes off her.

At the moment, he was also wondering what exactly was filling him with a unique sense of pride as he escorted her through the lobby and up the wide staircase to the second floor and their balcony seats.

"I can find my way to our seats by myself," she said near his ear.

"Why?" he asked quietly, because his mother, sister, and Jake were only a step or two ahead of them.

"Because you've been scanning the crowd like you've lost something since the moment we walked in the door."

"I was just noticing how many other women have nosegays," he replied.

She made a quiet scoffing sound before whispering, "It was very kind of you to surprise us with the nosegays, but I do not believe that is what you've been looking for."

"Well, it is."

"It is not."

"Is too."

Shaking her head, she huffed out a breath.

He grinned, and stepped aside, allowing her to follow the others through the curtained doorway of the private balcony, where six chairs were lined up along the half-wall of the open area that overlooked the stage.

They walked to their seats, and he held her chair as she sat before taking the seat between her and the wall. The chairs were padded, yet he wasn't looking forward to sitting here for the next hour. From past experiences, it was going to be long and boring. He wasn't disrespecting the actors, their abilities nor the work they put into their performances. It was his attention span that was to blame. He'd never been captured enough by a performance for his mind not to wander and wish he was someplace else.

Victoria's hand touched his knee as she leaned towards him and whispered, "It won't be that bad."

He chuckled at how she knew what he was thinking and leaned close enough that the ends of their noses practically touched. "That's a matter of opinion."

"Perhaps. However, I believe if you were to have an open mind, you might enjoy this performance."

"I have an open mind." In fact, his mind was so open, it was noting how the overhead lights were reflecting in her blue eyes, making them sparkle. It was also so open that it wondered why he'd never noticed such things about her in the past.

Her smile grew. "Good, because I can't believe you haven't heard of Robin Hood."

"What does Robin Hood have to do with anything?"

Her brows knit together and her smile disappeared as she asked, "You know that's the performance, don't you?"

"No." He went on to explain, "I never asked. It didn't matter. I knew we'd be here no matter what."

Her entire expression softened and her hand still on his knee increased its pressure, spreading a warmth over his leg.

If she'd been going to say anything, the dimming of the lights must have changed her mind. She removed her hand and turned her gaze over the balcony ledge as darkness overtook the theater.

The curtains opened, and the performance began in a market square where the actor playing Friar Tuck broke into a song declaring he was an honest man. Lincoln knew the Robin Hood story well, and had to chuckle at the content of the opening song. However, it was the coy glance that Victoria cast his way that truly sent happiness rushing through is veins.

She reached over and patted his arm, and before she could remove her hand, he covered it with his.

They remained like that, hands touching, and to his surprise, the stage curtain fell and the lights turned on signaling the intermission between acts long before he'd expected it. Leastwise, he hadn't yet grown bored or stiff.

Victoria's gaze was on him. "You can admit it," she said.

"Admit what?"

"That you are enjoying the performance."

He rose and held her chair with one hand while offering the other for her to hold while rising to stand. "Yes, I can admit that. You're enjoying it, too."

"I am, more than I'd imagined," she said. "The performers are wonderful."

His mother quickly responded to that, explaining how she'd seen some of the same actors in other performances. She continued talking, making comparisons to past plays as they exited the balcony and descended the steps.

As his mother saw friends amongst the other show-goers and shifted her attention to them, he asked Victoria, "Would you care for a refreshment?"

"I would, thank you, but—" She leaned closer and lowered her voice. "I believe Mr. Webster is attempting to gain your attention."

He lifted his head in the direction she nodded towards and made eye contact with John Webster on the other side of the room. His goal for the night was to speak to John, but an easy way to excuse himself wasn't immediately forming. Like purchasing a nosegay for Victoria, he hadn't fully thought this through. His mother never approved of business being conducted during social events, even though this conversation would only take a moment. He'd found a legitimate way to hold up any sale. John's father's will had never been probated. Though in this circumstance, it was merely a formality, it would provide the time needed to explore and prove who was behind the suggested sale and why. All he needed was John's agreement to go ahead with the probate.

"Go say hello," Victoria said. "I'll escort your mother into the refreshment room. You can join us there."

The sense of near disbelief washed over him. He could

almost kiss her for her offer. He knew enough about women to know most would never suggest such a thing. They expected a man's full attention to be on their wants and needs at all times. "You wouldn't mind?"

"No, not at all."

He gave her elbow a slight squeeze. "Thank you. I won't be long."

Victoria allowed herself a moment to watch Lincoln walk away and silently admire how handsome he looked in his black suit. She wondered if his handsomeness had something to do with the way her heart was still beating faster than it should. Or was it because she knew they were fooling all these people surrounding her. Making them believe there was more than friendship between her and Lincoln. That felt a bit devilish, and she'd never done anything devilish in her life. She could justify the reason behind it, but justifying the feelings inside her was becoming difficult. Fooling anyone should not feel good. Should not make her happy, yet she was happy.

Her gaze shifted and there was no limit to the number of eyes that were following Lincoln, just as her gaze had, and they weren't all those of young women. Many were older, mothers who would like to have their daughters courted by him. Married to him. That wasn't what Lincoln wanted, and she was certain that knowing that is what imbedded a sense of bravery inside her that had never been quite so strong. It gave her the ability to pull up a smug smile to display upon the sets of eyes that shifted from him to her.

As the onlookers shifted their gazes elsewhere, Victoria turned towards where Roseanne was still engaged in conversation with two other women. Jake and Audrey were nowhere in sight, leaving her to believe they had already entered the refreshment area. She also believed that John Webster was who Lincoln had been looking for upon their arrival this evening. A genuine smile tugged at her lips over his insistence that he'd been looking to see what other women had been wearing nosegays. Together, they might be fooling others, but he could not fool her.

However, she was warmed by his thoughtfulness for the flowers he'd purchased for all of them. A few other men had given her flowers, and she'd never been overly impressed by the action because she'd known the reason behind their actions—the hope of getting their hands on her family's money. Lincoln had done it just to be kind, and even though she wasn't the only one he'd purchased the nosegays for, it made her feel special.

"Where's Lincoln?" Roseanne asked with a frown as she scanned the crowd.

"He's visiting with someone," Victoria replied. "I told him we'd meet him in the refreshment area. I assumed you were thirsty. I know I am."

"I am quite parched," Roseanne said, looping their arms together. "All that laughing during the performance is to blame. It's been an entertaining rendition of an old tale, don't you agree?"

"I do," Victoria replied as they made their way through the crowd. "The actors are extremely talented."

As she'd expected, Roseanne began explaining the number of times she'd seen the same actors in other performances, which took her mind off her son's whereabouts.

It didn't take Victoria's mind off him. Not even the play, which had been excellent, had done that. She'd been excited to see how he had instantly become occupied by the performance. She would have too, if his hand hadn't been upon hers and squeezing it during certain times. That had sent her heart into quite a state, making following the storyline somewhat difficult.

Her thoughts had been on him, and were again now. She once again wondered if Mr. Webster was one of his clients. Not that it was any of her business, she was just curious. He certainly had been looking for someone and it had been evident that Mr. Webster had been discreetly attempting to catch his attention a moment ago.

It could possibly have something to do with the bicycles he'd purchased, but all Mr. Webster would have had to do was call Lincoln about that. Then again, all he'd have to do was call him if he was a client and had a question. She was just too curious, or perhaps too distrustful of men. All men. Which wasn't unexpected considering her history of would-be suitors. She couldn't remember a single one that she'd ever thought might have an interest in her for herself.

Lincoln wasn't interested in her, either, not in that sense. He didn't need her grandfather's money, and for a brief moment, she wondered if this, this happiness inside her, would be the same if he truly was interested her as a woman. Someone he wanted to share his future with, his dreams and goals. If he would welcome her to assist him in manifesting those goals and dreams.

It was a silly, fleeting thought. She shouldn't be wondering about that, nor imagining how thrilling it would be to work alongside him. Offering him support and ideas or suggestions that he'd welcome. He would thank her for being a part of his life.

She gave herself a clearing head shake. That was not what either of them wanted and she appreciated that, therefore, she shouldn't hold the same skepticism towards him as she did others. She certainly didn't when it came to other things, so why was she wondering so much about Mr. Webster? Which is where this entire line of silly thoughts had begun.

No answers to her own thoughts formed as she accepted a glass of champagne and sipped on it while listening to the others around her discuss the performance and actors. The fluttering sense of happiness returned as she recalled how Lincoln had laughed during a scene that they mentioned. He was in attendance because of family requirements, and had been prepared to be bored the entire evening. She'd recognized it because that had been exactly how she'd felt every time a suitor had been invited to her home for a meal or just a visit. There had been no fun, no thrill in any of that.

Nothing like what she'd experienced since arriving in the city this trip. Lincoln was the reason. She'd had fun on all of her visits with Audrey, but this time was different and that alone gave reason for her to know she was right in her goal of not getting married just because it was expected of her. She didn't want a dull and uneventful life.

That hadn't been something she'd thought of before, but every moment she'd spent in Lincoln's company had been anything but dull. Even when they bickered over a difference of opinions.

A soft touch on her elbow caused her heart to do a little loop-de-loop, and she instantly knew who was at her side.

"Thank you," he whispered.

"You're welcome." She scanned the room, looking for a waiter. "Would you care for a beverage?"

"It looks like they are collecting empties. It must be time to return to our seats."

She handed him her glass. "You can finish this one."

He took it, finished it, and set her empty glass on a tray that one of the many attendants were carrying.

Roseanne set her glass upon a tray as well. "Who were you visiting with, dear?"

"Just an acquaintance," he replied as he escorted both of them out of the room.

Victoria held her question until they were once again seated in the balcony and the lights were out. As the curtain rose, she leaned closer to him. "Did you cancel your order?"

"What order?" he whispered in return.

"The bicycles."

"No."

She attempted to stop herself from asking, but it didn't take hold. "Is he a client of yours?"

"He is now."

The smile that tugged on her lips seemed silly, yet she liked having her curiosity satisfied. She also liked that he trusted her enough to tell her that Mr. Webster was a client.

Her smile faded as she wondered why Mr. Webster had just become one of Lincoln's clients. That resulted in her giving herself a chiding. She didn't need to know everything, not about Lincoln or his clients, but she couldn't let it go.

Her thoughts refused to shift to the play, because his arm was resting along the back of her chair, making it impossible for her to concentrate on anything but him.

Long after the play was over and they were back home, she lay in her bed, staring at the picture, still wrapped in paper behind the chair near the window, wondering why Lincoln was willing to have Mr. Webster be his client but unwilling to help her with her case.

Even though she told herself that wasn't a fair comparison, because Mr. Webster probably had legal business issues that he needed Lincoln to take care of, whereas Lincoln had already told her that she didn't have enough information for a robbery case, she couldn't get it off her mind. Her goal was to make sure Elwood paid for his crime against her family.

However, she now had the new goal of keeping Lincoln safe from all the socialites, and in truth, that one was what was on her mind more than Elwood. Leastwise, it had been up until tonight. Was that because she'd realized how much she was enjoying Lincoln's company? Not just his company, but his friendship. He had many clients that he'd probably told people about for years, so why had she relished in him telling her that Mr. Webster was one of his clients? Because it made her feel like she was even more of a part of his life?

Attending a theater performance wasn't new. She'd lost count of the number of times she had attended one, yet she'd never been more excited about going to one than she had been today. Since waking up this morning, a thrill had lived inside her, knowing that she'd be attending with Lincoln. That same thrill had remained throughout the entire evening.

Truthfully, it was still there and the day was over. Furthermore, if she was being completely truthful with herself, she knew that thrill was going to remain right up to the wedding. She liked acting as if she and Lincoln were a couple. Which was completely unlike her. She'd never wanted to be part of a couple.

This was different, though. She wasn't really part of a

couple. Perhaps that's where the thrill came from, that she and Lincoln were only pretending.

However, when the pretending ended, nothing would have changed. Nothing about her life.

Unless she found a way for Lincoln to help her see that Elwood was charged for what he had done. She couldn't lose sight of that. After all, that had been a part of why she'd agreed to their pretending.

The main reason.

She had to set a precedent so in the future, men wouldn't believe she or Eva were easy pickings.

Chapter Eight

Despite her night of tossing and turning, and twisted thoughts, the following day brought another opportunity that thrilled Victoria beyond belief. Upon arriving home from church, where she and Lincoln had sat side by side, which had once again been enough to keep her pulse elevated, they discovered that the bicycles had been delivered.

While Audrey and Jake, who had accompanied them to church, were ecstatic over the gift, Roseanne was clearly aghast, and Victoria found herself once again whispering with Lincoln. "Did you know they were being delivered today?"

He shook his head, yet smiled. "If you recall, when we purchased them, Mr. Webster said they'd be delivered early next week."

She nodded.

"This is next week," he said, still grinning.

"It's Sunday."

"Yes, the week begins on Sunday."

"I know, but Webster's isn't open on Sunday."

"Perhaps that's why they were delivered today." He shrugged. "People were available to bring them over."

"Lincoln," Roseanne said sternly, capturing both of their attention. "Those things are not only unsightly, they are dangerous and a menace to society!"

"They are also increasing in popularity every day," he replied.

"For no good reason!" Roseanne replied. "It's just a fad that will soon fade away. I can't believe that you of all people bought into such tomfoolery!"

"Actually, Mother," Lincoln said, "alternate sources of transportation are the future, especially combustion engines, which is why Ronald Woodroof is working on attaching one to a bicycle."

Roseanne's mouth fell open, before it snapped shut with a huff. "That's the most ridiculous thing I've ever heard. Does his mother know that?"

"I'm assuming so," Lincoln answered. "She's always been proud of Ronald and his inventions in the past. I can't see why this would be any different."

"Well, I never!" With another huff, Roseanne marched towards the house, leaving the rest of them in the driveway where they'd discovered the bicycles upon stepping out of the carriage.

"How much do you want to bet she's on her way to call Ronald's mother?" Lincoln asked.

"I would be a fool to make that bet," Victoria replied, thinking she couldn't recall ever seeing Roseanne quite so miffed.

His agreement was little more than a chuckle as Audrey first hugged him, thanking him for the gift, then grasped Victoria by the arm.

"Come," Audrey said. "Let's go change our clothes so we can learn to ride the bicycles."

"They are for you and Jake," Victoria said.

In true Audrey fashion, she laughed. "I know! But we're

sharing! Jake can help me learn to ride and Lincoln can help you."

"Perhaps Lincoln has something else to do," Victoria said, glancing over her shoulder. Her heart flipped at the way he grinned and shook his head.

"No, I don't," he said.

"We will hurry!" Audrey told him, while tugging Victoria towards the door. "I love how the four of us are doing so many things together," Audrey continued excitedly. "And I've never seen Lincoln enjoy events as much as the play last night and the magician the night before, have you?"

Victoria had never had a lot of interaction with Lincoln prior to this trip, so had no opinion on that, but did admit, "The magician was amazing. I still don't know how he switched my nosegay for Lincoln's boutonniere."

"I still can't believe you and Lincoln bought Jake and I bicycles!" Audrey exclaimed, hurrying into the house and down the hallway.

"Lincoln purchased them," Victoria corrected.

"But you helped him, and now I know why the two of you were whispering all the time."

Victoria lifted the hem of her skirt as they quickly climbed the back staircase, and chose to remain silent because the bicycles were only one of the subjects she and Lincoln had whispered about.

Audrey didn't seem to need a response. "I was beginning to worry that you two didn't like each other. Now, well… Wouldn't it be wonderful if you and Lincoln truly became a couple?" she asked. "I get giddy thinking that we could not only be best friends, but sisters!"

Victoria's heart leaped so fast in her chest that she stumbled on a step, and luckily caught herself before tumbling.

"We are simply attending events together prior to your wedding in order to prevent any type of a scandal."

"I know, and I thank you for that. Everyone noticed you two at the ball, and it immediately put a halt to the socialites seeking him out. None of them even approached him at the theater last night, and that was such a relief. I was worried about him having to attend so many functions. He usually avoids them, but with father out of town, mother insisted that Lincoln fill in. I told her it wasn't necessary, because you and she would be at all of them, but she claimed it was expected that a male member of our family was in attendance, too. It's all worked out so perfectly for you and him to attend everything together."

Victoria was aware that she didn't understand all of the rules of society, nor was it her place to argue them, but it was her place to make sure that Audrey didn't get her hopes up over something that could never be. "Lincoln and I have simply become friends, because of you. Neither of us want anything to interfere with your wedding."

Audrey stopped in the hallway and embraced Victoria in a hug. "I know, and I'm grateful to both of you." Releasing her hold, she said, "I also know that Jake and I were friends before we fell in love." Spinning around, she grasped the doorknob of her bedroom door. "Now hurry, go change. I can't wait for us to learn how to ride bicycles! It's going to be so fun!"

As Audrey disappeared into her room, Victoria continued down the hallway to her room, wondering if she should have thought more deeply about the consequences of what others might perceive when it came to her and Lincoln. What had seemed so simple had certainly become more complicated than she'd ever have imagined.

Complicated and confusing. She knew the truth, and had to stop confusing things in her own mind.

Lincoln hadn't felt this excited for someone in ages. Helping Victoria learn to ride the bicycle felt almost as if he was mastering it himself. He'd already done that. While the women had been changing their dresses, he and Jake had tried out the bicycles. Figuring out the correct balance had been the greatest challenge, but once he'd done that, it had not only been easy, it had been exhilarating, and he was looking forward to her experiencing it.

After explaining how the bicycle worked, he'd encouraged her to keep her body straight and not lean to the left or the right while pedaling in order to maintain her balance. She'd followed his instructions and with only a couple of short panicked moments where she planted her feet on the ground to keep from falling, she'd mastered pedaling. Her steering was still wobbly, but he was confident she'd soon master that, too.

While holding on to the back of the bicycle seat, he jogged along beside her on the path in the park. "Relax your arms," he said. "Hold the handlebars like you do a horse's reins, with a firm grip, but giving them a little play."

"Absolutely not!" she shouted in return. "A horse has a brain, and it's not going to hurt itself. This bicycle has a mind of its own and it wants me to fall!"

"I won't let you fall!"

"Well, I might very well knock you over while I'm falling!"

"No, you won't, just relax your hold, the front wheel won't be so wobbly."

She planted her feet on the ground, bringing him along

with the bike to a halt. "If I relax my arms, it's going to go wherever it wants."

"No, it won't."

She wiggled the handlebars, turning the front wheel. "Are you sure?"

"Yes, I'm sure." He held the bike seat firmly, although his hand and arm felt as if they were on fire being in such close proximity to her hind end. He couldn't remember a time when a woman had affected him the way she did, and even after hours of thinking about it, he couldn't figure out exactly why.

"How sure?" she asked.

He grinned. "You'll have more control of the steering if you relax your hold. I promise. You're just being a little too stiff."

"Stiff?"

The look she gave him made him laugh out loud. "Yes, stiff." He released the seat and leaned in front of her, laying both of his hands atop hers that were gripping onto the handlebars. "See how easily it turns?" he asked, while turning the handlebars.

"Yes. It turns too easily, that's the problem."

He removed his hands and grasped a hold of the seat again. "You'll be glad it turns so easily once you start riding. Now, just relax, put your feet on the pedals, and let's try again."

She closed her eyes for a moment, and took a deep breath before placing her feet on the pedals.

He could see how her arms were relaxed at the elbows, and complimented her. "Good job, just keep your arms like that. I'll give you a push to get started."

She held up one arm. "All right, but after giving me a

push, let go. I think you're making me nervous. I don't want to hit you when I fall."

"You aren't going to fall," he said. "You know how to pedal. Just don't tighten up your arms."

"Right." She gave a nod and blew out a breath while taking a hold of the handlebars again. "Ready."

"On the count of three," he said. "One, two, three!" Along with a slight push, he ran along beside her for a few steps, just to make sure she had her balance, then let go.

She quickly figured it all out, and was pedaling at a quicker pace, making him run to keep up.

"I'm doing it!" she shouted. "I'm doing it!"

"Yes, you are!"

Jake and Audrey had been several yards ahead of them, but at the pace Victoria was now pedaling, the yards were being eaten up.

"Bicycle coming through!" Lincoln shouted as he ran.

Jake and Audrey laughed and cheered Victoria on as she whizzed past them.

Lincoln slowed his pace long enough to tell them, "She rides a bicycle like she rides a horse. Full speed!"

"I'll be catching up with her in a moment!" Audrey shouted.

Lincoln waved, but kept running after Victoria, who was pedaling along as if she'd been doing it for years. He was proud of her, and happy. "You're doing great!"

"Thank you!" she shouted in return without a wobble whatsoever.

He continued to run after her, all the while wondering when he'd stopped having fun like this. It had been years since he'd felt this carefree and enjoyed such simple things. He could easily point out that had changed the day he'd picked her up at the train station. That had been nothing more than a simple act, one of duty and courtesy, and despite what he'd thought at the time, he was now glad to have been the one to pick her up that day.

Suddenly, for no apparent reason, she stopped pedaling, let the bicycle coast to a stop and then put her feet down on the ground.

"Why did you stop?" he asked, arriving at her side.

"I didn't want you to run any further."

The warmth inside his chest was so great, it stunned him for a split second, then he laughed, and realized that she was definitely one of the nicest people he'd ever known. "A little running won't hurt me."

Before she could answer, a squeal filled the air.

"I'm doing it!" Audrey shouted, following her squeal. "This is so fun!"

"Quick, give me a starting push, so I can ride with her!" Victoria said.

For a moment he considered showing her how to push off with one foot, but changed his mind and grasped the bicycle seat. He waited until her feet were on the pedals and Audrey was near before he gave her a little shove.

The two women were quickly side by side on the path, and considering the way their front tires wobbled slightly, most likely due to their excited laughter, he wondered if riding side by side was safe for the two of them.

The look on Jake's face said he felt the same way, and side by side, they ran after the bicycles.

Amongst an excess of giggles, the women stopped their bicycles before the park trail curved to the left. All the running left both him and Jake somewhat breathless by the time they arrived beside the women, and Lincoln took a moment to brace his hands on his thighs as he sucked in air.

Victoria climbed off her bicycle. "I've used your bicycle long enough, Jake. You and Audrey can go for a ride together now."

Her obvious joy at learning to ride had Lincoln asking, "You're done riding already?"

"Yes," shc said, releasing the handlebars to Jake, who was still huffing.

"Why?" Lincoln asked.

"Because the bicycles are gifts for Jake and Audrey." Shifting her gaze to Jake, she said, "Thank you for sharing your bicycle with me."

"You're welcome to use it anytime," Jake said. "Are you sure you don't want to ride more now?"

"Yes, I'm sure," she replied.

Lincoln stepped forward and held Audrey's bike steady as she place her feet on the pedals, then gave her a push to get started as she and Jake began riding along the trail.

Victoria stepped up beside him and they watched as the couple turned the corner and pedaled onward. "You were right," she said. "I was holding on too stiffly."

Without a thought to his actions, he draped an arm around her shoulders and gave her a side hug. "I'm glad you figured it out. I'm thinking I should buy more bicycles."

She laughed. "I'm thinking that will make your mother twice as mad as she already is."

"Perhaps," he said, "or maybe she'll learn to ride one herself."

Victoria giggled. "I doubt that."

"One never knows." He dropped his arm and took a hold

of her hand. "Let's follow the path, make sure those two don't encounter a dog."

She shook her head. "Are we going to argue over that again?"

He chuckled. "No, we are just going to take a walk, unless you'd rather return to the house."

"I'd much rather follow the path, thank you."

Holding her hand felt right, practically natural, yet he questioned if he should release it as they started walking forward. There was no one watching, so it wasn't as if they needed to pretend to be courting, yet, they could encounter someone. The park was always busy on Sundays.

Was that why he felt so carefree? Because their pretend courtship had given him a freedom he hadn't known in years? It did feel as if a weight had been lifted off his shoulders. More than that, though, she was enjoyable to be around.

"Are you really considering buying another bicycle?" she asked as they walked around the curve.

There was no sign of Audrey and Jake, which wasn't unexpected since the path not only curved several times, but had several forks that led in various directions. "Yes," he answered. "I enjoyed riding one. Did you?"

"Yes, I did. I might consider buying one, too, although, my mother's thoughts about them could be close to your mother's." She glanced at him. "Have you seen the one Ronald is putting an engine on?"

"No, I have not." He shrugged. "Maybe we should go look at it."

"I'd like to see it," she said.

Although he hadn't thought much about it in the past, he was now more interested. "So would I. What do you say we go to his house after lunch today?"

"Do you think he'll be home?"

"I know he will be. Ronald only leaves his workshop when required."

"Why is that?" she asked.

"Because he loves his work. I've assisted him in obtaining several patents for his inventions."

"That had to be interesting."

He hated to see the shine in her eyes diminished, but had to admit, "Actually, filing for a patent is rather boring. It's all paperwork."

"But you've seen the inventions, haven't you?"

"No, not all of them."

"Why not?"

"It wasn't necessary to file the paperwork."

"But weren't you interested to know what they were?"

"Ronald told me about them."

She sighed and shook her head. "That's one of my downfalls. Curiosity. I'd have to see them myself."

"I wouldn't consider that a downfall," he said.

"My mother does."

"One more thing we have in common," he said. "Mothers who believe they know what's best for us." He stopped at the Y in the path. "We will go look at Ronald's bicycle this afternoon, but right now, which way do you think Jake and Audrey went?"

After looking left and right, she shrugged. "I have no idea, but let's go right."

"Why right?" he asked, as they started in that direction.

"Because this path will take us back around to the road in front of your house."

Feeling a slight disappointment, he asked, "You're ready to return to the house?"

"You should be after all the running you did."

"Are you still worried about that?"

"Not worried. I just feel bad that you had to do it."

"There's nothing to feel bad about. I wanted to do it. It was fun teaching you to ride a bicycle."

"It was fun learning to ride one," she said. "It was scary at first, but then easier than I'd imagined, and exhilarating."

He was about to tell her that's what he'd thought, too, but was sidetracked by a man on horseback who had stopped in the middle of the pathway a short distance ahead of them. Something about the way the man was staring at them stiffened Lincoln's spine.

"Let's go back the other way," Victoria said.

Lincoln's intuition kicked in stronger at how her hand trembled inside his as she turned about, as if not wanting to look at the man on horseback. Tightening his hold on her hand, he asked, "Is that Elwood Kelley?"

"Yes," she whispered as if someone else might hear. "And I'd prefer to not have anything to do with him, including saying hello."

Lincoln would prefer that she didn't have anything to do with Elwood. That was the catalyst behind him agreeing to their arrangement. Although he didn't know the man, he felt a strong loathing towards Elwood.

Casually, Lincoln let his gaze wander to the man on horseback, still staring at them. He not only didn't want her embedded with men like Elwood and his father, he was committed to it not happening. No matter what it took.

The thought that crossed his mind could complicate things far beyond what he wanted, but at this very moment, complications were not his first concern. While giving her hand a slight tug, forcing her to twist so they were facing each other, he stepped closer and used his free hand to catch her beneath the chin. He didn't hesitate, yet moved slowly so as to not frighten her as he lowered his face to hers.

A flash of excitement struck, and the heat that grew deep inside him was fiery For a brief moment, he questioned if he should worry whether it was the type of heat that would warm him or burn him.

Either way, he brought his mouth down upon hers.

Victoria's breath caught in her throat as Lincoln's lips touched hers. Softly, tentatively, yet warm and inviting. She felt her own hesitation. A mixture of surprise and not knowing how to react. That only lasted a moment before an instinct she didn't know lived inside her took over. Her hands landed on his chest, grasped a hold of the lapels of his jacket, and she used that hold to stabilize herself as she pressed her lips firmly against his.

Her heartbeat doubled, then tripled, as his lips slid across hers, and hers moved to match his movements, almost like a dance. One that fully consumed her thoughts. This is what she'd been afraid to think about. Kissing him. It had been in the back of her mind, but she'd never dared let it come forward. Never dared to dream of what it would be like.

One of his hands slid around her back, pulling her closer, and she willingly leaned against him, feeling the heat of his body merge with hers. There wasn't a single part of her that didn't feel alive, thrilled beyond all she'd ever known.

This wasn't a fast, quick kiss that she'd felt obligated to provide after a man had ask permission to kiss her, which had happened occasionally in the past. Lincoln hadn't asked, and there wasn't a hint of the obligatory floating through her.

This was a kiss. A real kiss. One that women wrote about in their diaries, vowing to never forget. It was all-consuming. Unforgettable.

The need that was growing inside her was as uncanny as it was wild and powerful. She felt the rumble of a pleasure-filled moan in the back of her throat. Much like one that happened unintentionally, uncontrollably, when she tasted something far more delicious than expected.

The rest of the world ceased to exist. There was nothing, no one, except for her and Lincoln at this moment in time. A moment that felt as if it should last forever, yet ended long before she was ready.

She swayed forward as his mouth eased off hers, and once again had to use her hold on his jacket to maintain her balance. It was as if the world was spinning around her, and she didn't dare open her eyes until the dizziness slowed.

That took more than a few moments, and then she was afraid to open her eyes for fear of what she might see. However, her curiosity to know Lincoln's reaction to their kiss was stronger than her fear and she lifted her lids, looked up at him.

There was not only a smile on his face, but also a brilliant shimmer in his eyes. Looking at him made her heart beat uncontrollably all over again.

He touched the side of her face, ran a single finger over her cheek. The touch was so soft, so tender, a soft sigh escaped her lips.

"Forgive me. I should have asked permission to kiss you," he said. "But there wasn't time."

Confused, she took a moment to make sense of that, but couldn't. "There wasn't?"

"No, Elwood had started riding towards us."

Elwood! How had she forgotten about him? She twisted

left and right, seeing nothing but an empty path in both directions. "Where did he go?"

"He rode past."

The sigh she huffed out was a mixture of frustration and gratefulness. She was glad that Elwood was gone, but frustrated that they'd run into him in the first place. At least that's what she attempted to tell herself while trying to think about something other than kissing Lincoln. The thrill of that was still pulsating throughout her body, even though she now understood why he'd kissed her. What she wasn't so sure about was why she'd kissed him in return. She'd had no control over that. It had been like jumping into a pool of water, where every instinct instantly kicked in and told her to swim. Her body, or maybe her soul, had told her to kiss him back and instantly knew how to do that.

"Are you afraid of him?" Lincoln asked.

She shook her head in an attempt to clear her head, to push kissing him into the recesses of her mind so she could think, clearly think, about other things. Taking in a breath of air, she lifted her gaze, met his. "No. I just want him to pay for what he did. I don't want him to get away with it."

Lincoln stared at her for what felt like an eternity, in which her mind went off wandering again, filled itself with questions. One concerning if he was regretting having kissed her, and the other if he was considering helping her prove Elwood had stolen from her family. She wanted to know the answer to both questions.

"How well do you know him?" Lincoln asked.

The quick wash of disappointment told her which question had meant more to her, and it wasn't the one about Elwood. "Not well. I'd only met him once before he came to the house."

He lightly grasped her elbow and began walking along the pathway. "Where did you meet him?"

"In Tarrytown. My mother and I had been at the dressmakers back in January and he helped us carry some packages to the carriage."

"Did you ask for his help?"

"No, he accidently bumped into my mother and then offered to carry her packages. It was cold and snowing and I didn't even remember the encounter until my mother reminded me of it when she informed me that he'd be joining us for dinner."

"Was that the only time he was at your house? The day he joined you for dinner?"

"Yes."

"Had your mother invited him to dinner when he helped with your packages?"

Victoria had never been questioned by a lawyer about anything, but imagined it was much like this. Lincoln's questions were not only clipped and precise, his demeanor had become serious in a way she hadn't seen. "No," she answered. "He contacted her later, asking for permission to call upon me."

"You hadn't seen him at any time between the shopping trip and the day he'd come to your house?"

"No, I hadn't."

Lincoln was quiet for more than ten steps. She'd only started counting them because she didn't know what to say or think about his silence and had reached twelve when he stopped. She bit her bottom lip, waiting on him to speak, hoping he'd offer to help her.

"His family is not one you would want to be associated with. They are unsavory, and though I do believe you've been wronged, that he stole from you…" He ran a hand through his hair. "Without a more solid history, without more solid proof, it just isn't a case that would make it to court."

Victoria pinched her lips together to hold in the disappointment.

"I'm sorry," he said. "If I thought we could win, I'd help you, but with what we have, it would do nothing more than annoy him and his family, and that wouldn't be good for anyone."

His voice and face was full of sincerity. "Thank you," she said. "I understand."

"I hope you do," he said.

She nodded. "I do."

He let out a long sigh and glanced up and down the road. "Well, hopefully, after what he saw today, you won't have to worry about him contacting you again."

Her heart, or maybe her stomach, dropped. It was hard to tell because everything inside her felt deflated. She'd known that Elwood was the reason Lincoln had kissed her and she'd known why, but hearing it made it one hundred percent true.

Not that it hadn't been true before, she just… Just what? Wanted to believe that he'd kissed her for a different reason? That he'd actually wanted to kiss her? That was silly. It was also something that she shouldn't want. Not at all.

Then why was she disappointed? Why did she want it to happen again?

Furthermore, why did she believe him that there wasn't enough evidence? She had fingerprints and she rarely, if ever, let someone else change her mind. Her mother called her stubborn to a fault, and that hadn't changed.

So what had?

Chapter Nine

Pulling her thoughts together as best she could, trying not to think about how the taste of his lips was still on hers, Victoria said, "I hope so, and thank you for believing me. What happened does sound unbelievable. I understand that."

"It's not unbelievable," he replied as they started walking along the pathway. "It's just difficult to prove."

She nodded, because her thoughts were still on their kiss. How unbelievable that had been, while at the same time, nothing had felt more natural. Furthermore, she could imagine kissing him again. He was the only man in the world that she'd ever had such thoughts about.

Those thoughts continued as they made their way back to the house. Upon entering, she excused herself to prepare for lunch, and once in her bedroom, she sat down in the closest chair.

She was thinking too much about the kiss, and not enough about why it had happened. Not once had she considered kissing would be a part of their agreement. Therefore, she'd never needed to wonder how she would react to it.

A knock on the door interrupted any time that she might have had to think about it, because following the sound, Audrey entered the room.

"I have never, ever, had so much fun as bicycle riding!" Audrey exclaimed. "Have you?"

"It certainly was fun," Victoria agreed.

Audrey walked over and checked her image in the mirror, twisting to check if her hair was still pinned in place. "I feel guilty, because I'd rather go bicycle riding again rather than go to Jake's grandmother's house for lunch."

Victoria rose from the chair and stepped close enough to replace a pin in the back of her friend's hair. "You'll enjoy your lunch with her. You always enjoy visiting with her."

"I know. I adore her, and Jake promised we'd take another bicycle ride this evening." Audrey sighed. "I wish we had four bicycles so you and Linc could join us. I already feel bad leaving you alone all afternoon while we're at Jake's grandmother's house."

Victoria met Audrey's gaze in the mirror. "Don't feel bad. Lincoln and I are going to go see the bicycle that Ronald is putting a combustion engine on. I'm looking forward to seeing it."

Audrey spun about. "You are?"

"Yes, we were talking about it after riding your bicycles and decided to go look at it." Once again, memories of the kiss were strong enough to make her breath stall in her lungs. She'd truly never imagined anything could be so wonderful, so consuming that she hadn't been able to think of anything else but him.

"That's wonderful," Audrey said. "I was worried that you'd be stuck with Mother all afternoon, listening to how terrible bicycles are, but I should have known Linc would have thought of something. You'll have to tell me about it."

"And you'll have to tell me all about your visit with Jake's grandmother," Victoria replied, trying hard to not think about how Audrey would react if she knew about the kiss. Victoria would never tell her, even though that kiss would live with her forever.

Lincoln followed behind Victoria in the very crowded workshop that Ronald led them through, answering all of her questions about far more than his latest invention regarding the bicycle. Lincoln wasn't sure who was more excited, her or Ronald. Her questions weren't silly, either. They were intuitive and thoughtful.

Somewhat like his silent ones. It had been hours since they had been in the park, yet he couldn't get his mind off kissing her.

Off doing it again.

A kiss had never lived inside him like this one was doing. From the moment his lips had touched hers, it was as if he'd found something he'd been longing for, which made no sense. He'd never longed for a woman in his life, yet he knew one thing. He could kiss a thousand women and never feel what he had while kissing her. It had been too unique, just like her.

He couldn't concentrate on anything else. Not even the paperwork that had been delivered with the bicycles this morning. John Webster had sent along the contract that Lincoln had slipped him last night at the theater. The one that gave him permission to probate the will and therefore slow the sale of the department store while he continued to look for a way to completely stop the sale.

He'd glanced through the paperwork upon returning to the house from the park, but even that had led him straight back to her, and that kiss. He was convinced that Alderman Kelley was somehow behind the sale, which had made him think of Elwood, stealing money from her, and that had made him think of the kiss.

Why had he thought kissing her would be a good idea? Why hadn't he scrutinized that thought more deeply? Why had the thought ever even occurred?

He didn't have answers for any of those questions, because none of them made sense.

Victoria's laughter brought his mind back to the moment at hand, and he glanced between her and Ronald, who was demonstrating one of his many inventions. It was a broom, with an electrical cord attached to it. She was laughing and waving a hand at the dust in the air.

Lincoln chuckled to himself. Like the magician, and horseback riding, and the theater and bicycle riding, she made visiting Ronald's workshop enjoyable. The only conclusion he could draw out of that was that it was her. That the activity didn't matter, *she* simply made life enjoyable. He'd never imagined that someone could do that.

Ronald disconnected the cord from the socket, which turned the broom off. "It doesn't work as I'd imagined."

"It is a good idea, though," she said.

"I think so, too," Ronald said, putting the broom back on the workbench. "The bristles going back and forth send the dirt into the air rather than into a pile, and I have yet to figure out a way to change that." He held up a finger. "But step over here, and I'll show you something that does work."

Lincoln nodded at the question in her eyes when she looked at him, and then he followed the two of them to yet another long workbench.

"This," Ronald began, "is a bread toaster." It, too, was electric, and Ronald inserted the end of the cord into a socket, then he pointed to a small metal rack. "If I had a piece of bread, I'd show you, but I don't, so I'll just explain it. You put a piece of bread on this rack, and the coil beneath it heats up, toasting the bread, then you flip the bread over and toast the other side. If you put your hand over here, just not too close, you can feel the heat."

Victoria held her hand over the rack for a moment. "I can feel the heat. That's a very interesting invention."

"Thank you," Ronald said, with a mini bow after he'd unplugged the toaster. "Lincoln has submitted a patent on it for me."

"What will happen then?" Victoria asked.

Because both she and Ronald were looking at him, Lincoln replied, "Basically no one else will be able to copy Ronald's invention. He'll be able to determine what happens concerning additional toasters being built, distributed, sold, and used."

"So you could make several of them and sell them at places like Webster's Department Store?" she asked Ronald.

"If I wanted to, or I could have someone else build them for me, and I could keep working on other inventions. Like this one." Ronald moved further down the workbench. "An electric kite."

Lincoln cringed at the idea and laid a hand on Victoria's arm, slowing her footsteps as she followed Ronald. He knew a kite was behind the discovery of electricity, but also had additional reasons to be cautious when it came to some of Ronald's inventions. "What would the purpose of an electric kite be?" he asked.

"I imagined it would release the string, so you could fly a kite out of a window," Ronald explained, holding up a large spool of string with an electrical cord attached to it.

"But even on windy days, the kite couldn't catch air out the window. You'd still have to run to get it going."

"You would need a long cord," Lincoln pointed out.

Ronald nodded. "I know, that's why I gave up on it. However, it works wonderfully when it comes to winding the string back up on the spool."

Victoria was staring at the spool of string. "May I see that?"

"Sure."

Lincoln intercepted the exchange of the spool by grasping Ronald's arm. "Is it plugged in?"

Ronald laughed. "No." Then he told Victoria, "He's helped me with a few inventions, and may have gotten an electrical shock once or twice."

Lincoln had, and always asked if things in the workshop were plugged in before touching them. He released his hold on Ronald's arm and watched Victoria's thoughtful expression as she examined the spool. Her beauty shone through no matter what she was doing and it never failed to have a profound effect on him. His blood warmed, pounded faster in his veins, and desires formed throughout his body.

"You know, Ronald," she said, with a frown demonstrating her deep thoughts, "if your broom bristles were on a spool like this, it could sweep the dirt slowly into a dustpan rather than just spewing it into the air."

Ronald frowned for a moment, then his eyes grew wide. "I'd never thought of that, and you're right, that could work!" With enthusiasm, Ronald hurried past them and back to the broom, while saying, "And I could attach a dustpan to the broom to catch the dirt. Oh, this is fantastic!"

"Very ingenious thinking," Lincoln told Victoria.

"Ronald is the ingenious one. He has so many wonderful inventions," she said. "I'm in awe over several of them."

Lincoln was in awe over her. He couldn't imagine very many women finding all these inventions and gadgets interesting. In his experience, they were more interested in fashion and social events.

"Victoria, come here," Ronald said. "I need your help for a moment."

"Don't touch anything," Lincoln whispered as they walked towards Ronald.

"You warned me about that before we'd entered the room," she whispered in return. "Remember?"

"Yes."

"Have I touched anything yet, without asking?"

"No," he replied.

She grinned at him and stepped up beside Ronald. "I don't know how I could be of any help."

Ronald was sketching something on a piece of paper. "I need your opinion. I'm thinking something like this, with a roller attached to the handle with a frame similar to a rake, with the bristles coming out of the roller."

Lincoln had seen plenty of Ronald's haphazard drawings, and was more set on watching her as she watched Ronald draw, wondering if she was going to be able to make out hide or hair. He never could.

"That could work," she said, "but I think the bristles need to be shorter and softer, more flexible." She held a hand out. "May I draw something?"

"Of course." Ronald handed her the pencil.

Lincoln stepped closer, watching over her shoulder as she drew. All the while smelling the subtle flower scent of her perfume. It made his desires grow, yet he couldn't step back.

In the end, she'd created a picture similar to Ronald's, but much neater and far more recognizable.

Ronald was clearly thrilled. "Yes, that's it! Exactly what I was thinking." Pointing to the picture, he went on the explain where he imagined the dustpan being attached, and soon the two of them were discussing the number of rows of bristles, and how it might work better if the rows were further apart, but angled.

Lincoln soon found himself pulled into their idea and the design, and began offering opinions as well. He also told Ronald if he was to ever ask for another patent filing, Victoria should be the one to draw it.

Ronald agreed wholeheartedly.

They were still working on the broom, taking measurements for Victoria to write on paper, when a knock sounded on the workshop door.

"Come in," Ronald replied.

Edwin, the Woodroofs' aging butler, opened the door. "Forgive the interference, sir, but I am to inform you that dinner will be served in half an hour."

"Thank you," Ronald replied. "I will be there."

"I'm also to inform Mr. Dryer and Miss Biggs that it has been arranged for them to join the family for dinner. The Dryer household has been informed."

Lincoln had dined with the Woodroofs many times over the years, and looked at Victoria, awaiting her approval. When she gave a slight shrug, followed by a nod, he said, "Thank you, Edwin, we're honored."

"Thank you, sir," Edwin replied. "Would you like me to show Miss Biggs where she can freshen up?"

Ronald set down the measuring tape. "We might as well all go and freshen up. I have all the measurements that I need."

Victoria handed him the paper and pencil. "You'll let us know when you start working on the broom?"

"I'll start on it tomorrow," Ronald replied. "And I will let you know when I have a model completed."

Lincoln retrieved his suit jacket from a chair and shrugged into it, smiling as she looked at him with a frown. He knew what she was thinking and what Ronald's answer would be.

She then turned back to Ronald. "What about the bicycle you're working on?"

"I always work on more than one project at a time," Ronald answered as he held the door and waited for them to leave the workshop. "Otherwise, I get bored."

"I would never get bored," she said. With an adorable grimace, she added, "But I would make a terrible inventor. All those electrical wires scare me."

"You get used to getting shocked," Ronald said.

"No, you don't," Lincoln disagreed.

They continued to debate that and laughed as they crossed the manicured backyard of the Woodroofs' residence and in through the back door, where Edwin invited Victoria to precede him.

Lincoln used a water closet off the hallway, and then made his way to the front parlor, where he greeted Ronald's mother, Doris, and his father, Darwin, and made small talk until Victoria entered, upon which he promptly introduced her to the Woodroofs. The pride he felt at that moment was distinct, and it stayed with him throughout the evening. Here, too, there was nothing about Victoria that was inept. She easily participated in conversations that covered a variety of subjects and her good-natured humor was enjoyed by all. He could tell that Doris was impressed by her, even before they prepared to make their exit long after night had fallen.

"Do come again, Lincoln," Doris said. "And you, too, Victoria. We've enjoyed your company very much."

"Thank you," Victoria replied. "It was a lovely evening, and a wonderful meal." She glanced his way before saying, "I do hope to return. I'm anxious to see Ronald's broom invention once it's completed."

"There you have it," Lincoln said to Doris. "We will be back."

"Oh, good!" Doris kissed his cheek and Victoria's. "I'm already looking forward to it."

"As am I," Darwin said, shaking his hand in farewell. The man leaned closer, and whispered, "You've done well there, Lincoln. Don't let her get away."

Lincoln felt a lump in his stomach. Their pretend courtship was to fool people, but he didn't like fooling people he liked and had respected his entire life.

Victoria sat beside Lincoln in the open carriage as he drove through the streets, which were the quietest she'd seen them. Normally, when she rode about at night, it was inside an enclosed carriage, with a driver, giving her no opportunity to notice the quietness.

She normally didn't notice the happiness simmering inside her, either. It was there now. Had been all day. "Thank you, for a wonderful day," she said. "I enjoyed seeing Ronald's inventions very much."

"I'm glad you enjoyed it," he replied. "Ronald was very happy for your help with his broom idea."

"That is a remarkable idea. It's not anything I would ever have thought of, but I can see people buying them, using them. Can't you?"

"I can't say that I've ever thought much about brooms, but yes, I can imagine people buying them." He glanced at her. "If they work. That's yet to be determined."

"Oh, it'll work, and I can't wait to see it." She laughed at her own thoughts. "I can't wait to see the bicycle with the engine attached, too."

"How about the electric kite, do you want to see that one, too?"

She giggled, because to her, that had been a silly idea. "Tell me about some of the inventions you helped him with."

"You mean the ones where I got an electrical shock, don't you?"

She bit her bottom lip before saying, "I'm sorry you got shocked, but yes, tell me about them."

He didn't just tell her about the inventions, he told her about many failed attempts and about being shocked in such a comical way that they laughed all the way home. Were still laughing when they walked into the house.

Audrey and Jake, as well as Roseanne, were in the front drawing room, and Victoria happily told them all about Ronald's inventions. Except for the bicycle, she purposefully left out that invention, even though she was excited to see it when Ronald had finished it.

That didn't slip past Lincoln. His grin said as much. He also leaned closer from where they sat side by side on the sofa and whispered, “Aren’t you going to mention Ronald’s bicycle?”

“No,” she whispered in return. “I’m leaving that for you.”

He chuckled, and leaned forward to pick both his and her empty glasses off the table. “Would anyone else care for a refill?” he asked aloud.

Victoria bit her lips together in amusement at how he was pretending they’d been whispering about beverages.

“No, thank you,” Jake said. “I must be heading home.”

“I’m afraid it’s time for me to retire,” Roseanne said. “It was a lovely day.”

Victoria couldn’t agree more. She’d enjoyed every moment of the day and wished she kept a diary, so she could write things down. Yet she knew that wasn’t necessary. This was a day she would never forget.

Audrey followed Jake out of the room, to say goodbye to him at the door, and Roseanne left as well. Victoria had risen from the sofa and stood beside Lincoln as they bid the others good-night, and now, still standing beside him, she wasn’t sure what to say.

Lincoln looked at her, and all at once, she felt a rush of heat throughout her body, poignant enough that she had to plant her feet firmly against the floor. She also had to lick her lips, which had started to tingle.

He didn’t say anything, just continued to look at her.

Her heart rate increased by the second, and she could feel the heat rushing through her rising up, into her cheeks. She knew why, too. Because of her thoughts. Of kissing him again. She was wondering what it would be like to be Audrey at this moment, free to kiss, hold hands, hug Jake whenever the urge struck.

Victoria knew she wasn’t Audrey and Lincoln wasn’t

Jake. Whatever there was between the two of them was pretend. To fool others. She swallowed the lump forming in her throat. There were no others here right now, and nothing happening inside her felt pretend.

"Well, I guess it's time to say good-night," Lincoln said, but didn't move.

She nodded and swallowed again in an attempt to collect her nerves. "Yes, it is. Thank you for taking me to Ronald's today. I enjoyed that very much."

"You're welcome."

He still made no effort to move, at least none that she could see. "And thank you for teaching me to ride a bicycle," she said. "That was also very fun."

"It was."

His gaze moved to her lips and she wondered if what happened at that moment was what an electrical shock felt like, because something so strong and powerful it stole her breath zipped through her like nothing ever had.

He reached up and touched the tip of her nose with a single finger. "Good night, Victoria."

She was proud of herself for finding the wherewithal to say, "Good night, Lincoln," and for being able to stand still as he walked from the room. Then the air gushed from her lungs and she sank onto the sofa that was still luckily right behind her. Her knees were trembling and it took several deep breaths before she didn't need to concentrate on pulling air in and out of her lungs.

What was happening to her?

Not wanting to be caught sitting, doing nothing but breathing and thinking thoughts that she shouldn't be thinking, she stood and collected the empty glasses from each of the tables and set them on the credenza for a servant to retrieve and wash, before she left the room.

Aware that falling asleep in her current condition was unlikely, she went to her room, collected her nightclothes then proceeded down the hall to the water closet. With its mahogany wainscoting and the wooden cabinetry enclosing the tub and sink, the closet was as luxurious as the rest of the house, and she soon sank deep into the warm bathwater, scented by her personal bottle of lilac-infused oil.

She'd barely had time for her body to relax, let alone her mind, when the door opened and Audrey walked into the room.

"I thought I'd find you here when you weren't in your room," Audrey said, sitting down on the stool in front of the mirrored dressing table. The two of them often shared the room while getting ready, and Audrey began unpinning her hair. "Did you see Ronald's bicycle?"

Victoria leaned her head back against the edge of the bathtub and closed her eyes. "Yes. I didn't want to mention it in front of your mother."

"I figured as much. I'm going to write an article about bicycle riding for the newspaper society page."

That didn't surprise Victoria, but what did surprise her was something that had never happened. She felt a sense of jealousy towards her friend. Audrey not only had found the love of her life, she had something else she loved, writing. Victoria didn't have any of that, nor would she. She'd already determined that she'd be happy being an old maid. Why was that?

Not needing something else to think about, she said, "I'm sure people will be interested in reading that. Have you ever seen Ronald's inventions?"

"No, Mother would never allow me to. She said it was too dangerous, but Linc's told me about some of them. Was it dangerous?"

Victoria didn't open her eyes as she contemplated how to answer. Some of the inventions could be dangerous if one wasn't careful, but Lincoln had warned her in advance. Furthermore, with Lincoln at her side, she hadn't been afraid. "His workshop is very cluttered and you had to watch were you stepped, but I wouldn't call it dangerous." Actually, now that she thought about it, what she should find dangerous was Lincoln, because of the way he made her feel.

"But you enjoyed it?" Audrey asked.

"Yes." Victoria knew one thing for certain. She wouldn't have enjoyed seeing the inventions without Lincoln. It didn't matter what she did with him, he made it fun by just being there. Needing time to contemplate what that meant, she changed the subject. "How was your lunch with Jake's grandmother?"

"Wonderful. She gave me a lovely embroidered handkerchief that she carried on her wedding day for my 'something old'."

"That's special."

"It is. I really like it. She is a real sweetheart and wanted to know every last detail about the wedding. When we returned from there, Jake and I took another bicycle ride through the park. I asked Jake to leave his bicycle here, so you and I could take a ride tomorrow, and he did, but he said he'd prefer that we not ride alone."

Victoria was only half listening, because her mind kept loitering on Lincoln. "Oh, why is that?" she asked, wanting it to sound like she was interested.

"Well, it was actually kind of strange. There was a man

in the hedges across the street from our house. Almost like he'd been watching the house or something. He scurried out of the bushes when we crossed the road, and tried to act like he'd just been walking along the pathway, but both Jake and I had seen him, and he'd been in the bushes, not walking past. Jake recognized him. Said he was Alderman Kelley's son."

Victoria's eyes snapped open and she sat up so fast the water splashed over the edge of the tub. "Elwood Kelley?"

Audrey set down the hair brush she'd been using and turned about on the bench. "Yes. Jake said Elwood is one of his father's henchmen."

"What do you mean henchmen?"

"Alderman Kelley represents the poorest districts in the city, and keeps getting elected because he uses mobsters to scare the men in his districts into voting for him. If they try to protest against him or campaign for someone else, things happen to them. Bad things. Jake had a reporter working on a story about Kelley who ended up missing last year. They still haven't found him. Or his body, which Jake believes was dumped in the ocean. He can't prove it. He can't even print an article about it in the paper, because we can't print something without facts to back it up."

Despite the warm water surrounding her, Victoria shivered. Lincoln had mentioned that Elwood's family weren't the kind of people to be associated with, but she'd never imagined anything like that. No wonder he hadn't wanted to pursue the theft. She was glad she hadn't told Audrey anything about it, and was now greatly worried that Elwood had been looking for her. She hadn't been rude to him when he'd been at dinner, nor had she told him that she'd be out of town. She'd simply declined his request to see her again, stating her calendar was full and would be for some time. Her mind was filling with questions about him, but Audrey wasn't the person she could ask. That would have to be Lincoln.

Audrey turned around and picked up the pins she'd removed from her hair. "I told him we wouldn't ride in the park unless he or Linc were with us."

Although her mind was on Elwood, she didn't want Audrey to know that. Victoria stood and lifted a towel off the shelf above the tub before stepping out of the water. "There are some lovely ladies' skirts created just for bicycle riding at Webster's you might like to see before writing your article," she said.

Audrey stood. "We could go look at them tomorrow, after our dress fitting."

"Sure." Victoria slipped her nightgown over her head, wondering when she'd have time to talk to Lincoln.

"I didn't mean to cut your bath time short," Audrey said.

"You didn't," Victoria said. It would take a lot more than a hot bath to get her thinking in order.

Chapter Ten

Lincoln smothered yet another yawn as he stood near the window in his downtown office. He'd had a hard time sleeping last night. Victoria's image had been too prominent in his mind. As had the desire to kiss her again. Not doing so when they'd been alone in the drawing room last night had been one of the hardest things he'd ever faced.

That's why he'd gotten out of bed and left the house, and come to the office hours earlier than usual. He needed to find a way to concentrate on something besides her. He shouldn't have agreed to this partnership or whatever it was between the two of them. Keeping the socialites at bay had been easier than controlling the thoughts and feelings that Victoria evoked inside him.

He certainly hadn't expected that.

Why hadn't he noticed all the things he was now noticing about her, before? It felt as if something had shifted inside him, like a door had opened and revealed things he hadn't known were there.

He'd also never felt so powerless. That was the bottom line. He was powerless when it came to controlling his thoughts and feelings about her. He'd never thought that possible. Had never had something consume him so deeply.

A knock on the door interrupted his musing. He turned

from the window and walked back to his desk. He'd never thought it possible that anything would take up more of his thoughts than work, either.

"Come in," he invited.

The door opened and Jake walked in. "Hope I'm not interrupting, but I need to talk to you about something."

Lincoln welcomed the interruption, but didn't admit that. "Sure." He waved at a chair. "Have a seat."

While Jake sat in a chair across from his desk, Lincoln sat down behind it. "Everything all right?" Lincoln asked.

"For the most part," Jake replied. "But there's something I can't get off my mind. I didn't want to mention it in front of anyone else last night, and just so you know, anything said is off the record. I'm not here looking for a story, but I need to know if you are working on a case against Alderman Kelley."

Lincoln leaned forward and braced his elbows on his desk. "Not directly, but I hope it leads to him."

Jake nodded. "Does his son, Elwood, know that?"

"No one should know it, but I can't say for sure," Lincoln responded. "Why?"

"Because yesterday afternoon, Audrey and I went for another bicycle ride and spotted Elwood Kelley squatting in the bushes across from your house. He acted like he'd just been strolling past, but he hadn't been. I saw him emerge from the bushes and from the way the leaves were smashed, he'd been there awhile."

The hair stood up on the nape of Lincoln's neck. "I saw him yesterday, too. In the morning, while Victoria and I were walking back to the house after she'd learned to ride your bicycle. Elwood was on horseback then."

"There was no horse nearby in the afternoon. He walked

as far as the cross-street corner and waved down a cab." Jake shook his head. "I don't have to tell you about his lack of trustworthiness. I told Audrey that I would prefer if she and Victoria don't go bicycle riding without you or me with them. I wanted you to know, because she doesn't always heed my advice."

"Does any woman always heed advice?" Lincoln asked in jest, while at the same time the concern over what Jake had just said was growing inside him. He could trust Jake, would trust him with his life, but wasn't willing to share Victoria's claim against Elwood. She could be in danger if even a hint of her accusation leaked out.

"Not that I know of, but there could be one somewhere." Jake leaned back in his chair. "If there's anything I can do to help with your case, just ask. A legal case would be the only way to get Kelley out of office, and getting him out of office is the only way to help the people in his districts."

Lincoln wasn't opposed to gathering information in any way possible, but having a newspaper reporter snooping about would tip Kelley off that someone was looking into his activities. That wasn't new, reporters were after Kelley all the time, but his hand in buying department stores outside of his districts was new, and it was being well hidden on purpose. So far, all the information that his sources had been able to dig up wasn't enough to pin anything on Kelley. The only solid case Lincoln had against the purchase was due to Webster's will, which wasn't much.

More importantly, Lincoln wasn't willing to endanger Victoria in any way. That was of utmost importance right now. He couldn't chance her safety by having reporters sniffing around. "Thanks, Jake, but right now, I don't want anyone knowing that Kelley could be involved in what I'm looking into."

"I understand that," Jake replied. "There was another fire in one of his housing projects two nights ago. Those apartments are death traps. It should be illegal for those builders to force people to live in such conditions. Kelley keeps boasting that he's putting new regulations in place, but they never come to fruition, because the builders are paying him to keep any new regulations tied up in red tape and his mobsters keep the residents from talking about how bad it is."

Frustration rose up in Lincoln. The horror stories he'd heard about the living condition of factory workers were the reason he'd started considering running for office, and having seen those quarters, he'd become even more convinced that's what he needed to do. Something had to be done. Soon.

"You're right about that, and about Audrey and Victoria," Lincoln said. "I'll reiterate that with them."

"Thanks. I knew you would." Jake sat silent for a moment, before saying, "And I know I don't have to remind you to watch your back when it comes to Kelley."

Lincoln nodded, and something he hadn't thought of before struck a note. Taking on John Webster's case right now, while in the midst of pretending to be in a relationship with Victoria, could put her in as much danger as her case against Elwood. Why hadn't he thought of that before agreeing to help Webster?

That thought stuck with him after Jake had left, and that led to other thoughts, which made concentrating on work fully impossible. He left the office, and upon arriving home joined his mother, Audrey, and Victoria for lunch.

The women were planning a shopping trip that afternoon and as they left the table, he stepped up beside Victoria. "We need to talk," he whispered.

"Is something wrong?" she whispered in return.

"Yes. Did Audrey tell you about seeing Elwood yesterday?"

"Yes, she did."

"Did you tell her about your picture? The fingerprints?"

"No."

They reached the doorway, and he took a hold of her elbow while addressing his mother and sister, who had already entered the hallway. "If you'll excuse us for a moment. I need to speak to Victoria. It won't take long."

Barely acknowledging his mother's or Audrey's responses, he led Victoria to his study on the second floor. As soon he'd closed the door behind them, he said, "I don't believe we should continue to be seen together."

"Excuse me?" Giving her head a slight shake, she added, "Because of Elwood? I haven't told anyone but you about the theft."

"It's not the theft."

"Then what is it? Audrey's wedding—"

"Audrey's wedding doesn't have anything to do with it, either." Flustered, he ran a hand through his hair. This, how women complicated life, was exactly why he'd steered clear of relationships and why he had to continue to do so. She was different from others, he'd admitted that to himself, and that was also the reason he felt she deserved the entire truth. "I told you that I'm interested in running for attorney general."

She nodded.

"I'm considering doing that sooner than I'd expected," he said.

"Why? What's happened?"

"Jake came to see me this morning, told me about seeing Elwood in the bushes in the park, and while he was there, he also told me about another fire in the projects. I'm sure it was in the paper, but I haven't read the paper the last couple of days." That was a fact he hadn't realized until after Jake had left. He'd been so focused on Victoria that he'd even changed his normal routines. Things he'd always done. "Another fire makes me think something needs to be done sooner than later."

"Like what?"

He drew in a deep breath. It had been his goal for a long time, but saying it aloud would make it something he needed to act upon, not just think about. "Like enforcing laws that are on the books. The current attorney general isn't doing that. The election will be this fall. If I run and if I can get elected, Kelley and others like him will have someone they need to answer to. Right now, they are running roughshod over everyone because they'd never been held accountable for anything."

Her thoughtful gaze was still on him as she nodded, as if waiting for him to continue.

"The fires in those housing projects are death traps," he said. "The apartments aren't built to code, and even when the codes change, nothing is done about them. The factories don't pay the workers enough for them to be housed anywhere else. It's a form of enslavement. The workers are paid just enough to keep their families fed, while the factory owners and the politicians they pay off are the ones who get rich. Kelley's had control over the factories in his districts for years, and now he's moving to take over the department stores. He wants to own the whole damn city and will if someone doesn't put a stop to him."

"How can he take over department stores?"

"By buying them," Lincoln responded. "He's forcing them into selling. He's bought out Blackwells and wants to form a monopoly by buying all others."

"Alderman Kelley is who bought out Blackwells?" she asked.

Lincoln stepped closer to her, leaned against the edge of his desk. "He's using a front company to do it, so no one knows, and he's using henchmen to coerce others into selling their stores. The problem is that I can't prove it. I'll be able to slow him down from taking over Webster's store by legalities with John's father's will, but it won't fix the problem. The only way to do that is by having someone hold him accountable. The attorney general can do that by having representation of the state agencies, boards, and commissions, but the one we have right now, is already deep in Kelley's pocket. As is the mayor and other politicians. He controls them as much as he does the factory owners."

She laid a hand on his arm. "He sounds dangerous."

"He is, and corrupt. So is his son." Lincoln bit the end of his tongue, and cursed himself. Scaring her wasn't his goal. He laid his hand atop hers and quickly continued, "John Webster said he's being watched at all times. It could very easily be Elwood watching him and he's trying to figure out if I've taken on John's case."

"You think he was watching the house for you, not me?" she asked.

That's what he was hoping. He didn't want her in danger. He also knew that no case would ever be strong enough to stop Kelley and his crooked ways. No single lawyer could do that, but as attorney general he'd have the full scope of the law behind him. That was the only way to stop the corruption.

"I'm honestly not sure why Elwood was in the bushes," he answered. "I just know that I don't like it, nor do I trust him."

"Neither do I," she said, "and I understand why you don't want to be seen with me."

"I never said I don't want to be seen with you."

"You said that we should no longer be seen together."

He had said that, but it wasn't what he meant. Or was it? He'd been thinking about her safety, and how being around him could be dangerous, but it could be more dangerous for her to not to be nearby. He wanted to stop Elwood's pursuit of her, not encourage it. They had to continue their ploy. He had to wait until after Audrey's wedding before he could do anything. "I did say that," he admitted. "But it's not what I meant."

Victoria watched as Lincoln dropped his hand off hers, then walked away from the desk. He was usually very self-assured, but didn't appear to be so now. That confused her, but also concerned her. "What did you mean to say?" she asked.

He shook his head as he sat down in an armchair near the fireplace. "I'm not sure. I left my office convinced that I was ready to throw my hat in the ring for attorney general. Now I realize this isn't the time."

She walked over and sat in the adjacent chair. "Why not?"

"For the same reason that we made our agreement," he said. "Audrey's wedding. I can't make an announcement like that right before her wedding. I'll have to wait until after that."

Leaning forward, looking directly at his face, she went with a deep sense inside her. "The fire you mentioned is what has you worried, isn't it?" Outside of the city, they were called shantytowns, because of the tar paper shanties that people lived in, but she was aware that within the boroughs, many of those factories had apartments built nearby to house the workers.

"Yes." He let out a long sigh. "It doesn't take much for a fire to get started in one of those places, nor to burn the entire structure to the ground." Shaking his head, he continued, "The fire departments are instructed to water down the factories, to prevent them from burning rather than putting out the apartment houses. It's sickening."

He wouldn't lie about something like that, which made her want to know: "How do you know that? About the fire departments?"

"Because I've seen it. I went to more than one of those fires with Jake, when he was a reporter on the beat. The firemen don't like it, but they take their orders from the higher-ups, and the higher-ups take their orders from Alderman Kelley." Lincoln's expression turned hard and cynical. "Kelley swoops in the next day, handing out bottles of milk to the children and blankets to the women, claiming he'll have a new building erected posthaste, a better one, built to code."

"But that never happens, does it?" she asked.

"No, it doesn't. Workmen cobble up a building within a few weeks or so, mainly using reclaimed wood. It's barely livable, but the city signs off on it, and the tenants are so tired of living in makeshifts tents that they move in, happy to have a roof over their heads. It's a recurring cycle. One that will never end, unless it's forced to."

A feeling that was growing familiar when she was near him increased with a powerful intensity. It was within her heart. She wouldn't call it love, because she wouldn't let herself love someone. Couldn't let herself, not even with him. She'd confirmed all of that to herself when sleep had avoided her until the wee hours of the morning.

Lying in bed last night, she had admitted to herself that if she ever were to marry, she wanted a life where she could support her husband in his business, work at his side, build it into something they both could be proud of. However, that had also been when she'd realized that she didn't want everything else that came with that. When a person loved someone else like that, so deeply that nothing else mattered, it consumed them. Every part of them. And when that love was lost, when that person was gone, it continued to consume them. Love and loss went hand in hand. She'd seen that with her mother, how the loss of her father had stolen the life from her, and wouldn't put herself in that position.

Couldn't put herself in that position.

Nor would she ever wish that upon someone else. Especially Lincoln. Not that she would ever expect him to fall in love with her. That wasn't what he wanted. He hadn't wanted a distraction either, and she wouldn't ever want to stand in his way.

At the same time, she did care for him, deeply, and it was obvious how strongly he felt about helping people. Those who were being oppressed to the point that they couldn't help themselves. Once someone started working for one those factories, they never got out of there, she'd heard that several times. She saw the shantytowns outside the train window every trip into the city, and often wished there was something she could do to help them.

On that, Lincoln was right, it would take changes in leadership, but until then, there had to be something else that could be done. "The wedding is less than three weeks away, then you'll be able to throw your hat in the ring, as you said." She drew in a deep breath, stood up and held out a hand to him. "Until then, let's go see what we can do."

He looked at her hand, and then at her face. "Go see what we can do where?"

"Wherever this latest fire was," she replied. "We'll see what the people need and figure out how we can get it for them."

He shook his head. "You can't go down there."

"Why?"

He stood, and took a hold of her hand. "I know you mean well, but I've seen those places after a fire. It's a shambles, a terrible sight."

"I imagine it is, but it's also a place where people live. Women with children, trying to do all they can while their husbands are off working all day and night." A flash of her former life became a vision. When Mr. Hanson's barn had been struck by lightning and the entire countryside had come together to help him rebuild it, including her father and grandfather. They'd shut down the mine for the day, so all the miners could help. She hadn't thought about it in years, but had to wonder why, in a city with so many people, help like that didn't happen here.

Lincoln squeezed her hand. "I can't let you go down there."

She laughed and shook her head. "It's not a matter of letting me, Lincoln, it's a matter of either joining me or not. Those people may need Alderman Kelley's bottles of milk and blankets, but they don't need his empty promises. My grandfather says that's all a politician is made up of, empty promises."

Lincoln looked at her with a slight frown.

She shrugged. "He doesn't say it quite that kindly."

"I'm sure he wouldn't allow you to go—"

"He wouldn't stop me," she interrupted. "He would say I'm stubborn, but he wouldn't stop me. Now, are you going to go with me, or do I ask Audrey to go with me?"

"My mother would never allow Audrey to go."

Determination grew within her. This was something she could do, and it didn't involve loving anyone, simply helping those who needed it. "All right then, I'll go tell her that I can't go shopping this afternoon, that you and I have some errands to see to."

He still had a hold of her hand, and wrapped his fingers tighter around hers. "Victoria—"

"You aren't going to change my mind on this, Lincoln, so please don't try. It'll just be a waste of breath and of time."

An hour later, Victoria fully accepted that she hadn't been prepared for the sights or the stories that she heard, but she didn't regret coming. The number of women, with children of varying ages, yet still very young—because the older ones were working in the factory, along with their fathers—were a wearied, wary bunch. Wary of strangers and weary from scraping together whatever they could to create makeshift homes for their families. Ropes were stretched between anything they could be tied to, with blankets draped over them to fashion tents. An assortment of furniture, some charred black, was used to hold the ends of the blankets down, and cookstoves were set near the tents, with their cast-iron legs sinking into the ground that was still soft with mud due to the water that had been sprayed on the factory, to keep it from burning.

The noise of the machines inside the factory—this one was a textile plant—reminded her of the stamp mill back in Colorado. Nothing else at the scene did. She'd told Lincoln about Mr. Hanson's barn, and other such events that she remembered, while they'd traveled through the traffic. He'd appreciated the story, but had also warned her that things were different here in the city.

She'd been aware of that before today, but refused to let it change her mind.

Her light green dress would never be the same, nor would Lincoln's white shirt, but that didn't stop either one of them from lending a hand wherever they could. It hadn't been easy at first, since none of the women were comfortable enough talking to them, until Lincoln asked a woman if he could help her move a trunk that she was struggling to carry through the mud.

Then, a set of strong arms seemed to be welcomed. Victoria felt a sense of pride that she'd never experienced. Lincoln was a kind and good man, and seeing him in action like that not only confirmed it, it cemented something deeper inside her. She refused to contemplate what it was, even as it filled her heart. He would be easy to love. Too easy, and that reinforced her determination to not let it happen. To never be the one standing in his way from reaching his goals. If she allowed herself the time to focus on that, she would admit that it saddened her to know she could never be an integral part of his life. There was already enough sadness surrounding them and no reason for her to add more, so she ignored all those thoughts, and focused on helping in whatever way she could.

Hours passed as they helped the women scrounge items from the burnt-out structure, pots and pans, dishes, and other necessities, including boards for their tents to have some sort of floors to keep the children off the ground.

The apartment structure had been small, only two stories tall, yet twenty families had lived in it, and thankfully, no one had lost their life in the fire. The tenants were so prepared for such a tragedy that at the first scent of smoke, they'd all run from the building. There were theories and suspicions, but no one knew exactly how the fire had started. Only that the entire building was ablaze within minutes.

The area didn't look all that different when she and Lincoln walked to their carriage, mainly because the sun was setting, but it was a different place than when they'd arrived. Families were still living outside, in makeshift tents, with hardly any provisions or supplies, yet there were smiles on their faces, and heartfelt expressions of gratefulness for the help that had been provided.

Lincoln rested a hand on the small of her back. "Tired?" he asked.

"Yes, and no," she replied. "It was a lot of work, but don't you just feel good inside? Feel good that we helped them."

His hand slipped around to her waist and tugged her up against his side. "Yes, I do."

She leaned her head against the side of his shoulder. "Me, too." Then, looking up at him, she added, "I also sincerely hope it doesn't rain."

He grinned and nodded. "Me, too."

"How long will it take until their apartment is rebuilt?" she asked.

"I don't know. Weeks, months." He stopped next to the carriage, and assisted her onto the seat, before he walked over to where he'd tied the horse in a small grassy area while they'd worked.

Once the horse was hitched to the carriage, he climbed onto the seat beside her.

Victoria's mind had been busy all day, and still hadn't slowed down. "Couldn't we gather a bunch of people and help rebuild it faster?"

"Well, that's one of the things I meant about it being different in the city. It's not like in the country where you'd be helping individuals, or families. That property is owned by the factory, so is anything built on it. They charge the tenants to live there, and while it sounds like a charitable thing to do, it's the factory owner who would benefit, financially, if that were to happen. Yes, the people would have a place to live, but the company wouldn't have been held accountable to provide it. It's confusing, I know, but that's how it is."

"I hadn't thought of it that way," she admitted. However, her mind was still turning. "If the factory charges them for a place to live, don't they have to provide it? Isn't it illegal not to? To charge for something they aren't providing?"

"Yes, but a fire is a calamity, and as long as they are working on replacing it, there's no law being broken. It's considered a hardship. I know it doesn't sound fair, and it's not, especially when no one forces the company to rebuild as quickly as possible."

"What would you change about that if you were elected attorney general?"

"The first thing I'd do would be to create a housing committee. As attorney general, I would oversee the legalities of that committee, and have them lobby legislatures to pass laws and rules to ensure all building codes were followed, making the homes safer and healthier, and include protection for tenants in the event of fires."

His immediate response made it clear that this had been something he'd put a lot of thought into already. "What else would you want to change?"

"Child labor laws. There are far too many children working in these factories and elsewhere, and..."

She listened intently as he talked, not just about the children working, but several other topics that he'd like to see changed for the benefit of the people, and society as a whole. Once again, it was clear as to how much thought he'd put behind his idea and his compassion to help others. She had to believe that even her grandfather would change his mind about politicians if he knew Lincoln the way she did.

Their arrival home didn't go smoothly. Roseanne was irritated that they'd been gone so long, because they were supposed to join Audrey and Jake at the home of Jake's uncle for dinner and card games—something neither of them had remembered.

"We will go change and be on our way," Lincoln said.

"Change!" Roseanne shook her head. "You both need a bath! You're covered in soot. You look like chimney sweeps."

"We were helping some families whose home burned down the other night," Victoria said, more than willing to take the blame. "It was a devastating sight and help was so greatly needed. Time simply got away from us. Please forgive me, for it was all my idea and Lincoln was kind enough to accompany me."

Roseanne covered a gasp with one hand. "A home burned? Whose? I had no idea. Is there something I can do to help?"

"There are some things that are needed," Victoria replied. "But you're right, we both need baths."

"Oh, by all means, go, both of you," Roseanne said. "The three of us can discuss it over dinner. I'll be happy to not eat alone tonight."

Lincoln hooked a hand around her elbow and escorted her to the stairway. "You amaze me," he whispered.

"How so?"

He chuckled. "You put a lid on her steam before it had a chance to start puffing."

Victoria giggled at that description. "She was just upset because she wants everything to be perfect for Audrey's wedding. I truly had forgotten about dinner and card playing. All of the other people in the wedding are there."

"Good, then we won't be missed," he said.

She giggled again. "That's one way to see it."

"The best way," he said, and stopped in the hallway, near the door to her room. "I'll see you downstairs later."

"Yes, you will," Victoria replied, and entered her room. This time, she wasn't thinking about a soaking bath to get her mind off things. She was looking forward to a good scrubbing, and then a conversation with Roseanne about some supplies that they could collect to take to the families tomorrow.

Lincoln was also on her mind. Because of him, she'd found a way to help people whom she'd wished she could help for years.

Chapter Eleven

The days that followed caused more changes inside Lincoln. Changes that he didn't mind. What man wouldn't appreciate having a beautiful, intelligent, kind, caring, and remarkably likeable young woman at their side every day? Not a day had gone by where they weren't together, and that was something he'd not only come to appreciate, he'd realized there was nothing terrible about it. He liked doing things with her, and discussing things with her, confidential things, like his goals and cases. Her insight and thoughtful ideas were incredible.

Within two days of when he'd first told her about the fire, she'd gathered and delivered needed provisions for the fire victims. His mother and sister had helped her with soliciting items, but just the two of them, him and her, had delivered everything because Victoria had let it be known that the families would not be exploited. He understood, as did she, how there was little that the elite liked more than to brag about the donations they'd provided to the less fortunate.

His family had always been involved in charitable work, but she added a new dimension to it, a very compassionate one. Most of the fire victims had been immigrants, with little understanding of the English language, yet she had found a way to communicate with all of them. She hadn't assumed what they might need, she'd asked what would help them the most, and those were the items they had delivered.

Though it would still be weeks, possibly months, before the new building was completed, he was convinced that the families were faring far better than any other fire victims in the city's history.

Other things had happened in the past two weeks, things he'd never thought of until she'd suggested them, and each one was proven to be effective. She'd done everything without interrupting Audrey's wedding plans and events. Other than the dinner and card games evening that they'd missed the day they'd first visited the fire site, they hadn't missed a single event on his mother's list.

That's where he was headed now, to yet another function. This one was a ball at the Luther residence. Due to circumstances beyond his control, he'd been held up in court and was now arriving late.

As he hurried up the steps of the Luther mansion, he couldn't help but think about the last time that had happened, when he'd been late to the Christie ball and had been swamped by socialites upon his arrival.

Moments later, when he entered the ballroom, he couldn't say if there was a crowd rushing towards him or not, because his gaze instantly landed on Victoria. She was wearing an elegant blue gown, and he felt an immediate inner electrical current, which was stronger than any shock he'd ever received from one of Ronald's inventions. This one wasn't painful, it was enjoyable. He liked the thrill that shot through him at the way her face lit up when their gazes met.

Unaware of anyone else, he crossed the room to arrive

at her side. The hardest part—the one thing that he didn't like—was the undeniable desire to kiss her. It lived within him day and night and he'd give up anything for the freedom to act upon it. Though it was extremely difficult and disappointing, he was able to control that urge.

Somewhat. Upon arriving at her side, he took a hold of her hand, kissed the back of it, and then tucked her arm snuggly around his elbow. "I apologize for my lateness."

"You're hardly late. We only just arrived ourselves." Her glance shifted to where his mother stood on the other side of the room. "Your mother wasn't the least bit upset by your delay."

"Because she was too excited to sing your praises about helping after that article in the newspaper." The article had been about the plight of tenants in the aftermath of a fire and how one unnamed woman had taken it upon herself to see that one set of fire victims had been given more than empty promises. He was proud of Victoria, and understood why she'd wanted to remain nameless in the article. She'd wanted it to be about the plight of the victims, and how others could help, not about her. She figured if enough people learned about the living conditions in those apartments, how they were tragedies waiting to happen, more people would want to see changes. He agreed, and the buzz that article had provided was still spreading more than a week after it had been printed.

Thinking of that, he shook his head, before whispering, "I still can't believe that Audrey's been writing for the paper for years and I never knew it."

Victoria lowered her voice. "Others still don't know it, and Audrey wants it kept that way. Your mother believes Jake wrote that article."

"I'll keep that secret, but will Mother keep your secret?" he asked.

Her giggle was soft and light. "She has so far. She likes hinting that it was her idea, which is justifiable. Without her, we wouldn't have been able to obtain all of the items that we did. And..." She gave him a coy look. "Your mother's statements have been known to spread far and wide."

He knew she was referring to what his mother had said about him getting married. "True." Leaning closer, which caused his heart to thud a bit faster as her perfume tickled all of his senses, he whispered, "Your other idea is working, too."

"The ads?"

He nodded.

She shook her head. "That was your idea, I just agreed with it."

"As I remember it, we came up with the idea together." She had become very interested in John Webster's plight about having to sell his business. Lincoln had told her that there wasn't any legal way he could stop a sale, which had led her to researching New York City laws pertaining to business ownership. Although none would help stop the sale, it had produced their idea.

"How do you know the ads are working?" she asked.

He'd purchased ads in all the newspapers, large and small, anonymously, that stated there were laws, regulations, and stipulations pertaining to buying or selling a business within the boroughs. Which was completely true. The ads also stated that people should contact city hall if they were in the midst of buying or selling and had questions. "It's the reason I was late. Judge Mattheson requested a meeting in his chambers this afternoon, but court ran late, so our meeting was pushed until early evening. He was curious as to why I'd submitted that John's father's will be probated when there are no other heirs. I explained that John was being solicited to sell his department store. Mattheson asked if I'd seen the ads in the newspapers, I said I had. He informed me that the mayor is fit to be tied over the number of phone calls and visitors coming into city hall over those ads." Lincoln was convinced that many of those callers and visitors were being forced to sell much like Webster, and was just as convinced that without her help, he wouldn't have come up with the idea of putting ads in the newspapers.

She grimaced. "Does the judge know you put the ads in the newspapers?"

Lincoln shook his head, then nodded.

She scowled at him while giving his chest a playful slap. "Which is it?"

He trapped her hand beneath his, forcing it to remain on his chest. One of the wonderful things about attending events such as this ball was that it was expected of him to be overly attentive to her. Unlike at home, where he had to remind himself to keep any interaction to nothing except friendly gestures. "The judge didn't ask, but I believe he didn't ask because he knows I would have told him the truth, and he doesn't want to know the truth, so he wouldn't have to tell the mayor the truth. He also said that he has a full docket and that it'll be at least a month or more before the will can be probated."

"That will give you more time to figure out how to stop the sale," she said excitedly.

"Hopefully." He glanced over her shoulder, where he felt stares coming from. "I believe people are starting to wonder what we are whispering about. Shall we dance?"

"That would be wonderful," she quickly agreed.

That was another benefit of these events, he could give in to his desires to touch her and hold her close, especially while dancing. Such desires were becoming harder and harder to fight against. How that one kiss they'd shared still lived inside him day and night continued to make him want more.

He led her onto the dance floor, and though he knew the distance between them was shy of what was socially acceptable, he chose to ignore that as they danced. There were too many other things on his mind. Like how the curve of her waist fit perfectly in his palm, and how the scent of her perfume was particularly intoxicating, and how he liked the way she gently rubbed his shoulder every now and again.

"I've been thinking about something," she said, looking up at him with those eyes that glistened like stars.

"Should I be worried?" he teased.

She giggled. "No. I've been thinking about more ads."

He lifted a brow and waited for her to say more.

"You are well-known in the city, but in order to win the election for attorney general, the entire state needs to know who you are. Between now and when you announce your candidacy, perhaps you should put some ads in newspapers. Like the ones telling people about the laws, you could tell people about their rights. How the Bill of Rights gives civil rights and liberties to all individuals. You wouldn't put your name in the ads, just information, until it's time, then you can tell them how you wanted them to know their rights, including their right to vote for the candidate of their choice."

"That's a good idea," he said, with his thoughts growing even more focused on her. On how she outshone all other woman. Not only in appearance. She outshone them with intellect and compassion and in so many other ways, he was unable to name them all. He credited their pretend courtship agreement for how he'd never noticed so many of her true qualities before now.

"I'm glad you think so," she said. "I wanted to mention it tonight, because you'll have more time to focus on other things after this weekend."

"Why do you think that?"

She frowned slightly. "I'm sorry, I assumed you'd heard that your father will be home this Sunday. Your mother received a message from him today. You will no longer be obligated to fill in for him at functions."

The reaction inside Lincoln was so quick, so sharp, he nearly fumbled his dance steps. Weeks ago, his heart would never have clenched like this. All of him would have rejoiced, but she'd changed that. He'd already accepted that she'd changed him, but he wasn't ready to accept not being paired with her. Yet, he had to, because this was Friday, leaving only Saturday until his father returned. Furthermore, Audrey's wedding was a mere week away.

He'd known this wouldn't last. Known that from the beginning. It hadn't been meant to last beyond the wedding.

He hadn't wanted it to last, and knew he still shouldn't.

Then why did he?

Hours later, while lying in her bed, with her mind once again keeping her awake, Victoria found herself contemplating the last few weeks in a different light. She wasn't thinking about Lincoln—not solely. Rather, she was thinking about herself, and how different this visit had been from all the others. She'd discovered things about herself.

Back home, her life was about her family, but here, it had been about herself.

Perhaps because this visit was longer than all others had been, and the circumstances were greatly different. She couldn't say for sure, yet found some things disconcerting about this visit.

She loved her family, more than anything, and always would, but it felt as if her eyes had been opened. By Lincoln. He loved his family, too, but that wasn't stopping him from pursuing other things. A political career.

Due to her grandfather's distrust and dislike of politicians, that was a subject that was never discussed. After seeing the fire destruction and meeting those affected by it, she'd started reading some of the books in Lincoln's library. About civil rights, and how the lives of so many were affected by the choices of governmental leaders. He would make an excellent attorney general, and she felt a powerful desire to help him succeed at getting elected.

She felt a powerful desire for him in many ways, but had determined that was because he'd been the catalyst that had shown her that she could become more than an old maid.

For years, she'd told herself that she'd be satisfied to have that happen. To never do more than oversee her family's needs and watch over her grandfather's money. With her grandfather aging, and her mother's dislike of managing money, the duties of taking care of her family had fallen to her, and it was all she'd ever known. During this visit, she'd discovered that she could do more. She could help others. She'd helped Audrey's family by pretending to be in a relationship with Lincoln, she'd helped the fire victims, she'd even helped Ronald with his electric broom invention. He'd told her at the ball tonight that the broom was working.

She wanted to continue helping, too, especially Lincoln, and was regretting that her time here would soon be over. Taking care of her family wasn't so consuming that she couldn't do both, and it was frustrating to think of going back home where her life would return to what it had been. Where she wouldn't be able to see Lincoln every day. It was amazing how just seeing him at the breakfast table made her days brighter.

He made life brighter, and it was getting harder and harder for her to remember some things. Like their arrangement. How they would part as friends. She couldn't imagine a *friend* would ever make her feel the way Lincoln did. It was growing impossible for her dismiss how strong her feelings for him had become. Feelings she'd never felt before, nor had known how strong they could become. All-consuming.

The list of engagements that Roseanne had given her was now something she cherished, knowing those were times when she and Lincoln would be together. She continued to tell herself that they were still just pretending, yet wholeheartedly looked forward to being paired with him. To dancing with him, to sitting beside him, to holding his hand and touching him.

The feel of his firm muscles beneath his clothing was a thrill that she'd never known and couldn't describe.

It saddened her to know that would all end as soon as his father returned. They had agreed to continue their ploy until the wedding, but Lincoln would no longer need to attend other events with her or the rest of the family.

That would make those events quite boring, as would be

her life be once she returned home. She would miss Lincoln when she went home. Miss him very much. She hated losing things. Anything. And deep down, she knew that's what it would feel like when she went home. That she'd lost something. That wasn't supposed to happen.

Rolling over, onto her side, she tucked her hands beneath her pillow. She hadn't forgotten her original goal of having Walter assist her with her case against Elwood, but that had faded into the background. She still wanted Elwood to pay for his misdeed, and she was still concerned about what might happen if he wasn't, but was now concerned more about Lincoln. She didn't want to do anything that might cause Elwood to learn about Lincoln helping Mr. Webster stop the sale of his business to Alderman Kelley.

Ultimately, every thought she had, every feeling she had, was focused on Lincoln. That had been the major change inside her, and she wasn't overly confident that she'd be able to overcome that.

No one had ever changed her thoughts and opinions like Lincoln had.

No one had ever lived so strongly inside her.

That was clear again the following morning, when at breakfast, Lincoln suggested that they make a visit to Ronald's workshop, to see the broom. The thrill inside her had very little to do with the broom. The idea of spending time in Lincoln's company filled her heart with such joy, she'd been unable to contain it while replying affirmatively.

The looks she received from others at the table—his mother and sister—caused her cheeks to warm, and she quickly began telling them about the broom, hoping they'd think that's where her excitement was initiated.

Shortly after the meal ended, they left in Lincoln's carriage. "Thank you again," she said. "I'm excited to see the broom working."

"You're welcome, again," Lincoln replied, giving her a sideways glance. "You were so excited when I mentioned it, that I'm convinced if I didn't take you, you'd go to see it by yourself."

She playfully nudged his arm with her elbow. "I would not have, and don't worry, I won't touch anything without permission. I have no desire to receive an electrical shock."

"Good to know," he replied.

"What's good to know? That I wouldn't have gone to Ronald's without you, or that I have no desire to receive an electrical shock?" In the past, after a visit with the Dryers, it was Audrey she missed the most. That wouldn't be true this time. It would be him. The way they bantered with each other was such fun, and his laugh… She sighed. His laughter was the best sound in the world. She'd never forget it. Not ever.

"Both," he said.

His response increased her happiness, and encouraged her to continue with the teasing. "You wanted to see the broom as much as I did, and you want to see if he has the engine attached to the bicycle yet, too."

"That is something else you shouldn't touch," he said.

"You can't get an electrical shock from a combustion engine," she said. Then, not sure, she asked, "Can you?"

"When it comes to one of Ronald's inventions, anything's possible."

She laughed, as did Lincoln, but as their laughter faded, a shiver tickled her spine and a sense of melancholy appeared due to a thought that had formed.

Lincoln frowned. "What's wrong?"

"Nothing," she said. "Except, well, don't you wish it was that way for everything? For everyone?"

"What way?"

"That anything was possible." She'd never disclosed that to anyone that way before, that everything wasn't possible for her. Much like his family, her family had planned out her life, one that she didn't want, all the while knowing that she'd have to settle for it. Claiming that she'd only marry the love of her life was an excuse. One she'd come up with to put off the inevitable. She now fully understood what that inevitable was. Losing someone you love.

He opened his mouth, then closed it and nodded.

She wished she hadn't said anything, but couldn't take it back. Nor could she take back the feeling that while she'd been fooling Manhattan that she and Lincoln were courting each other, she'd fooled herself. Or maybe it was the other way around. She suddenly realized that she'd been fooling herself for years. Believing that she could control with whom and if she ever fell in love. Why that thought struck now was impossible to know, but it had.

She didn't want to contemplate why, because it might try to convince her that she'd fallen in love with Lincoln. Mainly because she was wondering if that was indeed what she'd done. Or maybe she was still trying convince herself that she hadn't. That she still had the ability to protect herself. Protect her heart.

He shifted the reins into one hand and laid his free hand on her knee. "Perhaps anything is possible," he said. "It's just people who think it's not. I would never have believed it was possible for a boutonniere to be switched with a nosegay without anyone knowing it, yet it happened. Happened to me and you."

She appreciated his response, but had to point out, “That was merely a magic trick.”

“Well, then, maybe more people need to believe in magic.” His grin grew. “Hans the Magnificent made me a believer.”

A hint of joy crept back inside her. “He was quite the magician.”

“That he was.” Lincoln winked at her. “Maybe you are a magician, too.”

“Not hardly,” she replied, yet felt more joy returning. It was impossible to be unhappy when she was with him.

He shrugged and removed his hand from her knee in order to use both hands as he steered the horse into the driveway. “Time to see your broom.”

“It’s not my broom,” she replied.

“You helped design it.” He set the brake and nodded at the groomsman who walked towards them to collect the horse.

“I gave a suggestion,” she said.

“Or two.” He jumped out of the carriage and held a hand up to her.

She took his hand as used it as she climbed down. “That doesn’t make it my idea or my broom.”

Still holding her hand, he looped her arm around his elbow as they walked around the carriage and into the backyard without saying another word.

She tried her hardest to remain silent as well, but lost the battle. “No last word?”

“I’ll leave that for you,” he said.

Victoria questioned what he meant by that, but quickly forgot when Ronald opened the door of his workshop and welcomed them inside. The wooden building was just as crowded with inventions as it had been on her last visit, and she was just as careful about where she stepped and what she touched while Ronald showed them the progress he'd made on the bicycle. To her, it didn't look much different, but that was because all of the work he'd done had been on the engine. He and Lincoln had a deep conversation about that, while her mind went back to falling in love.

It didn't seem possible, but it didn't seem deniable, either.

Maybe it was magic. Maybe Hans the Magnificent had played a magic trick on her heart when he'd switched their flowers that night.

Even if that had happened, even if she had fallen in love with Lincoln, it wouldn't last. She couldn't let it. A week from now, she'd be back home. Living her dull life, which felt as if it would be even bleaker than before. Lincoln had goals to accomplish, and he would. As long as he was free to stay focused on them. That's what he wanted, and that's what she wanted for him, too. That's why they'd agreed to their plan, and had stuck to it.

She had to continue to stick to it.

"And now," Ronald said excitedly, "time to see what you came to see. It's right over here. I put a pile of sawdust on the floor to demonstrate how well it works." Leading them across the building, Ronald continued, "My mother claims this is her favorite of my inventions, and there have been a lot of them."

Lincoln leaned close to whisper, "More than I can count."

Victoria stifled a giggle at the expression on Lincoln's face.

"Not including the ones that I refuse to remember," he quietly added.

"Oh, stop," she whispered. This, whispering with him,

was one of the things she'd miss the most. It made her feel so alive and...special. He made her feel special in ways no one ever had.

"Allow me to introduce," Ronald said with great flare as he held up the electric broom, "the automatic sweeping machine, model V."

"Oh, my! It looks exactly like the drawing." Victoria examined the broom that now had a rotating brush and dustpan attached at the bottom of the handle. "Why is it model five? Did you try that many times since we were last here?"

"The V isn't a Roman numeral," Ronald said. "It stands for Victoria, because you gave me the rotating brush idea. I named this original after you, because if it becomes popular, I'll have to consider other models. Larger ones, or smaller ones, or..."

She heard Ronald's explanation as he continued, but was looking at Lincoln, who was grinning like a cat who'd just trapped a mouse.

"Your broom," he whispered.

"You knew the name, didn't you?"

"Ronald might have mentioned it last night."

Shaking her head at him, she looked at Ronald who had finished his list of additional possible models. "I'm honored. Thank you."

"This is the switch," Ronald said. "I'll plug it in so you can try it. It's safe, I promise."

"How about you demonstrate it first," Lincoln said while laying a hand on her arm. "Just to be sure."

Ronald laughed. "I knew you'd say that, and it's why I have two piles of sawdust. I'll sweep one first."

The next hour or more was taken up with trying out the broom and discussing the parts and functions. Even Lincoln tested out the broom, and Victoria could tell that he was impressed by how it didn't leave any sawdust on the floor even before he said it aloud. He also readily agreed to file a patent.

After they went over the drawings and written descriptions and functions, Ronald walked them to the door. "You sure you have everything?"

"Yes," Lincoln replied, gesturing with the stack of papers in his hand. "I'll have it written up and call you when it's time to stop by my office and sign it."

"I'm excited about this one," Ronald said. "It could be my first fully marketable invention, thanks to Victoria."

"I merely gave a suggestion," she replied. "You did all the work, and I believe your sweeping machines will soon be for sale at Webster's Department Store."

"The model V," Lincoln said.

She lifted her chin. "Yes, the model V."

Lincoln had a heck of a time not kissing her right then and there, in front of Ronald, and not for show, but because it's what he truly wanted to do. She was so adorable and full of spirit. Furthermore, the one kiss they'd shared had instilled a hunger inside him that had grown until he was now starving for another one.

The desire didn't ease as they told Ronald goodbye and walked to the carriage, nor did it lessen as they drove along the city streets, with her signing praises at having a sweeping machine named after her and teasing him about not telling her that in advance because he was jealous that he didn't have an invention named after him.

It was all in jest and fun. He'd thought of little else other than her all night, and how their fake courtship would end soon, and he'd come up with one conclusion. Between now and the wedding, he was going to make the most of their time together. He was going to miss her, greatly, and the memories of the fun they'd had would be all that were left behind. That alone was enough to make him not want to return home immediately.

"Do you mind if we take this paperwork to my office?" he asked. "It will only take a minute."

"No, I don't mind at all." She smiled at him. "I've never seen your office. Audrey's pointed out the building, but I've never been inside."

"No one will be there except the doorman, but I'll show you around if you want."

"I'd like that," she said. "Unless you have other things you need to do."

"No, nothing at all."

"Until tonight," she said.

"What are we doing tonight?"

"Your family is hosting Jake's family for dinner, to finalize any last-minute wedding preparations."

"What could be last-minute? They've been planning for months."

"I'm not sure," she said. "That's what it says on the list of events your mother gave me. Didn't she give you a list?"

"Probably, I really don't remember if I got an actual list." He was disappointed that it wasn't a public event, where he could hold Victoria's hand or dance with her. "I knew Mother would remind me of where I needed to be and when."

"You'll be glad when this will all be over, won't you?"

He drew in a breath and held it, wondering how to respond. Honesty was his only choice. "Yes, and no." He steered the horse out of traffic, near the sidewalk outside of his office building, and then set the brake. Reaching over, he took a hold of her hand and looked her square in the face. "I'll be glad when the wedding is over, but I'm going to miss you, Victoria. I've enjoyed getting to know you better, spending time with you."

"I've enjoyed those things, too," she said quietly, "very much."

The hunger inside him to kiss her hit a full-blown starvation stage as they sat there, holding hands and staring at each other. He could remember the feel of her lips against his, the taste of them, the curves of her body as she'd pressed close against him.

His breaking point was hovering, and he felt himself leaning towards her, when a voice sounded, shattering something around him like a glass bulb bursting from becoming overheated.

He turned, looked at the man standing there expectantly. "No, Herman, there's no need to take the horse around back." He responded to the doorman's question. "We won't be long."

"Very well, sir," Herman replied.

While the doorman tethered the horse, Lincoln assisted Victoria out of the carriage, then collected the papers from beneath the seat before he escorted her through the set of huge wooden and glass doors that Herman hurried to open for them.

"Thank you, Herman," he said.

"You're welcome, sir, miss," Herman said, including Victoria in his head nod. "A parcel arrived for you this morning. I put it on your secretary's desk."

"Very good, thank you."

"Would you like me to man the elevator?"

"I can do that, thank you." Lincoln nodded towards the caged door on the side of the foyer, as he told Victoria, "My office is on the fourth floor."

The building was old, had been in the family for many decades, but had been well maintained and modernized several times over the years. It was a place he was proud of, and told her how his great-grandfather had helped design it and opened the first office in it.

"How many lawyers work at your firm?" she asked as they crossed the room, their footsteps echoing against the high ceiling.

"Twenty right now." He pulled open the elevator gate and stepped into the cage behind her, then closed the door and engaged the motor. The elevator cage was small, and they stood shoulder to shoulder.

The sound of the mechanical gears rolling together, giving power to the chain drive lifting the elevator upwards, was loud, but the noise didn't diminish the desires in him building again due to the close quarters. He felt her standing next to him, smelled her perfume, and had to swallow hard to find the strength to remain still. Other than to glance her way.

The way she smiled at him increased the hunger inside him to an altogether new level.

Had a man ever died from self-deprivation?

If not, he might be the first.

Chapter Twelve

Lincoln forced himself to focus on the dial above the door, so he'd know when to stop the elevator. Even the ticker hand seemed to be plotting against him, making it the longest elevator ride he'd ever taken.

When the dial finally reached the number four, he pulled the lever to stop the chain gear, and waited for the shaking of the cage to settle before sliding open the door. "My office is at the end of the hallway." The strain inside him made his voice sound hoarse.

"This is a beautiful building, and it's so quiet," she said as they walked along the carpeted hallway. "Other than the elevator."

"It's not so quiet when everyone is here," he said, finding his normal voice. Which, at the moment, was the only normal thing about him. "The elevator runs constantly then."

"When you're elected attorney general, will you live here, in the city, or in the capital, Albany?"

"Both. For years politicians have been advocating to have the capital moved to New York City, but just as many have been set upon keeping it in Albany."

"I wonder why."

"Several reasons," he said, though he was at a loss as to think of one at the moment. The blood was pounding too hard through his veins for normal thoughts to form. "They change every time it's brought up for a legislative vote." He opened the door that led first to his secretary's office, and from there led to his office. Catching himself watching the sway of her hips as she walked in front of him, he quickly pulled his gaze off her backside as she turned about to look at him, wait for him.

This might not have been a good idea. Bringing her here, where they were completely alone. He crossed the room and threw the papers from Ronald on his desk.

She was scanning the room, slowly, as if taking in the shelves, pictures, desk, chairs, and other items. "Won't you miss working here while in Albany?"

He was going to miss her whether he was here or in Albany, or anywhere else in the world, and the starvation inside him had him wound tighter than the spool of string on Ronald's electric kite. It turns out that he wasn't as immune to women as he'd thought, especially this one. The desires inside him had been building for weeks and he was losing the small amount of control he had left.

She tilted her head slightly, all the while keeping her gaze locked with his. "What are you thinking so hard about?"

He was about to snap, and took a step back, hoping to relieve some of the tension.

It didn't help.

"Do you really want to know?" he asked, holding her gaze.

She nodded.

"You." His throat was thick, his voice hoarse again.

She closed her eyes and pinched her lips together.

Heart pounding, he stepped closer, and touched the side of her face with four fingers. "Specifically, kissing you."

The words were out, as if he'd lost control over holding things in.

Her eyes snapped open, and her lips parted as a small gasp escaped. "You are?"

He nodded. Licked his lips that were twitching with want. "Yes."

She didn't say anything for what felt like an eternity, then, with a tiny shrug, she asked, "Are you going to, or not?"

He was going to, had to, but at the same time, an ounce of control remained. He had to know if she agreed. "Do you want me to?"

The smile that appeared on her lips had to be the most seductive one he'd ever seen, and the way she laid her hands on the lapels of his jacket sent more than a single electrical shock through him. Every part of him was sizzling and snapping.

But it was what she did next that totally jolted him.

"Yes," she whispered, lifting her face upwards. "Very much."

The weeks, days, hours of restraining himself had been trying, but the moment his lips touched hers, he concluded every minute had been worth it. All those caged-up desires collided together and escaped into deep, fulfilling kiss.

He'd never considered himself helpless, but at this moment he was helpless in resisting a singular thought.

She'd stolen her heart.

No, that wasn't right. She hadn't stolen anything. He'd been wrong. He'd been consumed with his own thoughts, his own beliefs, for so long, that he'd never considered that he might be wrong. Totally wrong in believing he'd never feel this way towards a woman. Never want a woman more than anything else in the world. But he did.

She leaned against him. Her soft curves fit perfectly with his firm ones, and her lips, tasting sweet and precious, moved in time with his. Somewhat feverishly.

More than somewhat. They were as feverish as his, as if they couldn't get enough.

He couldn't, and grasped the nape of her neck with one hand, increasing the pressure, the need between them. His other hand roamed her down back, along the curve of her hip, up the side of her waist.

Her hands were around his neck, her fingers combing into his hair. A surge of renewed desire struck, and he used his tongue to part her lips, then explore the sweet, wonderful heat of her mouth.

There was no way to make up for lost time. Time past was gone forever. What he was doing right now, was reveling in the moment. A point in time that would remain with him forever.

He tasted her mouth, teased her tongue with a game of tag, and let his hand roam over and along her perfect curves, exploring them, memorizing them.

Their lips parted now and again, for brief moments, then reunited in another, long, heated kiss. That happened several times, and each time he found himself lost all over again in the taste of her, the feel of her, the sounds of her little moans and sighs.

It was as if nothing else existed, except the two of them, even though he knew that they were surrounded by the entire city of New York. People involved in the hustle and bustle of traffic, the sun glistening off the glass of buildings large and small, the wind blowing breezes that carried sounds far and wide.

That knowledge might have been what brought him back down to earth, back to where rational thinking was possible. Then again, it might have been because he suddenly realized that kissing her would never be enough. He wanted all of her, and he wanted that right, the ability to kiss her, to have her, whenever the desire struck.

He wanted her like he'd never wanted anything.

Slowly, he released her lips, and softly kissed the tip of her nose, then her forehead before holding her close in a long hug, all the while wondering what he was going to say, to do, next.

He knew what he wanted, but that didn't coincide with what she wanted. Love, the desire for it, or even the belief in it had eluded him for so long that he didn't have the slightest clue as to what it took, or would take, to be the love of someone's life.

Victoria held on to Lincoln for dear life, because a part of herself had slipped away. She'd felt it, knew she was never going to be the same again. Could never go back to her old self.

Right now, she couldn't even catch her breath. There wasn't a single part of her that she had control over.

The fact that she wasn't frightened half to death over that, should probably scare her, but she was too full of warm, crazy feelings and happiness to be afraid. There was no place she'd rather be than where she was right now.

She snuggled her head against his chest and did nothing but cherish the moment, and smile at the glory that he'd kissed her again. Nothing had ever felt so right. She'd never felt so right. So happy.

It may have been seconds, or minutes, before a flash of memory struck. Had she asked him if he was going to kiss her or not?

A tiny shiver tickled or spine. Yes. She had.

And he had kissed her.

More than once.

Or had she kissed him?

There had been a moment when she'd thought he might not, and had stretched up on her toes, because she had wanted him to kiss her more than she'd ever wanted anything. It had been even more wonderful than she'd remembered, but there had been no reason for him to kiss her. There hadn't been anyone around, no need for them to pretend that they were courting.

Then why had he kissed her?

Because she hadn't given him a choice?

She stopped a groan before it became audible. Had she turned into one of those silly, lovestruck females that he'd spent his entire life avoiding?

What should she do? Tell him that she wasn't?

Or would that be a lie?

She hadn't dropped her handkerchief, or poured punch on her dress, or acted as if she'd twisted an ankle, or pretended to faint. No, she'd been more brazen than any of that. She'd asked him if he was going to kiss her or not, and told him that's what she wanted.

That want had been so overwhelming, there hadn't been anything else she could've said.

Her stomach was sinking deeper and deeper. They'd discussed what they both wanted and didn't want before they'd agreed to their ploy. How they would part as friends after the wedding. She couldn't change her mind now, and most certainly couldn't expect him to.

She'd concluded all that before now. Why hadn't she remembered that?

He took a step back, and she willed herself to pull up a smile before lifting her face to meet his gaze.

"We probably should leave," he said. "The horse is standing on the street."

She must have changed in more ways than she knew, because she quickly found the ability to act as if all was normal. Dropping her hands from around his waist, she stepped away. "Yes, we should." Forcing her legs to work, she walked towards the door. "Thank you for showing me your office. It's very nice."

"You're welcome."

They walked along the long hallway in silence, and once in the elevator, she was grateful for the noise that hid the long, shaking breath that she released. That part of herself that she'd felt slipping away, had that been her heart? The love she felt for him? Or had it been the cage she'd kept around her heart. Like the elevator cage, she'd kept the door shut, holding things in, until he'd opened it. Just like he did the elevator door when it clanged to stop in the foyer.

Once in the carriage, she was grateful for the noise of the city street, until it dulled when they crossed over into the residential area of Manhattan. The fewer carriages would have made talking easier, but by then, they'd both been quiet for so long, she couldn't find a reason to speak.

Their arrival at the house went unnoticed by others except the servants who took the horse and opened the door, and Victoria felt a sense of relief as she retreated to her room. She was still trying to comprehend how the best moment in her life had turned into the most dreadful. It was her fault. Somehow, she'd forgotten their goal had been to fool others. Not completely forgotten, because she had reminded herself of that on an occasion or two. The problem was she'd never let her heart know that.

She'd never expected that was something she would have to do. It certainly hadn't been in the past. That was because she'd believed she'd had control over her heart. Could fully control when and with whom she would ever fall in love. Could control who would become the love of her life. That had never seemed irrational, nor had she ever believed it would happen.

It shouldn't have happened. Lincoln could never be that person. First and foremost because it wasn't something he'd ever want.

There was only one thing she could do. Keep pretending.

It was only a week. Then they would part as friends.

Then she would return to her old life, where she'd be able to keep the door to her heart closed. She had to, because she didn't want to love him. Didn't want to love anyone so deeply that she couldn't even mention their name. That's how it had been for her mother when her father had died. She'd taken to her bed and cried, cried until the baby was born, then she'd cried more.

A knock on the door was quickly followed with it opening and Audrey poking her head inside. "There you are." The door opened all the way. "We have to go shopping."

Victoria drew in a deep breath, and told herself to act normal. "Oh? For what?"

"You aren't going to believe it, but Mother told me this morning that my father has arranged for Jake and I to spend a week at the beach cottage in Florida for a honeymoon! Whenever I'd mention a honeymoon, she'd tell me that wasn't for me to decide, so would Jake. Well, it turns out they both knew my father was arranging it, and I need a new bathing gown!"

"That's wonderful," Victoria said, trying hard to sound excited, but was finding a hint of jealousy creeping in again. If only her life was as perfect as Audrey's. If only she'd never known the pain of losing someone she loved. If only she wasn't petrified of experiencing that again.

"I haven't been to Florida in years," Audrey said. "I can't wait to show Jake our family cottage. It's going to be so wonderful!" Audrey grasped Victoria's arm. "I wish you could come with us! You'd love it there!"

Victoria stood. "No, you don't. It's your honeymoon."

Audrey laughed. "I know! I'm so excited. Maybe you could come with us the next time. It's right on the ocean and the sun is always shining! Jake and I will be able to go swimming and take walks along the beach, find seashells. I'll bring you back one, I promise, then you'll really want to see it. You'll be welcome to join us anytime you want. That would be fun."

Victoria crossed the room to collect her purse, and another saddening thought formed. Everything was going to be so different after the wedding. It was selfish of her to be thinking about herself, but she just couldn't help it. Audrey would always be her friend, but that too was going to be different. Audrey would be living with Jake, and coming here to visit would no longer happen. What she'd said about herself was coming true. She was destined to become an old maid, doing nothing more than taking care of her family's finances. It was her fate and there was nothing she could do about it.

"We can eat lunch at that café next to Webster's," Audrey said. "Oh, and help me remember that I need some more rose water, and..."

Victoria nodded, half listening as she followed Audrey out of the room, trying her best to hide the sadness growing inside her.

She was convinced that Audrey hadn't noticed until they were seated near the window inside the café, eating clam chowder that was probably delicious, but she just wasn't hungry.

"Is something wrong?" Audrey asked. "You've barely said a word since we left the house."

Victoria slid a spoonful of soup into her mouth to give herself time to consider her answer. She couldn't tell Audrey that she was jealous, or how she felt about Lincoln, or how she was destined to become an old maid. Needing help as to what to say, she glanced out the window, at the people walking past, on their way to Webster's. A man instantly caught her attention and shiver shot up her spine as his gaze landed on her.

He continued walking, right past the window, but the shiver inside her didn't disappear. It shot down her arms, making her hands shake.

"That was Elwood Kelley," Audrey said. "And he was staring straight at you."

Victoria couldn't find anything to say about that, either.

"He's going into Webster's," Audrey said, leaning against the window to see down the sidewalk. "We should follow him."

A gasp made her cough, more than once. With watery eyes, Victoria said, "No, we shouldn't."

Pushing away from the table, Audrey said, "Yes, we should."

"Why?"

"To see if he talks to Mr. Webster, tries to convince him to sell."

Victoria shook her head. "Mr. Webster will tell Lincoln if that happens."

Audrey stood, leaned over the table, and whispered, "If we hear something, we could be witnesses, so it's not just Mr. Webster's word against Elwood's if it goes to court."

Lincoln had sequestered himself in his study since lunch, torn between regret and embracing the passion he'd felt from Victoria during their kiss. He'd remembered every moment of kissing her, every stroke of his hand over her curves, every sound of her soft moans.

He'd also remembered how his life hadn't changed. How he still wanted to run for office, still had goals that he'd set for himself years ago, and questioned what would happen to him if he gave them all up. Would he soon find himself disappointed, unhappy, remorseful? Would he come to blame her?

Was that when what he felt for her now would fade? Leave him wishing he'd fought these feelings harder, and considered the consequences more deeply?

He'd also questioned if she too would be disappointed, unhappy, and remorseful. Is that when she'd look elsewhere for the love she wanted? The love of her life?

There was no law book he could scour for answers to those questions. No precedence he could research to follow.

In the midst of his private thoughts, he'd found one more thing. He wanted her in his life, but he'd never forgive himself if she ended up being hurt.

He'd considered skipping the evening meal, just to put distance between the two of them, but knew he couldn't ignore her for the entire next week, so had dressed and made his way downstairs prior to the arrival of their guests.

Other than Jake. He'd arrived earlier, and had been in the drawing room with Audrey. What they told him had Lincoln changing his mind about keeping any distance between him and Victoria.

Jake's parents, along with a slew of aunts, uncles, married siblings and spouses, and his elderly grandmother, had all arrived before Victoria slipped into the room quietly, as if not wanting anyone to see her.

Lincoln knew who that anyone was. Him. Therefore, he remained standing beside the tall grandfather clock, where he was partially hidden from her view and waited until she'd made her way to the credenza. He also waited until she'd selected an already poured glass of sherry and taken a sip, while turning about to scan the room.

Her gown was a flowing mass of pale pink sink, almost the color of her skin, and for a brief moment, he remembered running his hand down her back, along her side. He balled his hand into a fist at how his palm began to burn, and that's what forced him to remember his anger.

The way her body, mainly her shoulders, drooped slightly, as if she'd relaxed, said she was relieved that he wasn't in sight.

Still, he waited, until she took a couple of steps, was almost directly in front of the clock, then he moved, stepped up behind her, and whispered, "Looking for someone?"

She jolted, then went completely stiff. "No."

"Not even Elwood Kelley?"

Shifting her stance slightly, she looked at him. This time it was more than her shoulders that drooped. She clearly knew that he knew. "Of course not."

"Really?"

She glanced towards where Jake and Audrey were talking with a cluster of his relatives, and let out a sigh. "He walked past the window of the café."

Full-fledged fear was embedded in his anger. Elwood was dangerous. Any number of things could have happened to her, and each thought made him madder that he hadn't been more vigilant in making sure Elwood kept his distance. "What were you thinking? Deciding to follow him?"

Her eyes widened at the harshness in his whisper. "We didn't follow him," she angrily whispered in return. "We went to Webster's so Audrey could buy a new bathing gown for her honeymoon in Florida."

Audrey had told him all that, and more. "But you couldn't stop yourself from saying hello to him. I told you that he's dangerous."

Her eyes snapped with anger, as she quietly hissed, "I know what you told me! We were in public! He said hello to me, I had to say hello in return."

"No, you didn't!"

"Yes, I did," she hissed. "It would have been rude not to. Give me some credit, Lincoln! I'm not an idiot! I didn't want to make him mad by not saying hello, and—" She huffed out a breath. "Never mind."

He grasped her upper arm when she took a step. "I mind."

Her lips narrowed into a tight line. "I mind, too! I've

been taking care of myself for years, and the rest of my family. I don't need you to tell me how to do that!"

Regret filled him. He wasn't mad at her, and didn't want her mad at him. Damn it! He wished her fingerprint picture would be enough to convict Elwood for theft, but knew it wouldn't. "I know that, but this is the city, things are different here and I don't like the fact that he was following you."

"He wasn't following me!"

"Audrey said you searched for him all over the store, then he suddenly was behind you."

She let out a sigh, but anger still flashed in her eyes. "We didn't search for him, we looked while walking up the stairs to the women's department, but didn't see him anywhere."

Elwood had been following her, he was convinced of that. "And there he was! Don't you find it odd that he was on the women's floor? I do!"

"For heaven's sake!" she hissed, glancing around the room to make sure no one was watching them. "You and I were on the women's floor."

That was true, but also very different. "We went there together."

"Yes, well, that will never happen again, now will it?" She tugged her arm from his hold. "Nor am I going to stand here arguing with you when there is a house full of guests."

Lincoln had no choice but to watch her cross the room and sit down on the sofa next to Jake's grandmother. He let out more than one muffled curse at how he'd handled that. He didn't want to be at odds with her, nor did he want to stand in the corners whispering with her. He hated the feeling that he was hiding something. Which he was. How long could he keep his love hidden?

Chapter Thirteen

Despite the fact that Victoria had barely spoken to him, or looked his way, Lincoln had survived the evening meal, somehow, and church services the next morning, where he sat beside her and came close to driving himself insane by trying to answer his own questions. When she was near, all his reasons to not love her failed to exist. He couldn't imagine a time would ever come when he didn't want her close, yet, when she wasn't nearby, he could remember all the reasons why he'd never wanted to even believe in love, let alone feel it.

Those reasons were losing ground. His ambitions to believe in them weren't as strong as they used to be, making him question just how wrong he had been. In another week, Victoria would be gone, and with Audrey moving into Jake's house, there would be no reason for Victoria to ever stay at his house again. She'd be at her house, with no one to protect her from Elwood, other than an elderly grandfather.

That knowledge took center stage and not knowing what to do about it was frustrating him to no end. He needed something against Elwood.

As unexpected as the first time he'd been shocked from one of Ronald's inventions, he realized he did have something. All of Manhattan thought he and Victoria were courting. They'd displayed that at all the social events and outings leading up to the wedding, but what if they were seen out together somewhere that had nothing to do with the wedding? A place where people went just for fun, an entire day on the town to really let the word spread beyond the social elites attending the balls.

He knew just the event, and hoped an apology would convince Victoria to attend it with him.

After helping her out of the carriage when they arrived home, he kept a hold of her hand, and waited until the others had entered the house. "I owe you a sincere apology for last night," he said. "I would like to make it up to you by taking you someplace."

She closed her eyes for a moment, then looked up at him. "Where?"

"I'd prefer to show you." He touched the side of her face. "I am sorry, truly. I didn't mean to upset you."

She pinched her lips together, then shook her head. "I'm sorry, too."

Not wanting to bring Elwood into the conversation, he quickly asked, "So you'll go?"

She nodded. "Yes."

Even overly excited, he withheld the desire to kiss her, even just a small peck on the forehead, and within the hour, he had William deliver them to the train station. The very one where, almost a month ago, she'd stepped off the train carrying her picture. That seemed more like a lifetime ago. Contrary feelings were still living inside him, crashing into each other. Although she'd agreed to accompany him, she'd barely spoken during the ride from the house.

"I have a suggestion," he said, once they'd settled in their train seats.

She twisted her neck enough to level a sideways glance on him. "Does it include telling me where we are going?"

"No, but it is pertaining to what we'll do once we get there."

Her dress was blue, with a matching waist jacket and a hat spouting a single short feather that dipped as she gave a slight nod.

He needed some solid facts in order to find the answers he was seeking, and this could be a way to get them. "For the rest of the day, let's just forget about everything else and have fun. No past or future. No rules, no worries, just a day of having fun."

A shimmer of a smile was forming on her lips. "Fun doing what?"

He chuckled. "I'm not going to tell you where we are going, you'll see once we get there, and I think you'll like it."

The whistle sounded, the iron wheels on the train began to turn. The train had chugged out of the station before she turned completely to look at him. "I truly had no choice but to say hello to—"

He pressed a finger to her lips, stopping her from saying more. "We're forgetting everything else." The feel of her lips touching his fingertip brought back memories and instilled hope. "Today is a day when anything is possible."

Her lips curled into a smile as she nodded.

He removed his finger, but not his eyes. He continued to soak in her beauty. The thick lashes surrounding her blue eyes, the tinge of pink on her cheeks that made her face glow, the petal shape of her lips that he'd never forget kissing.

Her eyes were on him, too, and she leaned closer as she whispered, "I could start having fun right now if I knew where we were going."

Laughing, he leaned forward and gave the tip of her nose a little kiss. She instilled a happiness inside him that was unmatchable, unconceivable, and that's what he wanted to do to her. Make her happy. So very happy. "Have you ever seen a lion?"

"A real one?"

"Yes, a real one."

"No, have you?"

Rather than answer, he asked, "How about an elephant? A live one."

She giggled. "No."

"How about a monkey?"

Her eyes took on a new shine. "Yes."

"You have?"

"A street performer had one in Tarrytown," she said. "It played a tiny set of cymbals while the man played the accordion. Why?"

"Because you are going to see all that and more today."

"Where?"

"Brooklyn."

She frowned, then let out a tiny squeal that she quickly covered with one hand, before she asked, "The circus? I saw the ad in the newspaper, but didn't think there would be time to see it."

"There is time today." He was also hoping that with no pressure to act a certain way, there would be time today for them to discover exactly what was between them. One day might not be enough to set a lifetime on, but it was enough to help him make life-determining decisions.

* * *

Victoria was in awe, enchanted, and terrified all at the same time as she watched the troupe of acrobats perform on the ropes and wires strung from the top of the huge tent. There were moments that she had to duck her head behind Lincoln's shoulder, because it was too scary to watch, yet she kept her eyes open because she couldn't completely look away.

It was that way with the lion and elephant tamers, too. With everything. The music and performers, animals, and sideshows were amazing and unbelievable at the same time. She could barely contain her excitement to see everything. It wasn't like the balls and performances she'd been attending this past month. Though parts of those had been fun, here there was no worry about who was watching them or what might be overheard. Today she felt free, and the attractions led her to believe that anything was possible. She certainly saw, heard, and tried things that she'd never have believed possible. Including riding a camel.

She and Lincoln had climbed onto the large, blanketed wooden saddle, while the camel was on its knees, and as it started to rise, she'd grabbed a hold of the arms Lincoln had wrapped around her waist.

"You're fine," he said. "I won't let you fall."

The camel's rise to its feet was a wobbly experience, and once it was standing, she fully comprehended how much taller a camel was than a horse. "That's a long way to the ground."

He pulled her back against his chest. "You're safe."

She did feel safe and secure, and wished every day could be just like this one. "I never imagined I'd ride a camel."

He rested her chin on her shoulder. "Actually, we are being led around a pen while sitting atop a camel."

She twisted her neck and didn't even attempt to stop the impulse that struck to kiss him on the cheek. "Actually, I don't care."

He twisted his neck and his lips touched hers quickly. "Neither do I."

A wonderful hum of pleasure filled her and she snuggled her cheek against his as they were led in two circles around the pen, following several other camels.

Lincoln kept his arms tightly around her as the camel wobbled back down to its knees, then he climbed off and lifted her out of the seat. She laid her hands on his shoulders and never took her eyes off his as he lowered her until her feet touched the ground. The things she felt for him were so strong, she knew that she'd never feel this way with another man. Couldn't. He was the love of her life. Even when she became an old maid, she would know that at least she had found him.

"What do you want to do now?" he asked.

"Whatever you want to do," she answered, because she knew something else.

When a person finds the love of their life, it's not about themselves. It's about the other person. About wanting them to have the best life possible. To have all their dreams come true.

He kissed her forehead and took a hold of her hand, led her out of the camel pen. "Let's get some popcorn."

After the popcorn, they watched jugglers, flame throwers, and a magician, who she declared wasn't as good as Hans, and several other performers before they walked to the train station to take them back to Manhattan. Dusk was falling and she let out a long sigh.

"Tired?" Lincoln asked.

"No, sad the day is ending. I wish we could do it all over again."

"It's not over yet," he said.

"It's not?"

He shook his head. "And don't ask where we are going, because I won't tell you."

"Not even a hint?"

"Not even a hint."

She laughed, simply because she was happy. So very happy.

He held to not giving her a hint as they rode the train back to Manhattan, sitting side by side and talking and laughing about the things they'd seen at the circus. They discussed other things too, but nothing of real importance.

William was at the station, with the carriage, and took them downtown, to where the buildings stretched high into the night sky and flickering street lights lined the sidewalks. William pulled the carriage to the side of the road and stopped in front of the tallest building in New York, maybe the world.

"This is Jake's newspaper's building," she said.

"It is." Lincoln climbed out of the carriage and offered his hand.

She laid her hand in his and climbed down. "Why are we here?"

He quietly spoke to William for a moment, then took a basket from the driver. "I thought we'd eat dinner here."

Glancing between the basket in his hand and the building, she asked, "A picnic? Here?" She loved picnics, but had only had them while living back in Colorado.

"Have you ever seen the city from the dome atop the building?" he asked.

"No. I came here with Audrey, but we met Jake in the lobby."

He took a hold of her hand. "I think you'll enjoy it." As they walked towards the building he continued, "Some of the newspaper offices are on the top floor, and from the terrace, you can see the entire city. It's a sight to see."

"Are Jake and Audrey here?" She felt a hint of shame at the silent admission that she hoped not. She didn't want their time alone to end.

"No, it's just me and you. However, others are probably in the offices. There's always a reporter or two working on a story, and their printing presses in the basement run all night, printing out the next day's paper."

"What's on the other floors?" The building was at least ten stories tall, if not more. She wasn't sure, and knew Jake's office was on the ground floor.

"Mostly apartments," he replied as they entered and walked across the shiny marble floor towards the caged elevator where an attendant was already opening the door.

The attendant greeted them by name, which said Lincoln had planned this in advance. That, too, thrilled her. Knowing he'd planned this just for them.

Like the elevator at his office, the cage shook as it began to rise, and the noise overtook the ability for conversation, which gave her mind plenty of time to recall her last elevator ride with him. It seemed like that couldn't have been just yesterday morning. Then again, the memory of kissing him was locked so firmly in her mind, that whether it was days, months, or years, she'd never forget it. Never forget him.

At the end of the elevator ride, Lincoln led her along a hallway that curved around the dome, lit by lamps, but also by the stars of the night sky that shone in through the glass windows of the dome.

He opened a glass paneled door, and waited for her to step out onto the terrace.

The night air was cooler than it had been down on the street, but not chilly, just a refreshing coolness that caused her to lift her face and feel it wash over her.

He set down the basket and took her hand, led her to the edge of the terrace, and the tall metal banister. "This isn't open to the public," he said.

"I can see why," she said, in amazement at the view of the city below, the river flowing past, and the tops of buildings stretched out as far as she could see. "Everyone would want to see this. It's like a different world."

"Where anything is possible," he said. "Everything we're looking at, the buildings, the electric lights, the streets and homes and businesses, where once mere thoughts in people's minds. Others may have thought it was impossible, but those who didn't forged onward. Through ambition and perseverance, they turned those thoughts into real things."

She smiled. "Making the impossible, possible."

He put an arm around her and she leaned her head against his shoulder as they stood there, silent, staring at the mixture of creations both natural and manmade. It was as incredible as it was inspiring.

"What would you like to make possible?" he asked.

She turned from the sight, because it suddenly pained her. "I don't know," she admitted. "I guess I've always just thought that my life is what it is, and there's nothing I can do to change that."

"That doesn't sound like you."

She walked away from the railing, back towards the

building. "It is me, though. I've never had goals and dreams like you."

He walked to the basket and knelt down, began unloading it. "What about finding the love of your life? That's a goal."

Thankful for something to do, she helped him spread the cloth on the terrace floor. She'd only recently discovered the truth herself, and if anyone else deserved to know it, it was him. "That was a lie. One I'd told myself, and others, for years."

"Why?"

She sat on the cloth to help unload the basket. "Because after my father died, and my baby brother, my mother was different. Not just sad, but hollow. Like she was living only because she had to. I tried to make her happy by doing things for her, and then that just became my job, to take care of everyone. When we left Colorado, it continued. Even while in school, I went home every weekend because there were things to take care of."

Setting a plate in front of each of them, she continued, "It wasn't hard, and I don't want to sound like I'm complaining. We have servants, and my grandfather taught me how to manage the finances long ago. When I finished school, my mother determined that it was time for me to marry. I have no doubt that she loves my sister and I, and that she wants to see us happy. But the only time she was happy, truly happy, was when my father was alive, because he was the love of her life."

"It's her who wants you to find the love of your life." He opened a bottle of wine and poured them each a glassful.

She took the glass he handed her and took a sip before answering, "I suspect so, but I didn't want that." Now that she'd found that, a man who could be, and in all aspects was, the love of her life, she wished she'd known then what she knew now—that it was impossible to not fall in love with the right person. And how that would never fit into her life.

"Why not?" he asked.

"Because I don't want to become hollow. To live just because I have to. That's when I started saying that I would only marry the love of my life, because I was convinced that I'd never let myself fall in love with anyone. I convinced myself that I'd rather be an old maid, taking care of my family, than being a shell of a person."

"Because you are afraid the love of your life will die, like your father did?"

"Yes. Everyone dies at some point." The melancholy shroud around her was becoming too strong, and she shook her head, tried to shake it off. "I'm sorry, I don't want to put a dark cloud over our picnic."

"You aren't," he said. "You're being honest, and if may, I'd like to be honest, too."

"Of course."

"I can't compare what you've lost. No one can, because everyone's life is different, and I respect your fears. We all have them. I swore I'd never get married because of my uncle Troy. He was like my older brother when I was young. I wanted to be just like him. He wasn't a lawyer. He worked for the family shipping company. On one of his trips, he met a woman in England and married her. I never met her, because on his only trip home after they wed, she was already pregnant and stayed behind. He promised to bring her with him on the next trip, but that never happened."

"Why not?"

"Because when he returned to England, he was accused of murdering her, and has been in prison ever since."

She covered a gasp with one hand, now knowing why no one in his family had ever mentioned his uncle. Not even Audrey.

"He didn't murder her, I'm convinced of that, but he was the one to discover her body and that of their groom, in her bedroom upon arriving home late one night. The authorities determined that she and the groom had been having an affair due to her being lonely because of Troy's long absence at sea, and that he'd murdered them both upon discovering them together."

"I'm so sorry," she whispered. "That's just so awful."

"It was awful," he agreed. "I was fourteen at the time, and decided that I'd never fall in love with a woman, and that I'd become a lawyer, which had already been decided for me so that was no different." He let out a sigh. "I'd wanted to become a lawyer so I could get him out of prison. It wasn't until later that I realized it didn't matter how good a lawyer was, how many laws were put in place, if those laws weren't enforced, even a lawyer's hands are tied."

"That's when you decided to run for office?"

"Yes. The more laws I saw that weren't enforced, the stronger that desire became."

A shiver, not a chilling one, but an intuitive one, coiled around her spine, making her thoughts grow deeper. Unlike her, who had decided she didn't want to change things because of the past, he was focused on changing them.

Other things grew inside her. Pride at how he was set on helping others, and love, because it was truly impossible to not love him even more. "You are going to be the best attorney general ever."

* * *

Lincoln busied himself by unloading the food out of the basket. That's what he always did when he was avoiding something. He worked. Consumed himself with his own goals so he wouldn't have to think about someone else. It had worked for years, until Victoria had stepped off the train, carrying her fingerprint picture. That's what today was supposed to have been about. A way for word to spread that they were courting so Elwood Kelley would leave her alone.

Yet he'd been so enthralled with her all day that he couldn't remember a single other face at the circus. Couldn't remember a single other face than hers. He could understand where her fears originated, why she didn't want to get married. Pain like that was impossible for some to get over. They simply lived because they had to, like she'd described her mother doing.

At the same time, he didn't want Victoria to live like that. Not even for a day. He'd told himself that he'd needed more information to determine what he was going to do, and had wanted today to tell him if he was truly in love with her or not.

Now he knew.

He'd never told anyone about Uncle Troy. Never talked to anyone about why and how he'd set the goals for himself. He'd kept them hidden inside him, because he'd never trusted someone enough to understand. Never loved someone the way he did her.

"I may not be elected," he said.

"Yes, you will." She folded back the cloths covering the bowls of food and used a fork to put slices of ham and cheese on both of their plates. "Have you thought about those newspaper advertisements I suggested?"

He add bread and fruit to their plates. "Yes, I have, but Audrey's too busy to write them now."

"We could write them." She broke off a piece of bread and ate it. "And mail them to all the newspapers throughout the state, by this fall, everyone will know you're the best candidate, and vote for you."

He sliced off a piece of his ham, ate it. "You'll be busy this week, too."

"Not that busy." Pointing to the cloth and food, she said, "This is wonderful. I haven't had a picnic in years."

"There are a lot of newspapers in the state," he said, before asking, "Why haven't you had a picnic in years?"

"Just never thought of one, I guess. We used to have one nearly every Sunday back in Colorado, after church the whole town would have a picnic in the churchyard."

"That must have been fun."

"It was. After eating the children would play and the women would visit while the men played horseshoes. My father loved playing horseshoes. In the winter, we would eat our picnics inside the church, and then play in the snow afterwards. One time, the men helped us, and we built a huge snowman. So tall that I had to stand on my father's shoulders to put on the face and hat." She laughed. "I haven't thought about that in years."

"It sounds fun."

"It was. There was a hill where we'd go sledding, too, but the men had to stand near the bottom, so we wouldn't sled into the trees."

They ate and shared all sorts of childhood memories, things he, too, hadn't thought about in years, until he checked the time on his watch, and knew that William would have returned, ready to give them a ride home.

Regretfully, he told her it was time to leave.

After they returned everything to the picnic basket, she walked over to the edge of the terrace, for another look at the city.

He stepped up beside her, laid a hand on the small of her back.

She twisted, looked at him. “I could stay a few days after the wedding. Until we get the advertisements mailed to all the newspapers.”

Taken aback by the suggestion, he asked, “You could?”

Turning, she scanned the view again, and nodded. “Yes, I could, and I should. You becoming attorney general is possible, more than possible, and I want to help make it happen.”

“I’d like if you could stay longer.” He wasn’t thinking about becoming attorney general, he was thinking about not having to say goodbye to her.

Not yet.

He wasn’t ready for that.

All the information he’d gained today still wasn’t enough. He’d fallen in love with her, but had no idea how to make her fall in love with him. She didn’t want to find the love of her life. He had to find a way to change her mind. For that was what he wanted, far more than he wanted to become attorney general.

Chapter Fourteen

It was late when they returned home, but the household was still awake. When William had dropped them off at the newspaper building, he'd informed Lincoln that he would be picking his father up at the train station and taking him home, before returning for them.

"Ah, Lincoln," his father greeted while rising from his chair as they stepped into the drawing room. "It's good to see you, son, and you, too, Victoria."

Meeting them in the center of the room, his father gave Victoria a hug and a kiss on the cheek, before embracing Lincoln in a hug, which he returned solidly. The trip to Florida was the longest his father had ever been gone.

"I hope you had time to get caught up on all the wedding plans," Lincoln said as they separated. "I figured Audrey would need a couple of hours for that."

"She did, and I'm afraid she's not done." His father shook his head. "Thank you for filling in for me, I knew I could count on you."

"It was my honor," Lincoln replied. "I hope all is well in Florida."

"You and I will discuss that later," his father replied quietly, before saying, "I am glad to hear that you've been thoughtful enough to get Victoria away from all the wedding plans once in a while."

"That, too, was my honor," Lincoln replied.

"Can I get the two of you a drink?" his father asked. "Your mother was going over the list of things that need to be completed this week, and it may take a while longer."

"I'll get the drinks, including one for you," Lincoln offered.

For the next hour or so, while the conversation was consumed with wedding plans, Lincoln's mind wasn't. Images of the day, of Victoria laughing and hiding her face behind his shoulder, of standing on the terrace in the night sky and telling him about building snowmen and sledding down hills, were flashing in his mind. He wanted to relive those moments, and live more moments like them. With her.

He was a collector of evidence, and his gut, his heart, told him that she'd enjoyed the day as much as he had, but feelings and thoughts weren't evidence. How could he know that for sure? She'd offered to stay longer, in order to help him. That wasn't love. She was a very caring person, liked helping others, he'd seen that with the fire victims.

She was so caring that he knew he couldn't tell her how he felt. Not after what she'd told him about why she didn't want to find the love of her life. She'd been hurt by love, so that was the last thing that she wanted. He had to treat this like a case, where he kept some evidence hidden until revealing it would guarantee a win.

What if there was no guaranteed win? Was he willing to risk his goals, his longing to make a difference for the masses, for something that might never happen?

His attention was brought back to the room by movement, and he rose, bade good-night to the women.

"I was glad to see that I wasn't the only one whose eyes glazed over during all that," his father said.

His astuteness is what made Walter Dryer one of the best-known lawyers in the state, and Lincoln wasn't surprised that his father had caught his inattentiveness. Sitting back down, Lincoln rested an ankle upon his opposite knee. "I always assumed a wedding was little more than two people and a preacher showing up at the same time."

His father laughed. "To a man, but to a woman, it's much, much more."

Lincoln wondered if it would be that way for Victoria. He doubted it. From her clothing to her thoughts and actions, she wasn't like other women. Those were only a few things that made her so appealing.

"I lied to you."

Lincoln looked at his father. "Excuse me?"

His father leaned back in his chair. "I lied to you. I haven't been in Florida this entire time. Your mother knew, but she and I were the only two, besides your uncles John and Frank, and decided that no one should know the truth. There were too many variables in the outcome, and with the wedding so close, we didn't need the gossip if word got out."

"If you weren't in Florida, where have you been?"

"England. Your uncle Troy was exonerated."

Shock had Lincoln sitting up straighter. "How? What happened? Where is he?" A flash of fear struck. "Is he—"

"He's alive, and well, and in Florida. He'll be staying at the summer beach cottage for a week, then will travel up here, after the wedding, when things have calmed down." His father shook his head. "Like you, I never believed he was guilty, capable of murder. Neither did John or Frank. Of us four boys, Troy had the softest heart. I remember once when he was little, and John, being a couple years older, punched him. Mother told Troy to punch him back, but Troy shook his head and said that he couldn't, because he loved John too much to punch him."

Lincoln rubbed at the smile that formed. He could see Troy saying that. All three of his uncles were good men, but Troy had been special to him. "I can't believe it. That he's free. What happened?"

"I've had English lawyers working on his case for years, searching for the smallest bit of evidence, and we finally got it."

"What was it?"

"Fingerprints."

"Fingerprints?" Lincoln asked, with his gaze quickly flying to a picture on the wall. Not Victoria's picture. Just a picture, but he was thinking about hers.

"Yes, fingerprints. The English have been using them for a while to solve cases, and I believe, before long, the entire world will be, too."

Lincoln listened with great interest as his father explained how another man had been a suspect in the murders, because he was a known thief who had broken into other homes during that time, but it could never be proven, until the man had been arrested on another charge. Then a magistrate agreed to listen to one of the lawyers. Upon hearing that news, his father had sailed to England to help at the trial.

"As impossible as it seems," his father continued, "the constable still had the murder weapon. A knife he'd retrieved from the scene and kept in his desk because he too didn't believe it had been Troy. The only two sets of fingerprints on that knife were the constable's and the thief's.

The thief broke down on the witness stand and confessed after the prints matched his. He'd broken into the house through Willamette's bedroom window, looking to steal jewelry. The groom had seen him, hurried into the house and up to Willamette's bedroom. The thief killed them both, then jumped back out the window, and admitted to seeing Troy riding up the street."

"Had Troy seen him?" Lincoln asked, wondering if that could have allowed this case to have been solved years ago.

"No, he'd been too focused on getting home, on seeing Willamette, to notice anyone. It was such a sad event, tragic, but I'm glad truth won out."

"The impossible, possible," Lincoln said, his thoughts going back to Victoria.

"Yes. Troy doesn't want gossip, because his return is sure to create some, to overshadow Audrey's wedding, so I won't tell anyone else, but once the wedding is over, he'll be home. Living just up the road from us."

"It'll be good to see him," Lincoln said, nodding to himself at one more thing that he'd been wrong about all these years. Not his uncle's innocence, but in how he'd thought marriage had ruined Troy's life. "Very good to see him."

With all that had been on her mind, Victoria had expected to be kept awake by wandering thoughts all night, but hadn't been. She'd slept so soundly that she woke up late. That was evident by only Audery and Roseanne sitting at the breakfast table when she entered the dining room.

She hid her disappointment at seeing Lincoln's chair empty and allowed herself to be drawn into the list of the day's appointments. Final dress fittings and alterations this morning, a trip to the florist's greenhouses this afternoon to choose flowers, and then an evening dinner at the Palace Hotel, where the wedding reception would be held on Saturday, after the wedding services at the church. Dinner would include both Audrey's and Jake's families now that Walter and two of his brothers were back in New York.

Victoria couldn't help but think of the fourth brother. Troy. The one no one spoke about. What had happened to him was so sad, and it seemed unfair that his family, except for Lincoln, had forgotten all about him. It didn't seem right, either, and she wondered if there was something that could be done about that.

She had met Audrey's other uncles, John, who lived up the road, and Frank, who lived down in Florida. Both of the uncles oversaw divisions of their shipping company, and were married with grown children, who would also be in attendance, as well as a number of grandchildren.

There had been a large number of children at the circus yesterday, carrying colorful balloons tied on sticks. She'd felt a tightening in her chest, knowing that as an old maid, she'd never know the sound of a house filled with children. Not her children.

It couldn't be helped, though. She was now completely certain that she didn't want to act upon the fact that she'd fallen in love with Lincoln. That had happened. There was no denying it, and that meant it was more important than ever for her to not give in to that love. If something were to ever happen to him, she would be worse than her mother. Worse than being hollow. She'd be dead inside.

However, even knowing that, she had decided that she would remain in New York long enough to help him with his advertisements. She wanted him to become attorney general, to help as many people as possible. When she did go home, she could be happy, knowing that she'd helped him make his dream come true, and that would be enough. It would have to be enough.

The fittings and alterations lasted all morning, and the flowers took up the afternoon, and neither did much to get her mind off Lincoln. It seemed that nothing could do that, and the skipping of beats that her heart did when she entered her bedroom to put away her purse and saw Lincoln sitting in the chair near the window completely stole her breath.

"Sorry to invade your privacy," he said, "but I need to talk to you."

Her hand had flown to her chest, and could still feel the rapid beat of her heart. "All right," she said breathlessly.

He had stood up and was also holding her paper-wrapped picture in his hand. "Let's go to my study."

"Has something happened?" she asked.

"Yes," he said.

She dropped her purse, not caring that it landed on the floor, and followed him out the door. His study was on the same floor, but on the other side of the large house, past the water closet and the main stairway.

Inside the room, she immediately asked, "What happened?"

He closed the door. "Someone tried to set Webster's Department Store on fire early this morning."

"Oh, no!" She followed him to the table, where he set down her picture, on the same table she had weeks ago. "Was anyone hurt?"

"One of his night watchmen ended up with some burns while putting out the fire," Lincoln replied. "The whole place would have gone up in flames if they hadn't been there. Webster hired additional watchmen recently, fearing something like this might happen."

"How did the fire start?"

"Alcohol bombs." He pointed to his desk, where a bottle sat with a charred rag sticking out of it. "That one hadn't broken when they threw it through the window and the watchman put it out."

"It didn't break when it hit the window?"

"The thugs broke the window out with rocks first, then threw in the alcohol bombs." He was carefully unwrapping her picture. "The watchmen heard the glass breaking, and ran to the area, saw two men toss in the bombs." He set aside the paper and turned, looked at her with a serious gaze. "One was Elwood."

An icy chill encased her. "Did they catch him?"

"No, the watchmen were too busy putting out the fires, but the one identified Elwood. He also works as a salesman, and was there on Saturday. Recognized Elwood as the man who followed you and Audrey, and said hello to you. He told the police, and they are looking for Elwood, to bring him in for questioning."

Filled with fright, she couldn't think of anything to say, or do anything except tremble.

"Come here," Lincoln said, wrapping his arms around her and pulling her close. "You're safe here. I won't let anyone hurt you."

She laid her head against his chest. The warmth and comfort of his arms made her feel more than safe, but her safety had never been her concern. "I know I'm safe, but others aren't, and that's my fault."

"None of this is your fault. Elwood was corrupt long before now."

"I should have known he was following us. I didn't think—"

"Stop," Lincoln said, leaning back to look at her. "It's not your fault. I told you that because I believe we have his fingerprints on the alcohol bomb. If we can get him arrested on an arson charge, I'll be able to bring up other charges, including your stolen property."

"I don't care about that anymore, I just want to see him arrested."

"The more charges, the more likely he'll be kept behind bars, which is where he belongs." He kissed her forehead, then released her. "I'm going to get a magnifying glass from my desk."

"Will that work?" she asked. "The article that I read said that they use a special powder to make the fingerprints visible, so the design could be seen by the jury."

"We'll see. I mainly want to examine the prints on your picture, so I know what to look for on the bottle. I used a cloth to pick it up this morning, and hope that no one else had touched it before then. The night watchmen said they hadn't, and I know the police didn't touch it."

She carefully lifted the thin protective board off the picture. "How did you hear about the fire?"

"John Webster called me early this morning, right after the watchmen called him. I went down there, was there and at the police station most of the morning. Then went to my office to draw up charges." He arrived at her side with a magnifying glass. "I was beginning to wonder if you were ever going to come home."

"We were picking out flowers, but you could have just looked at the picture. You didn't need to wait for me."

"Yes, I did," he said, touching the tip of her nose. "I like having your help." He leaned down and held the magnifying glass over the picture. "Point out exactly where they are."

She pointed to the prints, and took a turn at looking through them with the magnifying glass. "You can see every swirl."

"I know. Let's check the bottle, now."

They walked to the desk, and Lincoln knelt down to examine the bottle.

"Tell me if you want me to turn it," she said. "I'll use the cloth and only touch the very top."

"Thanks, but I've already found them. I can't say they are identical, but they look the same to me. Kneel down here and take a look for yourself."

She peered through the glass and was shocked and elated at the same time. "They do look similar. Very similar."

"I think so, too."

She stood. "Why were you at the police station?"

He grinned. "Convincing them that Europe is using fingerprinting, and they should, too."

"You did believe me."

"Yes, I believed you." He set the magnifying glass on the desk and took a hold of her hands. "I've always believed you. It was the fact that a set of prints wasn't enough proof to have Elwood arrested, not when you hadn't filed a police report."

"I didn't dare."

"I know." He tugged her a bit closer. "Fingerprints just had my uncle Troy exonerated."

"What?"

"It won't be known until after the wedding, but the real killer was found, and convicted because of fingerprints still on the knife, all these years later."

He went on to tell her the entire story, and her heart rejoiced for him and his family. She wrapped her arms around his waist and hugged him tightly. "That's such wonderful news."

"It is, and it's also great that we have an eyewitness identifying Elwood. If they find him, and if they fingerprint him, as they said they would, upon arrest, and if those prints match this bottle, it'll be enough to keep him in jail until his court date. If the judge agrees to no bail. That will be the next obstacle. Getting a judge who isn't already bought off by Alderman Kelley."

"Sounds like a lot of ifs," she said.

"There always are." He rubbed her back with both hands. "There are ifs in everything."

"Like what?"

"Like what would you say *if* I said I want to kiss you."

Happiness exploded inside her and she stretched onto her toes, so their lips were mere inches apart. "*If* you said that, I'd say yes."

"You would?"

She nodded.

The moment his lips met hers, she wondered *if* she truly could be content to become an old maid. He made her entire body come alive. She'd never felt so many things all at once, or in so many places.

Lincoln had always enjoyed his family. And Jake's for that matter. They were good, fun people, but he'd be lying to himself if he didn't admit that he'd much rather be having a simple picnic with Victoria than sitting at the hotel, eating the five-course dinner that was stretching the meal into hours. She was at the table too, but clear down at the other end, on the same side as him, so he couldn't even catch a glimpse of her. His mother was slacking in her matchmaking. She'd insisted all the women sit together so they could discuss wedding plans.

How many times could the same subject be discussed?

He also wondered how many times a man could kiss a woman before the thrill wore off. Before the desire to repeat it eased. That certainly wasn't happening. The more times he kissed Victoria, the more he wanted.

Some flavor of dessert was put in front of him, and he took two bites before setting his fork down. "Excuse me," he said to those sitting next to him. "But I have a need to stretch my legs."

It was as if he'd just given permission, because nearly every other man at the table set down their forks and pushed their chairs back, while verbally agreeing with him. They were in a private dining room, and clusters soon formed of those who hadn't been able to converse with each other while seated at the long table.

Jake was beside him, and said, "That was the longest meal of my life."

Lincoln nodded. "You can say that again."

"The pomp and circumstance of the wedding is for the bride," Jake's uncle Roy said. "The wedding night is for the groom."

Others chuckled, and slapped Jake on the back, ribbing him with more wedding banter, before the subject changed to the new horse track, the stock market, and other subjects that men preferred. Lincoln joined in, offered his opinions now and again, but was more focused on glancing towards the tables where the women still sat. Mere seconds had passed between two glances when he noticed Victoria's chair empty. He stepped sideways, to see around the cluster of men surrounding him, and his heartbeat kicked up a notch as he saw her walking towards him.

He didn't bother to excuse himself, just left the group, meeting her halfway from the table. "Is something amiss?"

Her expression was dull as she leaned closer and whispered, "I'll deny ever saying this, but I'll be so happy when I don't have to comment about dresses, shoes, flowers, gifts, guest lists, food, cake, vows—" She sucked in a breath. "The list just goes on and on."

"Your secret is safe with me," he replied.

"Thank you," she said, sounding as if he'd just saved her from a truly dastardly deed.

"Do you want to take a walk?"

"I would, but..." She glanced around the room. "Think we can sneak out without being noticed?"

He laid a hand on her back to steer her about. "I truly don't care if we are noticed."

That became Lincoln's mantra the rest of the week, because it was true. He didn't care what others thought. Other than Victoria. They formed a silent communication. All one or the other had to do was catch the other's eye, and the other would find an excuse for them to take leave together, right up to the wedding day.

It was a grand affair, synonymous with prestige, status, and old money that would be talked about for years to come, which had been his mother's goal. He was happy that she'd got what she wanted, and that Audrey and Jake got what they'd wanted. There was one thing that he'd got, that he had wanted—to meet Victoria's family.

Her mother was personable and pretty, yet quiet, almost like a piece of fine china that everyone was afraid to touch because she might break. Her younger sister, Eva, was also quiet, but in a shy way, like she didn't know exactly where to step, but her grandfather made up for the quietness of the other two. Emmet Biggs was the kind of man that dime novels had been written about. He spoke his mind whether it was what others wanted to hear or not, yet did so in such a way that no one was offended, but rather befriended, and left wanting to hear more. To know more about this gruff old man and his adventures.

Lincoln could instantly tell that was where Victoria had gotten her spirit, and her diplomacy, along with her caring nature. Her grandfather adored her, and her sister, as well as their mother. That was clear by the way he looked at them, and spoke of them. It was also why Victoria was so devoted to them.

That hadn't slipped past Emmet, though. He'd made a point of telling Lincoln that Victoria being in New York the past month was the best thing that could've happened to her, and her mother. "It's the only way Ramona will ever break out of her shell," Emmet said. "She was always delicate, but sadness turned her into a turtle who barely sticks its head out. I respect her pain, but it's not right the way she became the child and Victoria became the mother. Victoria needs to have her own life. That's why I sold out, moved us all back here. I was afraid I'd been wrong, until tonight. Victoria has a shine in her eyes, a light in her soul." Leaning closer, he whispered, "And you, young man, are what put it there."

"We have become good friends while she's been here this time," Lincoln admitted.

"Good friends, my ass," Emmet said. "You're in love with the girl, and she's in love with you."

Lincoln opened his mouth, but a denial wouldn't emit.

"You can't fool an old man, and a good lawyer can't lie, that's who's sitting right here, now, isn't it? An old man and a good lawyer."

Lincoln nodded. "Yes, sir."

"She's afraid," Emmet said. "Afraid of love, because she lost a lot at a young age. I always knew it would take a good man in order for her to find it. So did Ramona, and that's why she paraded a gaggle of men before Victoria, like she was the golden goose, but Victoria wasn't looking for a gander, do you want to know why?"

"Yes," Lincoln answered.

"Because Victoria's a swan."

Lincoln grinned. "You're right about that."

"She's afraid to risk losing anything again, even a hairpin," Emmet said. "It's up to you to show her loving someone isn't a risk, it's a refuge. That she won't be losing anything, while gaining everything."

"Do you have a suggestion as to how I can do that?" Lincoln asked, hoping he'd finally found someone who could answer that.

"You know."

"No, I don't believe I do."

"I believe you do." Emmet touched his hand. "Ambition isn't created, nor is it destroyed, it just changes form. Whether it's family, career, or business, it's there, and it will manifest."

"Make the impossibe, possible," Lincoln said, merely remembering conversations with Victoria.

"See, I knew you knew," Emmet said. "Now go, I've taken up enough of your time, ask her to dance."

Lincoln still didn't know. The old man made sense, yet hadn't provided any answers, and Lincoln knew he wasn't going to get any. "I will, and I thank you for our conversation."

Chapter Fifteen

Victoria felt as if she was traipsing across a rickety bridge, where the ropes could break at any time and she'd plunge into a dark abyss below. For the last month she and Lincoln had fooled the upper crust of Manhattan into believing they were courting, yet tonight, at the wedding of the year and the very reason for their plan, she suspected that she should be doing the exact opposite. Her family was the reason. They had arrived shortly before the ceremony. Having them in attendance at the wedding hadn't caused her any concern. She'd truly been excited to see them, for she had missed them, but the reception, where there was dancing, was a completely different game.

She hated the feeling inside her, almost as if she had to choose between Lincoln and her family. Hated it because she knew, if given the choice, which one she'd choose. Her mother, her sister, her grandfather, they needed her, but she wanted Lincoln.

Touching him, and him touching her, with their gazes locked, as they waltzed across the dance floor, she felt higher than when she'd been on the terrace of the tallest building in New York. While in his arms, she was on top of the world, where nothing was impossible.

But as soon as the music ended, it was as if she was

dropped back down to earth, where the impossible wasn't possible, not for her, because she didn't have a choice.

Although her grandfather had suggested they stay at the hotel, Roseanne wouldn't hear of such a thing, not when they had so many spare rooms at their home. William had delivered their luggage to the house upon picking them up at the train station, and though it was only for one night, it made Victoria even more nervous.

She had to find a way to tell them that she was staying in the city a while longer. Both to help Lincoln with his advertisements and the case against Elwood, who as of yet hadn't been arrested. There was also the fact that she couldn't tell them about either reason, not with her grandfather's dislike of politicians and no one but Lincoln knowing about the money theft.

All in all, by the time they arrived at the Dryer home following the reception, she had a pit in her stomach the size of a horseshoe.

Lincoln kept looking at her, and she knew all she had to do was give him the slightest signal, and he'd come to her rescue, make up an excuse that would result in the two of them taking a walk together, and sharing a kiss or two. That had happened several times during the past week, and she knew it was yet another sign that she was breaking the rule she'd set for herself.

The rule of not letting her love for him grow any deeper. She'd been given a role in life that she had to fulfill.

She didn't give Lincoln a sign, but instead escorted her mother and sister upstairs to the rooms they'd use for the night, and saw that they were both settled in, before she made her way along the long hall, past Lincoln's study, to the room her grandfather would be using.

He was already wearing his blue-and-white-striped nightgown, and in the bed, albeit propped up by a stack of pillows and wearing his wire-framed glasses to read the newspaper.

"I just wanted to see if you had everything you needed," she said, "and to say good-night."

He set the newspaper on his lap and patted the bed beside him. "Sit down a spell. We barely had a chance to say hello today."

She sat down and patted his knees that were under the covers. "I know, and I'm sorry. It was a busy day. The entire month was busy, and made me not want to ever plan a wedding."

"You don't say?"

"I do say. It was never-ending, and quite costly."

"I have enough money to pay for several costly weddings," he said.

"I know you do, but some things just seemed overly frivolous."

He chuckled. "You get that from your grandmother. That woman was a penny-pincher. I swear, she could pinch one penny into two." He lifted his gray brows. "That's probably the reason we ended up with millions."

She'd always liked the way he talked about Grandma in fun, happy ways.

"Speaking of money," he said. "Are you ever going to tell me about the money missing from my safe?"

The pit the size of a horseshoe in her stomach shot up and landed in her throat, leaving her incapable of speaking for a few moments. Yet she finally managed to admit, "I should have known you'd notice it."

He nodded. "And the picture."

The pictures in the room had been close, but not identical. "I should have put hinges on the one I replaced it with," she said, "but there wasn't time." She huffed out a sigh. "Why did you open it in front of him? You'd never done anything like that before. He watched you and got the combination."

"No, he didn't. I left it unlocked. I'd done it to others. Tested them, seen if they'd steal anything."

Flabbergasted, she opened her mouth, but no words would come out.

"He was the first one who took anything." A sneer formed as he added, "Figures, being a politician's son."

Victoria pressed her fingers to both temples, where a headache was sure to form soon. "How many other times did you do that?"

"A few." He reached out and took a hold of her hand. "I know ten thousand is a lot of money to a lot of people, even to us, but you are worth a whole lot more than that. The way your mother was inviting men over like she was collecting stamps had to stop, and I knew a theft would do it. She's not addled, she was just doing what she thought a mother should do, find you a husband."

"I didn't want one," Victoria said.

"I know you didn't, honey, because you've got a powerful will. You get something in your head and you just won't let it go, but there is a life out there for you. A wonderful life, that can include marriage and children." He squeezed her hand. "Just not to one who stole money. That one was a shyster, and sly, he didn't take it all so that when questioned, he could say, *why would I only take ten thousand if they're claiming there was fifty thousand in the safe?* Trying to make us look like the fools, that's what he figured. I guarantee it. He'll get his due, his kind always do."

She huffed out a breath, and knew she had to tell him the truth. It took time, but she explained about the fingerprints, about asking Lincoln to help her, about Mr. Webster being forced to sell, and who had bought Blackwells, and about the fire, the alcohol bombs, and how the police were looking for Elwood.

Her grandfather's laughter as she finished her explanation surprised her.

"It sounds like you've had quite an adventure," he said. "Tell me more."

She did. She told him about the circus, the fire, bicycles, Ronald's inventions, and the terrace on the newspaper building, and then she told him that she was going to stay longer, at least a week.

"Good for you," was his response to that. "I'd be packing my bags and moving down here full-time if I was you."

"I could never do that," she said.

"Why not?"

"Because of you, and Mother and Eva. She still has two more years of schooling, and Mother, you know how much she depends on me, and you. I love you."

"I love you, too, darling, but what about Lincoln?"

Her nerves kicked in and she fought to not let any emotion show. "What about him?"

"What if he doesn't catch Elwood in a week, or even a month?"

She shrugged. "Then I guess I come home, and forget about it. I know it's a lot of money, and I'm sorry—"

"Darling girl," he said, interrupting her. "I could lose all my money, and I'd still be a rich man. I have been since the moment I met your grandmother. Money made me wealthy, but she made me rich, along with you, and your sister, and your mother. Love is what makes a man rich. With the love of a woman, a man can reach for the stars, grab them, collect them. Mark my words, behind every successful man is a loving woman."

Victoria wasn't sure if he was saying she needed to stay long and help Lincoln catch Elwood, or something else. Did he know she'd fallen in love with Lincoln, just as he'd known about the stolen money?

She didn't have a chance to ask.

"Well, now, I best be getting some sleep," he said, while he pulled off his glasses and set them on the table beside the bed. "You, too, my darling girl." He kissed his fingertips and blew the kiss at her, then snuggled down under the covers. "I'll see you in the morning."

She turned out the light and left the room, relieved that she'd told him about the money, but confused by what he'd said, or hadn't said. She still wasn't quite sure about that.

She wasn't quite sure what happened the following morning, either, but somehow her grandfather made it sound like she was staying an extra week, or more, to have Lincoln help her take care of some family business, and everyone was excited about that. Didn't even question it.

Other than Lincoln, who with one look knew that she'd told her grandfather about Elwood. He wasn't upset, either. After her family had departed and a quick visit with Audrey when she and Jake stopped by to pick up her luggage for their honeymoon, Victoria showed Lincoln the list that Jake had created for them.

"It's all the newspapers in the state, along with their addresses and phone numbers. I will call each of them, ask their advertising rates and mail them a copy of the ad, along with payment."

"Jumping right into work, are we?" Lincoln asked.

They were in his study, and for the first time in weeks, she felt nervous. Their pretend courtship was over and she didn't know what that meant. Walking to the desk, she said, "That's why I'm here."

"Your family are really good people."

"Thank you. It was good to see them."

"Your grandfather is quite the character. He didn't seem to be ailing to me."

"We all try to make sure his heart spells are few and far between." She sat down at the desk. "I was thinking the advertisements should be short, and eye-catching."

He leaned over the desk. "I was thinking we should go for a bicycle ride. Jake and Audrey's bicycles are still here."

She looked up at him, at his face that was so handsome, his smile that was so charming, and wondered how long it would be before he destroyed her will. Destroyed the only piece of her old self that she had left. And what she'd do then.

Lincoln stood in the jewelry store, staring at the rings, wondering if he should pick one out, or let Victoria pick out her own. He had no idea which would be more appropriate, nor did he have any idea about diamond rings.

Nor did he know if that was what Victoria wanted. The past few days had been wonderful. She had come to work with him, used the empty office next to his to call the newspapers and mail off the advertisements. She was excited about them, and he'd decided that even if he didn't decide to run for office, it wouldn't hurt for people to be educated on their rights.

Emmet Biggs had been right about ambition changing forms. It was still there inside him, but had shifted to a different goal. That of marriage and family. To her. With her.

A giggle sounded, and he turned, looked towards the door, where two young women entered the store dressed in ruffles and bows, with clusters of feathers and flowers adorning their hats.

"Is there a ring you'd like to examine?" the jeweler asked.

The giggles still emitting from the socialites reminded Lincoln of the Christie ball, the night he and Victoria had struck their deal. She hadn't faltered on their deal. He had. And there was no way of knowing that he wouldn't change his mind again.

That was a lie. He wouldn't change his mind. But if he bought her a ring, and she didn't want it, would that push her away? Ruin everything? She'd said she didn't want to find the love of her life, and though she returned his kisses, she hadn't said she'd changed her mind about that. About anything. He couldn't force her into wanting something that she didn't want, no matter how badly he wanted it.

Shaking his head, he looked at the jeweler. "My apologies, I just remembered an appointment, I'll return another day."

"Very well, Mr. Dryer. Have a good day."

"You, too."

The girls giggled again as he nodded towards them on his way to the door.

How the hell was he supposed to make the impossible,

possible? There was no guarantee that the impossible he wanted was what she wanted.

Impulse control. He'd once claimed others needed to find some when it came to marriage, and now was his time to heed his own advice. He'd give it a few more days, find a way to discover what she wanted.

Furthermore, he did have an appointment. He'd been on his way to see John Webster when the jewelry store had caught his eye.

Maneuvering around and through the never-ending traffic, he made his way across the street and into Webster's store. The windows had been replaced and it was as full of customers as ever. He took the elevator up to the top floor, and nearly ran straight into John as soon as he stepped out of the elevator.

"I just called your office," John said.

"I said I'd drop these papers off to you," Lincoln said, pulling the papers out of his pocket that held the court date for the will. "I just picked them up at the courthouse."

"The police just called," John said. "They've arrested Elwood."

Shocked and elated at the same time, he said, "Let's go. I want my own copy of his fingerprints."

"Will they give them to you?" John asked as they hurried into the elevator.

"There's no law saying they can't." There weren't any laws pertaining to fingerprints as of yet. There would be soon, he had no doubt on that.

The fingerprints were a match and the court date was set, and all hell broke loose at city hall. Alderman Kelley was demanding the mayor have Elwood released, and the mayor was demanding that the police chief find a way to make it happen, and Lincoln was there citing laws that had to be upheld despite Elwood being the alderman's son. The place was also swarming with reporters, jotting down every shouted word, and snapping pictures.

Amongst the chaos, Lincoln found a phone and called home, to tell Victoria that Elwood had been arrested, and what was happening. It was exhilarating to share it with her, to share everything with her. "I'll be home soon, and tell you all about it," he said before hanging up.

He wasn't home soon, because the chaos got even stronger. Word had spread about the arrest of Elwood, and shopkeepers, business owners, and factory managers soon arrived, wanting to file charges, not only against Elwood, but against the alderman for misdeeds done to their businesses. There was even a mob boss trying to file charges, claiming that the alderman was trying to take over his territory.

The whole thing came to a stop when Alderman Kelley, who had been shouting, red-faced and pounding on the counter, suddenly collapsed. An ambulance wagon arrived and though the alderman was awake and talking, they quickly whisked him off to a hospital. Not even that stopped the people from demanding their charges be filed. It just all became more civilized without the alderman barking orders. People also wanted legal advice, and Lincoln was obliged to answer their questions. The time for the alderman to face his misdeeds was past coming.

Therefore, it was late, well beyond dinnertime when Lincoln arrived home. The adrenaline was still racing through him when he entered the house, and he picked Victoria off her feet, hugged her tight and kissed her right in the middle of the drawing room, in front of both of his parents. Then, keeping an arm around her until she was seated back in her chair, he told them about how the mayor had stepped down and turned state's evident against the alderman. The chief of police hadn't been far behind the mayor.

Lincoln proclaimed this was going to be the case of the century.

"We'll put every lawyer we have on it," his father said. "Once this hits the papers, we'll have clients coming out of the woodwork."

"It'll be the news story of the century, too," Lincoln said. "Jake's going to be disappointed that he's out of town."

"He'll have time to make up for that," his father replied. "This isn't going anywhere anytime soon."

He and his father continued talking about possible charges and cases, that could go back years, ever since Alderman Kelley had first been elected, long after his mother and Victoria had left the room to retire.

When he finally made his way up to his room, he considered walking down the hall, to her room, but didn't, due to the hour, she'd probably be asleep. He wouldn't fall to sleep anytime soon. A case that would bring down the corrupt ways of Alderman Kelley had been a dream of his, but he'd truly never thought it possible.

The impossible, possible.

Awake early, excited to get started on the case of the century, Lincoln made his way down the hallway towards Victoria's room. She may not be up yet, but he wanted to tell her that he was going into the office early.

Surprised to see her door was open, he increased his speed, but skidded to a stop when he encountered William and Curtis carrying out a trunk. "What are you doing?" Lincoln asked.

"Miss Biggs is returning to Tarrytown today, sir," Curtis replied, with a glance over his shoulder.

Lincoln had to wait until they were out of the way before he could see into, and then enter the room. Victoria was buttoning her waist jacket, the same blue one that she'd worn to the circus.

An inability to say anything other than one thought overcame him. "You aren't returning home today."

"Yes, I am. The last of the advertisements were mailed out the day before yesterday, and Elwood was arrested yesterday. There's no reason for me to stay."

"Yes, there is." His thoughts were returning by the dozens and he wanted to say he was a reason, but stopped himself.

She picked her hat off the bed and walked to the mirror. "It's what we agreed upon."

"There's still more that needs to be done. You'll need to testify at Elwood's trial."

"That could be weeks from now, or longer." She used two pins, one on each side of the hat, to keep it in place. "By then, you'll have so many other charges, mine won't matter."

"Yes, they will." He crossed the room, and grasped her shoulders to turn her about. "You're the reason the case got started. Your fingerprints."

"They aren't my fingerprints, they are Elwood's."

"I know that, but it's because of you that we found his fingerprints on the glass bottle. No one would have thought of doing that. You're the one who knew about that."

"Not the only one, your uncle Troy was exonerated because of fingerprints."

"In England, not here." Frustration was growing inside him. "The fingerprints don't matter. The case doesn't matter. I don't want you to go."

"I have to, Lincoln."

"Why?" Worry formed. "Is something wrong with your family? Your grandfather?"

"No." She wiggled from his hold and walked to the bed, picked up her purse. "Our agreement has ended. It's time for us to part as friends."

"Friends?"

She nodded.

"We aren't just friends, Victoria, and you know it."

Shaking her head, she closed her eyes and pinched her lips together. "Please don't make this harder than it needs to be, Lincoln."

He took a hold of her hand. "It doesn't need to be hard at all. You don't have to leave."

"Yes, I do." She opened her eyes, where tears welled. "Because I can't stay. I can't do this."

"This?" he asked, although knew what she was referring to. "You mean what we feel for each other?"

"Yes." She covered her mouth with a hand for a moment, then shaking her head, she continued, "Last night, when you didn't come home, after I'd heard all the commotion in the background, I was afraid that you wouldn't come home, and I can't do that."

He pulled her close and wrapped his arms around her. "I'm sorry, I didn't mean to worry you. It won't happen again."

"Yes, it will." She pushed away from his chest. "You won't be able to help it, and I know that. I even understand it. Your dedication and ambition are all so admirable. I'm proud of how committed you are to helping others, and you'll be just as committed to being the attorney general. But I also know myself and I can't take the chance of losing someone I love again. I just can't." She rested a hand on his cheek. "Please, let's just part as friends. Friends who have wonderful memories of the time they had together."

A dozen arguments came to mind, but the tears slipping from her eyes made his throat thick.

"Please don't hate me," she whispered.

"I'll never hate you." He might hate himself, but he would forever love her. Love her so much that he couldn't force her to stay. Couldn't make her live a life that she didn't want. Planting a soft kiss on her forehead, he said, "I'll see you to the train station."

"There's no need for that."

"Yes, there is. It wouldn't be proper."

The ride to the station was the longest one of Victoria's life. Her heart was breaking in two and telling herself that it was only temporary, that this was the only way she could protect herself from living with a broken heart the rest of her life, wasn't doing any good.

She'd known it was going to be hard. Very hard. She loved him. Very much. This handsome, strong, dedicated, honorable man. Giving in to that love would be easy, but she couldn't do that, because it would be opening herself up to a life of always being afraid. He was full of his ambitions and goals and dreams. She wanted him to fulfill all of them, and knew if she stayed, she'd only be in his way.

The carriage stopped, and he helped her down.

"I'll see to your luggage, Miss Biggs," William said.

"Thank you, William, for everything."

With his hand on the small of her back, Lincoln escorted her to the depot door, then stopped. "Would you be opposed to me calling on you?"

She drew in a deep breath, pulled up her last bits of willpower. "I would prefer that you didn't." Wrapping her hand around his fingers, she gave his hand a squeeze. "I don't want you to change, Lincoln. I want all of your dreams to come true, and that won't happen if you're worried about me."

"You could go with me, then you'd never have to worry about—"

"Don't, Lincoln," she said. "We both know that wouldn't be possible. You don't need the pressure or the responsibility of someone else's fear, or happiness. No one does. It would become nothing but a burden. I know that, because that is my life, and I wouldn't wish it on anyone else. Especially not you."

"I don't want that for you, either."

She stretched up on her toes and kissed his lips, softly, quickly. "It's not your choice. Goodbye, Lincoln."

Forcing herself to not look back, she walked into the depot, then to the train heading north, to Tarrytown. Her footsteps echoed off the floor, and they echoed inside her heart. Some people would consider her foolish or selfish for the decision she'd made.

They would be right. She wasn't too stubborn to admit that. Nor could she deny that it was a decision she'd have to live with for the rest of her life.

What others wouldn't understand was that she had to be selfish when it came to Lincoln. She had to hold on to what they'd had to protect herself from ever giving in to the longing of having more. What if they had children, a family? What she felt for him was already overwhelming, but then she'd have more people to be terrified of losing.

Not one to succumb to tears, she blinked them away, and climbed aboard the train, took her seat, waited for it to start rolling. She was returning a different person than when she'd left. Stronger in some ways, weaker in others. That was to be expected when she was leaving part of herself behind.

Arnold, her family's driver, was at the station when she arrived in Tarrytown, and when he asked how her trip was, she told him it had been wonderful. For it had. In so many ways.

Chapter Sixteen

There was no great fanfare when Victoria arrived home, nor had she expected any. After sharing a loving embrace with her mother and a peck on the cheek with her grandfather, she excused herself to change her clothes.

She chose a gown that hadn't gone to Manhattan with her. One that had no memories whatsoever, and then she went to the ground floor library, to go over the household finances, expenditures that had occurred in her absence.

The loss of ten thousand dollars also needed to be recorded, and though it had caused no significant issue to their wealth, it still irked her. She hated losing anything.

"How'd we fare during your absence?" her grandfather asked as he walked in the room.

She closed the ledger and replace it in the bottom drawer of the desk. "Fine, everything is in perfect order."

"Did you expect differently?"

"No."

"Good, you shouldn't." He sat down in his favorite chair and hoisted his feet onto a matching footstool. They were both covered in a green velvet that was starting to show wear. "Read about Elwood getting arrested in the *Daily Beacon* this morning. Read about Lincoln, too. Sounds like it was quite the tussle. Been a long time since I was involved in a good old argument, when men lose their tempers, would have been fun to see."

"I'm just thankful no one was hurt," she replied. "That can happen when men lose their tempers."

"It can. I also read that the alderman is going to be fine. Didn't give himself a heart attack or stroke. Just fainted."

His disappointment was clear in his tone. "We shouldn't wish ill will upon anyone," she said.

"Don't need to, he'll get what's coming to him." He pointed towards the door. "The paper is in the parlor if you want to read it."

"No, thank you, but I do need to let you know that I left the picture in New York, for Lincoln to use in the case against Elwood. I will purchase a new one to replace it."

"No need. I already did that."

Still finding it hard to believe what he'd done, she asked, "Did Elwood ask you to put a watch in the safe that day?"

"Yes, I knew right then that he must have heard that I'd left the safe unlocked when other suitors were here." He frowned. "Is that something Lincoln should know for the case?"

"I don't believe so, but I do request that you refrain from doing it again." She pointed a finger at him. "That was a very dangerous game you were playing."

"I know that, and it's why we have two butlers, not one."

"Neither of them stopped Elwood," she pointed out.

"Because I told Bart not to." He planted both hands behind his head and held his arm akimbo as he leaned back. "So, how long are you home for?"

Not wanting to get into any explanations, she stood. "For good."

"Ignoring something doesn't make it go away," he said.

She walked to the door. "I'm not ignoring anything."

"You're ignoring me."

"I'm talking to you."

"And making a fast exit."

She refused to comment on that, because it was the truth, and walked out the door.

"If you never lose," he said in her wake, "you don't know what it feels like to win."

She kept walking, because she did know what it felt like to lose.

Lincoln slid the paper Ronald had signed into the envelope, while ignoring the pinch of his heart. It was just a little pinch. He'd felt much stronger ones when it came to thoughts of Victoria.

"Thanks for taking the time to send in the patent with all that's going on right now," Ronald said. "Can't pick up a newspaper that isn't filled with your name."

That was because work was the only thing that would get him through this. "The deeper I dig, the more I find on Alderman Kelley," Lincoln said. "False leases, fake vouchers, padded bills, he was pilfering money from everywhere, inside and outside of his districts. Including from his associates, which is why they are willing to sing. Even his own son is indicting his father in everything."

"So, is Victoria coming back anytime soon?" Ronald asked.

There wasn't a day in the two weeks since she'd left that someone hadn't asked him about her. They had fooled Manhattan well, more convincingly than he'd imagined. "No. She's busy with her family. Her grandfather has heart spells." That was his given excuse, and he would use it as long as it took. Took for what? To forget her? That would never happen.

"That's too bad, I have a new invention I'd like to show her. It's an electric fan."

"The electric fan has already been invented," Lincoln said.

"Not one like this," Ronald said. "It blows so fast that it can dry your hair. Just don't have long hair and stand on the wrong side of it."

Lincoln nodded while pointing a finger at Ronald in a gesture that said he could be right on that one.

"Well, maybe I could tag along on your next trip Tarrytown, tell her about my fan."

If he were welcome, Lincoln would have already been there, but wouldn't have asked anyone to tag along because he was selfish when it came to her. "Hard for me to get away right now, but I'll let you know."

"All right, I'll let you get back to work," Ronald said, walking to the door. "Don't be a stranger."

"You, neither," Lincoln replied.

The door closed and Lincoln leaned his head back, let out a long sigh. He should be glad things had worked out the way they had. That he hadn't been completely wrong. He didn't have time to worry about a wife and if she was sitting home lonely or not. Worried or not. This case was becoming so complex, he was wondering if he should put a bed in his office, so he could just sleep here.

If. There were a lot of ifs in life, just like he'd told her.

Such as, if he loved her, as much as he thought he did, shouldn't he be happy for her? Happy that she was living the life that she wanted, even though it wasn't one that included him.

If he really loved her, shouldn't he be happy for the time they'd had together? That's what Troy had said. That he was happy for the time he'd had with Willamette. That was fine for Troy to say. Willamette had died loving him.

If he really loved her… Lincoln shook his head. There was no if in that. He did love her. And he was so selfish that he wasn't happy to not be in her life and he wasn't happy that they weren't together now.

There was no reason. No precedence. No law.

Therefore, he had reason to be selfish. He had reason to show her, too. Show her that he'd put both Kelleys in prison. Show her that he'd run for attorney general and win.

Show her…

His entire being went still, except for his heart, he could feel it opening as the last thought struck.

Show her that he didn't want any of that without her.

He shot out of his chair and out of his office.

Three doors down the hall, he opened his father's door. "I'll be gone for a while."

"All right," his father replied. "How long?"

"I don't know."

"Where are you going?"

Done fooling anyone, he said, "Tarrytown."

His father grinned, and nodded. "Take as long as you need."

He didn't even pack a bag, just went to the train station, and boarded the first train heading north. Less than three hours later, he knocked on her front door.

It was a big house, made of stones and wood, on the outskirts of town, with a vast expanse of green grass and full-grown trees.

The man who answered the door, the butler, he assumed,

was more than what he'd call good-sized. This one was big enough to throw two good-sized men out the door at the same time. "I would like to see Miss Biggs," Lincoln said.

"May I tell her who is calling?"

"Lincoln Dryer."

The butler gave a slight nod. "Please wait here."

"He doesn't need to wait anywhere," an old voice said.

Lincoln grinned, hoping that he did have an ally in Emmet.

"Come in, Lincoln, I was wondering when you'd show up." Emmet waved a hand at the butler. "Shut the door, Bart, and Lincoln, follow me."

Lincoln obeyed, walked down a long hallway, through a sitting room, and out a door onto a covered porch, that hosted several chairs and small tables.

Emmet pointed towards a line of evergreen trees. "She's out there, on the other side of the tree row. She bought herself one of those new-fangled bicycle things and takes it for a ride every afternoon. I think it's making Maize jealous, that's her horse. She rides the bicycle on the same trail she used to ride Maize. Just follow the gravel, you'll eventually run into her."

"Thank you, Emmet."

"Yeah, well, don't blame me if she bites your head off. She took mine off a time or two already this week."

Lincoln could relate. He'd snapped at a few people himself the past few days. He and Victoria weren't so different. "I won't."

He followed the gravel pathway, out to and through the row of trees, and continued to follow it as it twisted and turned around bushes and trees, until he saw her.

Actually, he saw the bicycle first, lying on the ground.

She was sitting on the ground, with her back leaning against a tree trunk. The gravel beneath his boots alerted her and she turned, jumped to her feet.

She didn't say a word, just shook her head.

He kept walking towards her, stopped when she was little more than an arm's length away. "Hello, Victoria."

"Lincoln." She was still shaking her head. "You shouldn't be here."

"I think you're wrong," he said. "I should have been here before now."

"Why?"

"Because I love you. I want to marry you. I want you to be my wife. I want to see you at the breakfast table every morning and the dinner table every evening. I want you to have my children. I want so many things, and they all include you."

She pressed the back of her hand over her mouth, while shaking her head again.

He knew it was going to take some hard work to convince her, and that was something he'd never shied away from. "We are very much alike, Victoria. In a man it's called ambition, and in a woman, it's called stubbornness. At least I believe that's what's happened in our case. I'm considered ambitious, because when I set my mind to something, I believe I'm right, and rarely change my opinion. That's true for you, too, but you're called stubborn when you refuse to change your opinion. Can you agree to that?"

She nodded.

"Good. Now, for a few facts. I love you, and you love me." He waited and let out a silent sigh of relief when she nodded again. "I can't promise that I'll never make you worry, and you can't promise that you'll never make me worry. That's part of loving someone, you care about them in every way. That is what I can promise, that I will love you, I will care about you in every way. Fully, completely, without reservation, I will love you above and beyond all else, for the rest of my life." He stepped closer, touched her cheek with the palm of one hand. "I know you're afraid of being hurt again, and there, too, we are alike. Because I'm afraid, too. Of losing you. I'm afraid of living the rest of my life without you."

Victoria swallowed a sob, but couldn't stop a second one. Nor could she stop the trembling of her hands, her body. "No. No." All her hours of thinking, all her fears of losing him, she'd never considered his fears. Never considered what her actions were doing to him. "You can't be afraid."

"I am," he said. "I've never been more afraid of anything in my life."

She took a step back, needing the space to think. To remember why she couldn't give in to the overwhelming desire to be wrapped in his arms. Her heart was pounding. Faster now than it had been when she recognized him on the walking path and realized she wasn't seeing things.

He was here. In person, and she'd missed him so much. So, so much.

She had to remember why loving him was worse than the fear of losing him, but she couldn't. Because it wasn't worse. The love she felt for him was stronger. More powerful. The part of her she was afraid of losing, couldn't ever be lost, just shared. She'd given it to him freely. Her love, all of it, and sharing it with him is what had made her whole. She'd just been too blind to see it. Too stubborn to see it. "I've been such a fool," she said.

"No, you haven't. You were just protecting yourself."

A plethora of emotions washed over her. "In doing so, I hurt you."

He grinned, shrugged. "You could kiss me and make it all better."

Pinching her lips together, she tried hard not to smile. Tried harder to find a reason why she shouldn't kiss him, but nothing formed. It couldn't. She was too excited and leaped forward, looping her arms around his neck, and pressing her lips against his.

There it was. All the happiness she'd known in Manhattan was back.

She kissed him with all the love filling her heart. All the love filling her world.

Her love collided with his, intertwining their hearts, as much as their lips, their arms, and bodies. She couldn't tell where she ended and he began. Encompassing her to the point where there wasn't any room for anything else. Certainly not fear. There never would be room again. She'd been so focused on losing, that she'd failed to see what she was gaining. What she was winning. Him. His love. His forever love. That made her a winner.

The winner.

For the rest of her life.

A week later—because neither of them were willing to wait—in a small, private ceremony of family and a few dear friends, at the community church in Tarrytown, she became Mrs. Lincoln Dryer.

Proof positive that they hadn't fooled Manhattan, they'd shown the entire world what love could do. Make the impossible, possible.

After a short reception, she and Lincoln checked into the small local hotel, for their wedding night. They would embark on a honeymoon in the morning. He wouldn't say anything more than where they were going was a surprise. She accepted that, because she loved his surprises, loved him. Every day with him would be an adventure that she would live to the fullest.

Lincoln removed his jacket and tossed it onto the chair, before taking a hold of her hands. "There's nothing to be afraid of," he whispered, kissing her softly.

She looped her arms around his neck. "I know."

"We'll take it slow."

She grasped the front of his shirt with both hands. "We've already waited too long for this." They had, the past week of loving each other and not fully acting upon that love, had taken a toll on her patience. She ripped the front of his shirt open, not caring how buttons flew in every direction.

He laughed. "I love you."

"Show me," she whispered.

His strong, deft, and loving hands made short work of removing her wedding dress, and the promise of what was to come powered through her, leaving her incapable of thinking about anything else.

Kisses, hot and strong, that stole her breath and left her begging for more, told her he felt the same, and she loved it. Loved being his.

She kissed him, touched him, and savored the friction of his body against hers. He knew what she wanted, when she wanted it, and she enjoyed herself fully, knowing he was hers as much as she was his.

Like their love, how it grew every moment, so did the passion between them. She couldn't get enough, wanted more, and wasn't shy about admitting that. Wasn't shy about demanding that.

Neither was he, and when the moment struck, when there was no higher that they could climb together, she cried out his name as an explosion of pleasure erupted inside her. It felt like she was flying. Flying high above the world, locked in his arms.

She eventually floated back down to earth, but was still breathing hard, her heart still beating wildly, and filled with happiness. "That was—"

"Worth the wait?" he asked.

"I was going to say amazing, but yes, it was definitely worth the wait."

Epilogue

Victoria smiled as Lincoln lowered down beside her on the warm sand, and leaned back as he stretched out, using her lap as a pillow. She used her fingers to comb his damp hair off his forehead. "It's going to be hard going back to New York after all this warm weather and Florida sunshine."

"We can stay as long as you want," he said, eyes closed.

She let her gaze roam over the blue ocean water, watched how the waves rolled onto the beach, then retreated, leaving the sand with a glossy sheen. It had taken well over two years, but Alderman Kelley was now in prison. So was Elwood. People all across the boroughs of New York were safer and healthier because of her husband. He'd worked tirelessly and hadn't lost a single case against the Kelleys. She was so proud of him.

She was also proud that he wasn't done. Not by a long shot.

The length of the cases and his commitment to see them through, had meant that he hadn't ran for attorney general, but he would next year, when the term of the current one was up. Everyone was as excited about that as she was. Even her grandfather. He claimed it was past time to get some politicians people could trust.

She leaned down, kissed Lincoln's lips. "We can stay as

long as you want." The plan was for everyone on both sides of their family to stay for a week, but she wasn't opposed to lengthening that. She was never opposed to anything he wanted, because like their love, they shared dreams and hopes, and many times, ideas. Including buying a model V automatic sweeping machine for the beach house to sweep up all the sand that was tracked inside.

He twisted his neck, and kissed her stomach, where deep inside, their love was growing into a new human being that no one knew about except the two of them. Not because they were keeping secrets, but because other family news had needed to be celebrated first.

"It was a nice wedding yesterday," he said.

"It was," she agreed.

"I'm happy for them."

"Me, too." She let out a sigh that was filled with happiness. "You Dryer men are hard to resist."

"So are the Biggs women." He cupped the back of her neck and tugged her face down for another kiss. "Maybe we should have gotten married on the beach."

"Neither of us were willing to wait long enough to plan something like that."

"I planned the honeymoon."

"You did, and Niagara Falls was wonderful." She shook her head in partial disbelief. So many things had changed the past two and a half years. So many wonderful things. "Our wedding is where my mother met your uncle Troy, and now they're married, spending their honeymoon sailing to the Caribbean."

"And we are enjoying an extended stay at the beach cottage." He glanced up and down the beach before he looked at her. "Do you think anyone will notice if we sneak away? Up to our room?"

She kissed him. "I don't care if they do notice."

He leaped to his feet and tugged her to hers. "Neither do I."

Hand in hand, they ran across the sand, laughing, and happy, because they were both winners.

Always winners.

Making the impossible, possible.

* * * * *

If you enjoyed this story,
be sure to read Lauri Robinson's
latest historical romances

A Dance with Her Forbidden Officer
An Unlikely Match for the Governess

And why not pick up her
Southern Belles in London miniseries?

The Return of His Promised Duchess
The Making of His Marchioness
Falling for His Pretend Countess

Enjoyed your book?

Try the perfect subscription for Romance readers and get more great books like this delivered right to your door.

See why over 10+ million readers have tried Harlequin Reader Service.

Start with a Free Welcome Collection with free books and a gift—valued over $20.

Choose any series in print or ebook.
See website for details and order today:

TryReaderService.com/subscriptions

RSBPA24R